The Kitchen

ELIZABETH FELLERS

Johanna,
Happy reading
happy cooking!

E. Fellers
2016

The
Kitchen

A NOVEL

ELIZABETH FELLERS

PAPER
BIRCH
PRESS

THE KITCHEN

© 2016 Elizabeth Fellers

PAPER BIRCH PRESS

Edition ISBNs
Trade Paperback: 978-09892855-2-0
E-book: 978-0-9892855-3-7

First Edition 2016

This edition was prepared for printing by
The Editorial Department
7650 E. Broadway, #308
Tucson, Arizona 85710
www.editorialdepartment.com

Book design by Morgana Gallaway

Dedicated to the memory of my mother

Hulda Bertram Fellers

*Her wonderful cooking and delicious recipes
live on with her children and grandchildren.*

Her special ingredient was love.

ACKNOWLEDGEMENTS

WRITING a novel is not a one-man show. Family and friends are valuable counterparts.

First on the list has to be my Critique Group. I am forever indebted to Louise Boost, Joyce Sanford, and Rosemary Simpson. They offered wise, honest, creative criticism every Tuesday morning. The completion of this book belongs to them.

My dear friend Gail Caggiano shares my passion for cooking, cookware, cookbooks and attending a culinary school anywhere in the world.

Early readers, Linda Gallaway, Linda Hallgren and Evie Rohling said to keep writing; they wanted more.

I can never forget Alexis Powers. She continues to inspire.

Beth Lake with Input Creative Services even made house calls.

My sons and their families are my rock. My husband supports this crazy habit. They are the best.

Once again, it is a true pleasure working with Morgana Gallaway Laurie, and The Editorial Department in Tucson, Arizona. Morgana put it all together to make an amazing-looking book. Much gratitude to a fellow foodie!

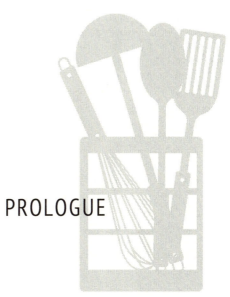

PROLOGUE

The thin morning sun woke her. In those first seconds, Julianne basked in the cool autumn light, remembering nothing, stretching her long arms upward and flexing her slender feet. She was totally in the moment.

Then it came back. Alone in the king size bed, the comforter and pillows next to her undisturbed, she remembered. Julianne counted the days. Today was the twenty-first morning of widowhood. Jock was really gone. Jock was dead.

There were no more tears to cry, no more shouting about life being unfair, no more thinking it was all a bad dream. It was time to get up and face another day as a middle aged woman. Alone.

Hastily pulling a gray sweatshirt over her silk pajamas, Julianne made her way down the back staircase, into the kitchen, and over to the coffee station.

Jock had always made the coffee, first thing, every morning. He usually rose by five o'clock, never one to wait for the sun to come up. On his way down the stairs, he would flick on every light making his own sunlight as he went. Jock had a million things to do. Every day. Retirement meant nothing to him.

As the coffee brewed, Julianne looked wistfully around the high-end gourmet kitchen, her favorite room in the custom built house. Even as a young girl, cooking with her mother and grandmother was one her favorite things. As an adult, it became a well-honed hobby. She had traveled to France and Tuscany to attend culinary classes. The shelves lining the center island held a hundred or more cookbooks. Her husband indulged her passion, giving her carte blanche to design this gastronomic domain. Julianne felt the kitchen was the heart and soul of the home.

Before pouring her first cup of coffee, she wandered around the kitchen. Stroking the highly polished granite counter tops, straightening the five empty mahogany bar stools, and dusting off the red knobs on the Wolf cooktop. Julianne felt the empty, hollow, echo of a house with only one resident. She hadn't cooked a meal in weeks.

The coffee maker gave a final burp and quick beep to signal it was done. Julianne filled the same mug and stood in the same spot she had twenty-two days ago.

Twenty-two days ago her life was steady, predictable, and running just fine. Now it was derailed, off the tracks, and turned on its side.

In the past, Jock and Julianne had shared this valued quiet time each morning. Julianne would make her way to Jock's office. He was always there. Seated behind the massive desk, busy on the computer, shuffling files or reading the Wall Street Journal. He would look up and greet her with a hearty good morning as she took a seat across from him. They would chat about the day ahead, talk about the previous day, and make future plans. The room was filled with Jock; his personality, his essence.

Julianne took the steaming mug and left the kitchen. She walked down the front hall, standing stoically in front of her late husband's office.

The double doors were tightly closed. Briefly, she let her left hand flutter down to touch the brass doorknob, then quickly pulled it back.

From the detective's report, it was clear there was another Jock. He died in a downtown Chicago hotel in the middle of the day. No one was with him but the police found evidence a woman had been there. After days of investigation, homicide and suicide were ruled out. The autopsy proved it was a heart attack. There was no evidence of recent sex. But still, why was he there? Who was the woman?

The loss, the pain, pure anger, and the unresolved issues haunted Julianne. Did her husband have another life? Was that secret identity hidden in this room, his sacred office?

Soon she would find this man and know this other Jock. But not today. Today was too soon.

CHAPTER ONE

As the days rolled into one another, each day felt the same. Julianne did her best to keep busy. She managed to grocery shop a bit. Occasionally she baked a chicken breast or lamb chop, sautéed a fresh vegetable and opened a bottle of Merlot. Even though she hadn't touched a thing in Jock's closet, she dragged home six flat boxes from the UPS store, telling herself, *someday soon,* just not today.

One morning in mid-October, Julianne took her coffee to the three-season porch. She walked through the family room, stopped to turn off the security system, 5-5-53, Jock's birthday, stepped through the French doors, leaving them wide open to allow heat from the house to trickle in.

Fall was settling in. The mornings were brisk but northern Illinois would hold on to balmy afternoons and bouts of Indian summer for several weeks. The sunroom felt chilly.

The cold travertine floor bit through her slippers as she headed for her favorite rattan rocker. Twelve years ago, this room had been added to the house plans prior to the start of construction. Jock balked, preferring a deck or blue stone terrace. Julianne was the new bride then, she won. Little did she realize future victories would be harder to come by.

Oh, yes, the furniture issue, that had been a little tricky. But before Jock realized it, Julianne had the room furnished in white wicker with cushions sporting red geraniums on a polished cotton fabric. She loved it.

Her husband wanted solid wood, something in teak, and gruffly asked, "Can't you return this stuff?"

Was it then? Was it at that moment she knew this marriage wasn't going to be easy? Where were the pampering, sweet nothings, and constant endearments that had peppered the short courtship?

But in the end the furnishings had stayed and the sunroom was hers.

By now Julianne's coffee was cold but her feet were warm and toasty as a patch of bright sunlight settled on her slippers and crept up her bare ankles. Julianne called it a sun porch, five foot tall windows covered three walls. Each one could be cranked open to catch summer breezes in the humid Midwest or latched closed in cooler weather but radiating solar heat throughout. The gift of the sun made it cozy this morning and the warm glow soothed Julianne.

Rocking slightly, she thumbed through a *Gourmet* magazine then put it down. Julianne took off her reading glasses and set them on top of the publication. She closed her eyes, let her head fall to the back of the chair, and quietly said to the empty room, "I used to love this time of day. You were upstairs showering and dressing. I was planning our dinner. Trying to decide between a recipe for beef tournedos or veal Marsala. Wondering which wine you would pair with the beef. Then you would come in and kiss me, saying you'd call on your way home."

Tears rolled down her face. "I miss that. But you bastard," she continued, her voice rising, "I did wonder what you did all day after you sold the business and there was no office to go to."

When the phone rang, Julianne jumped. Her first instinct was to ignore it. But several insistent rings later, she left the porch to make her way to her small desk in the kitchen where she grabbed the receiver. *Oh No!* The caller ID lit up with the name of Jock's daughter.

"Good morning, Shelby."

"You sound strange, Julianne, are you okay?"

"Yes." Julianne cleared her throat. "I haven't used my voice today. Maybe too much coffee. How are you doing?"

"Really? I'm surprised you ask. I haven't heard a word from you since my father's funeral."

Why did her stepdaughter never fail to start a conversation without a thinly disguised condescending remark? She decided to ignore it. "I know, dear, this is a very difficult time for you, too. I hope you're holding up as best you can."

"I suppose I am. All things considered with Daddy leaving me the way he did."

Jock denied his daughter nothing. Deep down, Julianne believed Shelby was dealing with little grief. She was angry that Daddy was no longer present to take care of any slight travesty. Julianne thought most women by the age of thirty-one were established, independent, and self-sufficient, but maybe not.

Shelby continued, "I'll get right to the point. Several months have gone by and I think it's high time I go through Dad's things. Today would be good for me, I'm off." Shelby paused, mustering up steam to go on. "I want several pieces from his office. Things I know he would want me to . . ."

"First of all, it's been five weeks, exactly thirty-five days, not MONTHS! And I just woke up. I'm not, well, to be honest, Shelby, I'm not ready." Distraught, Julianne paced the length of the kitchen.

Shelby practically screamed into the phone. "Ready for what? For God's sake, Julianne!"

"Not today. Let me think." Julianne pulled out a stool from under the counter, perched on the edge, and rubbed her face. *Please leave me alone.* Of course, this was Jock's only child. She needed time. And she wanted answers.

"No, Shelby, I'm not ready to go through your father's desk or clean out his office. I understand where you're coming from, I don't mean to be insensitive but please understand my position. Honey, it takes a while, you know, to do all this."

Shelby softened her tone. "Okay, Julianne, have it your way. I'm going to let you go now. I'm saying good-bye."

"Wait! I am sorry. I promise to get in touch with you soon." Julianne wasn't sure Shelby heard any of it.

Shaking her head, Julianne knew this was the last thing in which Julianne would involve Shelby. There was no way Jock's daughter would be the one to uncover his other life. If his office held those secrets, Julianne would be the only person to find them.

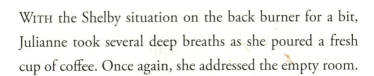

WITH the Shelby situation on the back burner for a bit, Julianne took several deep breaths as she poured a fresh cup of coffee. Once again, she addressed the empty room.

"I can't bear another day in this empty house. I have to get out! I can't turn into a blubbering old lady sitting and rocking and talking out loud."

Adela, her best friend, was the only other person who had seen the police report. She could hear Adela telling her to take time with all of this. *Think of yourself first. Take care of yourself first.* That is who she needed right now. She needed Adela. Without giving it another thought Julianne grabbed the phone again.

"Adela, it's me!" Julianne was surprised her best friend didn't recognize her voice.

"I'm sorry." Adela had her on speakerphone. "Really, you don't sound like yourself. Everything okay?"

"I don't? I sound like a crazy person? Well, maybe I am."

"Oh, come on. Good to hear from you." Adela closed the file with the sales contracts she'd been working on. "It's been too long. I wanted to call you all last week but I'm probably the loony one. I can't believe business is this good. Halleluiah, the recession is over. I sold three houses last week and I'm booked solid this week-end."

"Oh." The disappointment was heavy in Julianne's tone. "I suppose today, too."

"Actually, no," Adela said, picking up on her friend's mood. "I need to take a break. Shall we play a little?"

"Yes! I have to get out of this house. I want to wash

my hair, put on something nice, eat something delicious, drink something potent, and act like a girl again."

"Well, you are talking to the right person for all of that. First we shop. Nothing like retail therapy to put everything right with the world. Then we have lunch, then we shop some more, and before you know it, it's cocktail time."

Julianne laughed out loud. "Oh, my God. I laughed. Adie, I laughed!"

Smiling into the phone Adela said, "I'll pick you up at ten thirty. That way we'll only have one car left at some bar to rescue in the morning. I have a feeling we'll be Ubering home."

"You are the best girlfriend in the world."

"Yea, well, don't forget your credit cards."

"You are so buying those!" Adela whispered loud enough for almost everyone in the store to hear.

"Oh, my god, they're eight hundred forty-five dollars," Julianne exclaimed, standing in front of the mirror, never taking her eyes off her feet. "Plus, you've already forced me to buy that leather jacket and Lauren cashmere sweater. Hey, can you see the red soles when I walk?"

"So what? You'll wear them for years." Adela leaned

out of the posh brocade chair. "I don't know about the red. I wasn't looking. Strut your stuff. Walk over there so I can see if the red shows. I mean, really, they should. I always saw Oprah's. But you know what I heard? She never walked in them. Came on stage barefoot, put 'em on when she sat down."

"Adie, look now." Julianne took off down the aisle between the racks of shoes. Placing one foot in front of the other, abs sucked in, shoulders back and dropped, chin parallel to the ground, she was once again a runway model, albeit three decades later.

"Good grief, girl! You still got it. Look at your legs. When's the last time you had on a pair of five-inch heels?"

"Probably twelve years. Jock didn't like me to be taller. But, oh, I've always wanted a pair of Christian Louboutin's." Julianne collapsed in the chair next to Adela. "My legs are a gift from my mother. I wish you had met her. She was the true definition of a lady. Very French. Did you know she never became a citizen, even though she left France as a toddler?"

"Then this is a perfect match. Gorgeous French shoes for your gorgeous French legs. You're not taking those off." Adela signaled the sales clerk. "We've decided on these shoes and my friend will be wearing them out, please bag her other ones."

Two hours later they were still seated on the curve of the

long horseshoe shaped bar at Casey's, each carefully sipping their second dirty Sapphire martini. Adela had called her man-friend, as she liked to describe him, proclaiming she had long outgrown *boys,* and cancelled their dinner date. Having ordered a large selection of bar appetizers that would do for dinner and hopefully soak up some of the excess gin, the women smiled. The other choice was throwing in the towel and calling Uber when the evening ended.

"I'm feeling a bit guilty, you know?" Julianne mused, sipping from the stemmed glass.

"Why, because you got out of the house? Forgot to be in mourning for a couple of hours? Had some laughs with an old friend? Got some new rags? This was a small dose of therapy."

Julianne nodded, "Thank you, it was good." Nervously twirling her cocktail, she quietly added. "That attorney called again."

"Who? What about? And . . ."

"I don't know. I can't face it. I haven't even set foot in Jock's office. I haven't looked for his life insurance papers. I know there is a Schwab account. Somewhere. What about his profit sharing? 401k's, his checking . . ."

Adela interrupted, "Hold on, honey. What did you do for money? I mean you, personally. When he was living. Gracing us with his divine presence."

"Well, I'll tell you. He put five thousand dollars a month

into my household account to run the house, get my hair fixed, pay my credit cards, and whatever. Plus, I have my own money, some I inherited, my IRA. It worked." Julianne stared for a moment at her friend. "You never liked Jock, did you?"

"Let's not go there. Not now. But who is this attorney? Yours, his? Who is he?"

"Adela, I've never heard of him. His name is Maxwell H. Marconi. It's his voice, or maybe the messages he leaves. I don't know but there is something that scares me to death."

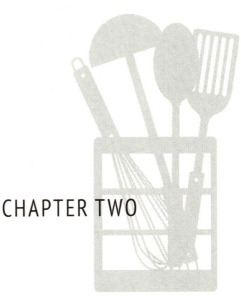

CHAPTER TWO

"Mom, where were you yesterday? I called home. I called your cell. I was scared stiff."

"Natalie, what are you saying? I talked to you last night."

"Really? Telling me you were sleeping and call in the morning. It was fricking 8:30. Hey, were you wasted?"

"Well. Maybe. Just a little." Julianne enunciated carefully so her daughter wouldn't suspect she was still in bed.

"Mother! You can't sit home and drink. Really? That can't be you."

"Of course not. Adela picked me up. We shopped, stopped for a cocktail or two. Wait till you see my new shoes. You are going to d . . . Oh, I mean be surprised."

"Cool. So. Mom. What is with Shelby? She called me yesterday and said you were like, real mean, and wouldn't let her come over and get her dad's stuff."

With a deep sigh, Julianne continued carefully. This was a difficult dilemma, which needed to be solved soon. Yes, her daughter and stepdaughter were grown women, but did she want them to know the truth about Jock? *Only if she knew the truth herself.* Should she fling the police report at them? Let them deal with the facts? All of them share in the pain? Probably not.

"Mom! Are you still there?"

"Come tonight for dinner, honey. Let me cook you a wonderful meal. I would love to see your pretty face at my table. Not much fun eating alone."

"Sorry. I've got a class tonight where I can use the credit toward a Master's degree. Just an hour after work I have to be at the U. Not much fun eating a hamburger in the car, alone, driving."

Mother and daughter laughed together, shared a moment, before Julianne asked, "This weekend?"

"Sure thing. Hey, plan on all day Saturday and most of Sunday. I'll sleep over. Got to run now. Love you."

"That's perfect. Love you too."

Seven in the morning was usually not too early for Julianne to take a phone call. But this morning was moving slower than usual. A couple of drinks didn't usually cause a bad headache. Thank heavens Natalie didn't suspect she was still in bed.

Sleep had been elusive. It was that damn office. That damn report. What was it all about? Well, enough already. Today was the day to cross the threshold, shove open Jock's office doors, and get to it. What was that old Bible verse? *Ye shall know the truth and the truth shall set you free.*

Once the decision was made, Julianne was up and out of bed, in the shower, hair pulled back in a ponytail, dressed in gray sweats and a Bears jersey, down the stairs, reheated yesterday's coffee in the microwave, and heading toward the front of the house.

This was her old self. Before husband number two, and for years after husband number one. As a single mother, sole provider for her daughter, she put the pedal to the metal, got an insurance license, and went after the big commercial clients. Back then every office door was a great, heavy barrier. Businessmen wanted to do business with another man. But perseverance paid off. Right along with absolute knowledge of the product, a beautiful smile, long legs, and a firm handshake, the good-ole-boys could relate to. That was how she met Jock. Cold calling was gruesome. But that day it all changed. She thought it had all ended well. The ending being their marriage and the fairy tale of *happily ever after.*

"FINE, I'm fine with that." Natalie muttered as she threw her iPhone in the general direction of the tote bag she was packing before leaving for the day. The idea to spend the weekend with her mother was a sudden impulse, but the more she thought about it the more pleasing the plan became.

Two years ago, Natalie graduated with honors and a solid degree in business from Roosevelt University. With several stellar letters of recommendation, portraying a serious young woman with a strong desire for success, she found employment in a world where forty-eight percent of her fellow graduates returned home to live, living their post-graduate life as if college never happened. Natalie decided early on that would not be her fate.

NorQuest Labs was an international pharmaceutical company struggling to find a foothold in the United States. The pay was low, the benefits lousy, and the perks minimal. Natalie secretly scoffed at the tedious training seminars and pep rally sales meetings. Her sights were set much higher. But a job was a job. The first rung of the ladder was usually a mundane position. She planned to super excel, hang onto the job for a couple of years, and then let her glowing resume speak for itself.

"Fluffy, come here. Come on out." Natalie scolded as she threw back the down comforter on her bed and tried to look sternly at the white longhaired puffball curled underneath. The kitten and the cover were the same creamy color. "I should have named you Princess. Look at you!" Fluffy looked up, ice blue eyes shining in her round face, and yawned. Persian cats thought they were royalty, unable to fathom why those silly humans didn't get it.

"Oh, shit, I don't think Mommy is ready for feline company in her perfect palace. Plus she would wonder about spending money on a cat when I'm supposed to be a struggling career girl."

"Too many questions, Ms. Fluff." Natalie scooped up and cuddled the kitten. "What to do with you Saturday and Sunday? I know. How about we ask your boyfriends Bruce and Troy? You'll be right next door."

Natalie gently put Fluffy down, grabbed her Coach purse and business bag, double-checked to confirm the money transfer was tucked in the side pocket, and locked the apartment behind her. The elevator door opened as she rounded the corner and she joined the cluster of young warriors descending twelve floors. Nodding quickly to the doorman, the group dispersed through the glass revolving doors before pouring out onto the streets of Chicago, ready to conquer another day.

The unbelted long Burberry trench coat flew out behind Natalie as she hustled the half block to the corner to hail a cab. Several men hurrying past her, going in the opposite direction, took the time to glance her way and give a brief smile of approval. Her sleek, glossy, full head of rich dark black hair caught their attention first. A peripheral scan didn't disappoint. Natalie was a little over medium height, with an athlete's toned body, the grace of a ballerina, and the poise of a worldly woman.

At the cab stand a middle aged man stood aside to let Natalie take his cab. Men tended to do this often. It pleased Natalie "to cab it" rather that catch a bus for work like so many of her struggling coworkers were forced to do. She had learned early that money was nice.

The naiveté her mother assumed Natalie still possessed was long gone. Even at twenty-four her mother thought of her daughter as somewhere south of nineteen. Natalie chose not to share the fact that her biological father still wired money directly into her checking account every month. In addition, her paternal grandmother Rose's estate dispersed thirteen thousand tax-free dollars into a money market fund the first of every year since her eighteenth birthday.

Jock had been the father figure in her life. During her formative teens and college years, he'd been a much closer advisor than her biological father out in California. More than a daughter-father relationship, they were buddies. She called him Jock-o and he called her Natty.

Between seeing her biological Dad two weeks a year and with constant emails and phone calls, Natalie never felt unloved or unwanted by her father. But it was about presence. Dad couldn't be present. Plus, he had a young wife and the young twins.

Julianne appeared content with the rapport her only child shared with her second husband. Natalie enjoyed the bond and so did Julianne. Jock was proud of his stepdaughter's business sense and for her birthday or special occasions, Jock would press a folded check into her hand and whisper clandestinely, "Make me proud, partner." Those were the code words for *read, research, buy low, sell high, keep the profits, and return the principle.*

Natalie had great fun with this brokerage project. In her sophomore year, with the declaration of her major, the two begin playing the game. Never once had she failed to deliver. The celebration was just between the two of them. Jock would meet Natalie at an award-winning restaurant, order a fine vintage wine, and they would dine in style, often depleting a fair part of the original investment. It was great fun. Natalie considered it the mainstay of the relationship, seeing no need to include her mother, even though Julianne might have approved. Plus, the extra money was wonderful.

Jock changed all that on the day Natalie saw him with that other woman. He never so much as glanced his stepdaughter's way.

CHAPTER THREE

"When one is opening doors that could be life changing, let them open!" Julianne exclaimed grabbing the brushed pewter double handles to fling open the doors to Jock's office. Inside it was dark and dank. Wrinkling her nose, Julianne wondered who had closed the wooden louvers. *Had someone been in here after the funeral?* The reception at the house was well attended and Julianne couldn't remember a single thing about the configuration of the office doors or windows. That entire day was a surreal blur.

After a minute, the darkness settled and the room came into focus. The first order of the day was to find the rod on each blind. As she twisted open the slats, dust mites bounced off the heavy furniture and the temperature rose as sunlight poured into the stale room. Julianne stood still.

Frozen in time and unable to move, she let her eyes take it all in. The huge mahogany desk, occupying half the room, with everything in place, neat as always, the back credenza hosting a row of family pictures, each tilted at the perfect angle, and a brass humidor filled with fine Cuban cigars.

The walls were lined with Jock's ego. An enlarged photo of him and Mayor Daly, a signed poster of the 1985 Bears Super Bowl team, another photo of Jock with Michael Jordan, and a diorama carefully arranged with memorabilia from the November 11, 1976 Eagles concert in Chicago Stadium, his favorite group and the music he played for years afterwards. The "Hole in One" plaque, honoring a lucky golf shot at Medina Country Club, was the newest addition to his walls of fame. All this, Julianne thought, *the things that defined the man he aspired to be.*

The fireplace angled in the far corner faced the desk and was flanked on either side with a leather tufted wing back chair. A small side table held several cut glass decanters filled with fine bourbon, double malt scotch, and expensive Russian vodka. This was a man's room in every sense of the word.

"Let's start at the beginning. I think it all begins at the desk." Julianne walked around it carefully, swung out the heavy black leather chair, and sat down. Without hesitating, she pulled out the center drawer. None of the side drawers, file drawers, or bottom drawers, produced anything extraordinary. What she found in her frantic search were bank statements, tax returns, car titles, health insurance records and their marriage license.

Beads of sweat lined her forehead. Julianne sank into the back of the big chair. Swiveling, biting her lower lip, and contemplating pushing on, she took a moment to breathe deeply. *What am I really looking for? Truth be known, I don't have a clue. All I know is that my husband was found dead, in a hotel room, fully clothed, on top of a made bed. A woman had been there!*

An iron curtain in her mind dropped down to shut off the possible rest of the story. *I will not think of that now. I will not accept the obvious. But I will stay here, in this room, and learn about this man. And, Jock, if you had secrets to hide, I will find them!*

Hours passed. The sun was sinking. The office darkened. Julianne's hand shook as she closed the last manila file from the final remaining cabinet of the credenza. When she noticed her hand, she noticed the waning light, felt dizzy and slightly nauseous. The gold clock on Jock's desk shocked her. Had she really been at this for almost eight hours with nothing to eat and little to drink?

It was time to quit. She wrapped her arms around the tall stack of files she intended to return to the credenza. That had been a very interesting history lesson. The story of Jock's business and the final buy-out was laid out in the original contracts, correspondence, and memos between his partners, their attorneys, and investors.

But the batch was too heavy, and as Julianne attempted to bend down and lower them into the credenza, they slid from her grip and scattered on the floor.

"Well, damn it all." Julianne slid off the chair and sat on the floor in front of the open cabinet picking up one file after another to stack inside. It was from that angle that she saw it. Hanging on a slim nail in the far top corner, deep in the back, was a brass key.

"Ha, what do we have here?" Julianne cradled the flat key in her hand, turning it this way and that way. Her palm grew sweaty around it and she knew then, in her heart, there were secrets to uncover and a key to unlock them.

IT wasn't light yet but Julianne was up. The hot shower made Julianne's skin tingle and cleared her head as she set the course for the day. As she blew her hair dry, she pacified herself by putting together a plan to search Jock's office again. Had the key been there all along or just since Jock took the buyout on the business, retired, and no longer had his office across town? Since it was meant to be hidden, it certainly would open a Pandora's box of some magnitude. All the normal suspects, household and business files, had been accounted for yesterday. So there was something else, somewhere.

Making her way downstairs and entering the kitchen, she flipped on the overhead lights, the under cabinet lights, the lights inside the glass cupboard doors, and the bulbs incased in the stainless steel hood over her six burner Wolf commercial range. There would be no darkness in this house this morning. There had been way too much of that these past weeks.

Julianne started the coffee, put her favorite Scanpan on a lit burner with a pat of butter, and walked to the double door Sub Zero refrigerator. Pulling out fresh spinach, basil, white cheddar cheese, heavy cream, and a carton of eggs, Julianne couldn't remember being this hungry for a very long time.

"No need, no need to hurry," Julianne said to herself as she cracked three eggs into a glass mixing bowl and grabbed the wire whisk out of a canister of utensils next to the range.

"I'm doing this my way today. Who was that crazy woman in there yesterday?"

Even though she had fallen into a deep sleep the minute her head hit the pillow last night, Julianne clearly remembered the dream. *Jock was in his Jaguar, in the driveway, beeping the horn, smiling, waiting for her to come out of the house and get into the car. His white hair was beautifully groomed as always, and he had on the dove gray leather jacket, the one she bought him last May for his birthday. He looked so handsome, so cheery. Julianne was excited to go with him but couldn't get to the car. Something kept pulling her gently back. Finally, Jock drove off, waving goodbye.*

In the brief moments after waking, a peaceful, easy feeling, like a lightweight blanket descended on her. The agitation of yesterday was gone.

The old familiar feeling of composure and self-control pleased her. After her shower, she had carefully dressed in designer jeans, a silk shirt, applied make-up, and made the bed.

"Mmm, you look so delicious," Julianne said, taking a deep whiff while sliding the omelet onto her white Mikasa plate.

CHAPTER FOUR

Thirty minutes later, standing in the center of Jock's office, Julianne looked around. Turning a full 360-degree circle she started then stopped to face the Landon stone fireplace and the floor to ceiling bookcases behind the leather tufted wing back chairs on either side. The brass key, tucked into the front pocket of her jeans, was reassuring.

Finally the decision was made. Julianne went to her pantry off the kitchen, took the utility step stool, a clean dust cloth, and a can of Endust back into her husband's office. She would hunt and clean. Starting at the top of the shelves on the left side of the fireplace, taking down one book at a time, Julianne worked her way across. She wiped off each book, paged through it, reached behind to dust the back of the shelf, and then moved on. The work was slow and tedious but somehow satisfying. It felt good to clean, eliminate, and move on. Somewhere in this office, something was hidden. Two hours later, nothing.

Next was the fireplace itself. Julianne stood back to contemplate the massive blocks of stone and the deeply burled wood mantle. "Will you look at that dust?" Julianne complained out loud running her finger over the wood. "Well, it's no wonder. He would never let the cleaning lady touch this mantle. Not with his precious antique clipper ship sitting up there. Said it had been his uncle's. Someone named Uncle Tomasz, a man that had been a huge part of his early life. I guess I'll make sure Shelby gets that damn boat."

Not being too careful, Julianne reached up with both hands to bring down the old craft, dusted it off, and went to return it to its long-standing position. Just as she was about to nudge it back into place, she saw it.

"What the hell?" There was no mortar around the bulky stone that sat directly behind Jock's precious boat. Almost dropping the ship, she regained her balance, set the darn thing on the floor, grabbed her step stool, and got herself up to eye level with the loose stone.

After several attempts to wiggle the rock out of its tight fit, Julianne gave up, found Jock's letter opener and used it to pry out the rectangular block.

"Oh my God!" Pushing the hefty rock off to the side revealed the hole behind was deep and dark. Without giving it another thought, Julianne was off the step stool, back to the pantry, grabbed a flashlight and climbed back up, clicking on the light. She shrieked. At least a foot back in the hole, the light caught a gray, rusty, metal fireproof box. Standing on her tiptoes, Julianne bravely thrust her arm in, clawed at the corner of the box, and gradually scooted it forward, placing it in the center of the mantle. Julianne backed off the stool, collapsed in a wingback chair, let her head rest against the high back and took several deep breaths to calm herself.

Julianne was still perched on a bar stool at her kitchen counter after one in the afternoon. She sipped a glass of ice water as she spun the little key in a circle in front of her. When the phone rang, Julianne jumped, shouting, "What?" The bell tone was such a loud intrusion to the hollow room and to Julianne's intense thoughts, that she almost fell getting to the kitchen desk.

"Hello, yes, I'm fine," she answered, out of breath."

Adela wasn't convinced. "I'm out running errands. How about I stop by? Would you like a little company this afternoon?"

With a pause that grew uncomfortable, finally Julianne blurted, "No! I mean, sorry, it's just that I'm about to go out myself. More loose ends to tie up, you know. And Natalie's coming for the weekend, need to grocery shop, probably gone the rest of the day."

Not feeling guilty about the lies Julianne rushed on, "Let me call you next week. No, haven't heard anything more from that lawyer. Yes, next week would be better."

Minutes later, Julianne was back in Jock's office, the key clenched tight in her hand, her reading glasses perched on top of her head. With one swift move, she scooped up the old box, seated herself at Jock's desk, and placed the box directly in front of her. After several frustrating attempts, she was able to open the rusty lock. Once the lid was thrown open, Julianne carefully laid out each item.

On one side of the box, she piled three yellowed envelopes. On the other side, a stack of old black and white photos, circa 1950s or older, she guessed, and next to those, several pieces of antique jewelry, including a man's gold watch.

After examining the address, return address, and postmarks, Julianne chose the oldest envelope. The paper crackled. When the envelope was slit open, she saw that the pages inside were neatly folded. Gently, she pulled them out and straightened the pages.

"Oh, my god!" Julianne gasped. The further she read, the greater the shock. The document was a court petition for a name change dated June 14, 1975. Moving through the pages, she found a copy of an original birth certificate. Although the ink was faded and hard to read in the folds, the message was clear.

Her husband wasn't always Jock Bernard Girard. He had been born Slavomin Jakab Kochevar. Her hand trembled holding the paper. It took several minutes to calm herself and continue to read.

"Well, at least he didn't lie about his age. He was an American citizen, born in Chicago, like he always said, thank God." The names of his parents were difficult to pronounce. "Wow, his mother was forty-four and his father fifty-two when he was born." Julianne had never met them but was told they died early. His father from COPD as a result of working in the coal mines in southern Illinois as a young man. His mother died from breast cancer at age sixty-six. Were his parents immigrants? Had Jock deserted siblings along with his name? Such a late-life baby!

The next envelope contained his old social security card and driver's license. In spite of being in shock, Julianne smiled at her husband's picture on the license. He was so handsome and with surprise, she noted that his hair was blonde. She had only known him with silver gray hair, which stayed as thick and full as on this picture.

The third envelope produced a thick folded paper that opened to a diploma. Once again Julianne gasped. Another lie. The diploma said a person by the name of

Slavomin Kochevar graduated with an office management degree from Central Illinois Community College in 1973.

Stunned, Julianne looked up at the framed diploma in his office, showing him to be an alumnus from the University of Michigan, with a double major in Economics and Business. He told her he graduated in the top ten of his class. Did it in exactly four years. Jock had been proud of Natalie when she did the same and so terribly disappointed when his older daughter, Shelby, dropped out after eight months.

It was all so much to think about. Julianne was exhausted and felt a terribly strong urge to get out of the office. Hesitating, the photos were tempting. She scooped them up, carried the bundle to the kitchen, and laid them on the cold granite countertop in front of her favorite stool.

Two hours later Julianne woke up on the sun porch realizing that it was late afternoon and she was chilled. It took a moment to clear her head and remember. Yes, she had come out here after eating a yogurt for lunch, decided to lie down for a minute, and closed her eyes. The tension in her neck had been awful but after a few deep yoga breathing exercises the muscles relaxed and she drifted off. Sitting up, taking in the waning light of a hazy fall afternoon, Julianne decided to make a cup of tea before going through the photos that awaited her.

Just as the kettle whistled, the doorbell chimed. "Now what?" Julianne didn't want or need company.

Opening the glass beveled front door, Julianne stood with her hand on her hip and scolded, "Okay, hello yourself, but what are you doing here?"

Without being invited, Adela crossed over the threshold and gave Julianne a hug. "I knew you were blowing me off this morning. Hey, Hon, I was worried. I won't stay long. Just want to give you a little company. It's not good. All alone. All day." She stepped into the foyer and dropped her purse on the Bombay chest in the wide hallway. Then Adela stopped short. The double doors to Jock's office were wide open. "Really?"

"Yea, I did it. And, now that you are here, well, what the hell. Come on in to the kitchen. Have some tea with me and I'll tell you *all about* my dear, departed husband." It surprised Julianne that she felt lighter and somewhat relieved to know that this burden was no longer hers alone to bear.

Seated at the round kitchen table, in front of a bank of windows looking out over the deep backyard and sipping hot tea, it didn't take long for Julianne to pour out the whole disturbing story. Talking about finding the key to the cleverly hidden box, she speculated that the box had been buried in the wall of the fireplace since the house was built. She told Adela how the box contained the paperwork for a name change, an original birth certificate, old driver's license, and some antique jewelry.

"But, Adela, come here." Julianne picked up the remains of the tea service and carried it to the big farm sink before pointing to the end of the island. "These photographs were in the box. I haven't touched them. We might as well look at them together."

Seated at the island counter, the women poured over the pile of photos. Most of the pictures were of elderly people dressed in unfashionable drab clothing, obviously grandparents, or Jock's parents. No names or dates were written on the backs. Not only were the photos confusing, but without dates, they were also irritating, leaving more questions unanswered than answered.

As they rummaged through the photos, Julianne found several odd shaped professional prints. Two different shots, taken at two different times, were of a chubby, very blonde baby boy. A third one, taken later, was of presumably the same baby, now a toddler. "This must be Jock," Julianne whispered more to herself than to Adela.

Pulling herself together, she exclaimed, "Oh, God, no, excuse me, Slavomin. Can you fathom a name like that?" Julianne traced the boy's face with her index finger before flipping the picture over several times searching for a name or date. But each time the back was as blank as the time before.

Adela, visibly shaken but trying not to over-react, fumbled through another pile. Without thinking she cried out, "This is so weird. Oh, Julie, look." In her hand were four or five colored snapshots, much more recent than the other photos. They were stuck together. As Adela carefully pulled them apart, her mouth dropped open.

"Let me see, Adela, hand me those."

Passing them over, Adela was afraid to ask but did anyway. "Do you think this is Jock, or whatever the hell his name was? Look at the baby he's holding. Is that Shelby? I don't think so. He would have been about thirty when Shelby was born. Right? This guy looks like he's nineteen, if that."

Julianne spread the prints in front of her. "No, no. I've seen tons of Shelby's baby pictures. She had brown curls and big brown eyes, her mother's features. This little guy, or gal, who can tell from these clothes, is either bald or blonde. You're right. Jock looks like a kid."

"Maybe a new brother or sister?"

"Adela, no, I didn't tell you. On his birth certificate, his mother was forty-four."

The two friends sat in silence. Neither one knew what to say. The situation was overwhelming with too many shocking facts and speculations to absorb. Julianne, blindsided by all the revelations uncovered in the past eight hours, was numb.

Finally, Adela broke the silence. "Now what?"

"Now what? I'll tell you now what!" Julianne pulled herself up and pounded the counter. "Give me those." She piled the prints together like a stack of cards and took them to the kitchen desk, opened the top drawer, and dumped them in. With just a moment's hesitation, she reopened the drawer, removed the top picture of Jock with a baby, slipped it into the front pocket of her jeans, and turned to Adela.

"I'll tell you now what! Now, you stay for dinner. You sit right there and I'll put together a nice pasta primavera, we'll drink a nice Chianti, and have a nice evening. I'm done for today. I can't take another minute of this."

CHAPTER FIVE

O ctober was wasting away. The Illinois weather was turning cold, days were getting shorter and shorter. Most of the leaves in the Girard yard were down or about to fall with the next strong wind. Daylight savings time would soon end and darkness would begin earlier and stay longer. Autumn was Julianne's favorite season but this year it came and went without her noticing. Her world was inside the house, in that office, captured in the photographs, the old lockbox.

It wasn't like Julianne to sleep late but she couldn't stay up after nine at night. This morning, when she turned over and saw it was almost eight, she bolted out of bed. It was Saturday and Natalie was coming. "From now on I set the alarm." Maintaining her old self and the old routines had become a constant battle. Hopefully her daughter would take the time to do her carefully choreographed workout this morning before leaving the city. Natalie was fanatic about her toned body and Saturdays were usually an extended session.

With no time to spare, Julianne rushed to start the day. Thank heavens she grocery shopped yesterday. Having planned to cook the Panna Cotta this morning, she needed to hurry. Natalie had asked that they prepare the dinner together, saying it was time to learn some good basic recipes. *You know*, Natalie had joked, *the kind that are boyfriend-over-for-dinner good.* They decided a simple Bolognese made with beef chuck would be man-friendly, especially if served over pappardelle noodles. Julianne smiled, remembering the conversation and then smiled again, remembering how good it felt to smile.

NATALIE decided to skip the Saturday morning workout and headed directly to the parking garage two blocks away from her apartment. Her neighbor, Bruce, convinced Natalie to leave the cat in her condo, promising to check on her faithfully throughout the next two days.

She dressed in a pair of Lucy yoga pants and matching hooded jacket, planning to get her mother out of the house for a long walk. Natalie looked forward to shuffling her feet in the dried colored leaves filling the sidewalks. There were only good memories of growing up in Oak Grove. The big McMansions sat back on large lots filled with mature oak trees. Sidewalks on both sides of the street connected the kids to friend's homes and the school five blocks away. The sidewalks were their highways to freedom. Oak Grove was a safe place to grow up. Trick or treating, Christmas caroling, riding bicycles everywhere, they never gave it a thought. As Natalie pulled the four year old BMW out of the assigned parking space, she wondered if things were still like that in the old neighborhood.

As much as she loved the city's high octane pace, there were times a quiet dose of suburbia was good for the soul. Easing the car onto the tollway, Natalie wondered if she should call her mom and let her know she would be early. *Oh why? I'm just going home. It's not like I'm a houseguest.*

Instead, Natalie pushed the phone icon on the steering wheel connecting the blue tooth and called her stepsister. "Hey, Shel, glad I caught you. Got a minute . . ."

"Mom, Mom, I'm home." Natalie came in through the side door off the garage. Even though there wasn't a space for her car, she had never relinquished her automatic garage door opener. Knowing she always had a home to go to and a way to get into it gave her a deep sense of security.

"Geez, Mom where are you?"

"Honey, is that you? Already?" Julianne came to the top of the back stairs, blow dryer in one hand and a round brush in the other. "I'll be right down. Or, better yet, come up and keep me company. I still need to make my bed and put on a little make-up."

Dropping her bag, Natalie took the steps two at a time. Greeting her mother at the top of the stairs, she wrapped her arms around her and breathed in the familiar scent of Chanel body lotion. "It's good to be here. How are you? You know, we haven't seen each other since . . ."

"Yes, dear, that's right." As Julianne held her daughter and stroked her hair, a tear leaked out of the corner of her eye. "I do miss you."

"Okay, we had our moment," Natalie said, laughing as she pulled away, finding it strange her mother was not dressed and the bed still unmade at midmorning. "Are you doing all right? Sleeping nights?"

"Well, I think I am. Considering everything." Julianne turned, hid her face, and walked into the master bathroom.

Natalie followed, pulled out the vanity stool from under a long counter, watched her mother lean into the mirror, and line her eyes. "I think you've lost a little weight." It wasn't often Natalie saw her mother without makeup and she looked older or maybe it was sadder. "Hey, Mom, are we still on with the sauce tonight?"

Julianne nodded, never moving her eyes from the make-up mirror.

"I have something to tell you." Natalie rushed on. "And, I've already done it. Just hear me out. It will be nice."

With a smile in her daughter's direction, Julianne picked up a lipstick and said, "I'm listening. Go on."

"Well, I called Shelby. You know, she's sad too. And she's more than a little miffed she hasn't heard from you in over a week. She said she didn't want to keep hounding you but she'd like some keepsakes from her dad and she can't understand why you turned so cold . . ."

"That's not true, I've just been . . ."

"Mom, don't interrupt. Let me finish. So, I told her I was coming out this week-end and I asked her to . . ."

"Today, she's coming today?"

"Mom! No. Tonight's our night to cook. I asked her to brunch on Sunday at the Chart House. We can all meet there. We all love the food. My treat. Then maybe, it might be a good idea to ask her back here and we can, together, go through a few things of her dad's. Like old pictures, his watches, trophies, those first edition books in his office, whatever. Maybe sort a couple of items out for her to take to her apartment." Natalie watched her mother's body language. Julianne straightened up, took a deep breath, and put a neutral expression on her face before turning toward her daughter.

"Well, I can't see the harm in that. Let me think a minute." Julianne disappeared into the master closet and dressing room at the far end of the bath. She emerged wearing brown alligator loafers and fastening a matching belt over an ecru cashmere tunic that flowed on skinny russet jeans. "How about this? This afternoon we'll put together some stuff, like his jewelry box, that bag of those old coins, maybe his fountain pens, cuff links, I know where his wedding ring from Shelby's mom is and those pewter German beer mugs. Yes, all that. We'll make a collection on the dining room table. Right on the dining room table! Really I don't care, I'll throw a cloth on it, won't hurt a thing."

Natalie never said a word but she did wonder. It was perfectly clear there would be no going anywhere near Jock's office. And, if she had to guess, anything that would be in the office her mom would take out late tonight, after she went to bed, or early tomorrow morning. Natalie decided to wait and not say a thing.

Yes, she thought, *I'll wait, watch, and then I'll see. Soon, I'll know how much she knows and then maybe it will be time to tell her what I know.*

CHAPTER SIX

"I'm sitting right here, Mom." Natalie said, perched on the middle stool at the counter in her mother's kitchen. It was late afternoon and the day had flown by. The pair had shopped in the village, lunched in their favorite tearoom, and finally took that walk Natalie had planned all along. Now it was time to cook. "I can see everything from here, I'll take notes and I'll be in charge of the wine. This Chianti looks wonderful. Jock's got quite the stash down in the wine cellar."

"I say, lets drink it." Julianne replied, lighting a flame under the Le Creuset cast iron Dutch oven, coating the bottom of the lapis blue pan with olive oil. "He was so persnickety about every occasion, was it good enough for his wine, and then matching the price of the bottle versus whom he was trying to impress. Heck with it. Take a couple of bottles back with you. I don't care." Julianne surprised herself with that tone. *Where did that burst of anger come from? Not tonight, no upsetting thoughts about Jock or whomever he was. Tonight is just for my daughter and me.*

"Cool. I will." Natalie settled back at the counter and watched her mother, directly in front of her, at the center island, assemble several vegetables, pull out a cutting board, small cleaver, and spices.

The gourmet kitchen that Julianne had so carefully designed was an ergonomically correct wonder. The windowless back wall bore a long marble counter top lined with cabinets on the bottom and open shelves above. This was the baking station, with marble as the perfect work surface for rolling out dough and cutting pastries. Mixers, baking sheets, cake and pie pans of all sizes and shapes, rolling pins, molds, cutters, measuring cups, spatulas, and whisks, were housed behind the doors and in the drawers. Above, on the lower open shelf sat glass canisters filled with flours, sugars, grains, chocolates, extracts, and leveling agents of all kinds. The top shelf was lined with beautiful serving pieces. Several tiered cake plates, some with dome tops, stood next to fluted edged platters, tureens, and crystal compote bowls.

The four casement windows on the adjoining wall created wonderful light with a panoramic view of the back lawn and made for a pleasant space for working at the massive farm sink that sat beneath them. Twin dishwashers were installed on either side of the sink. The remaining wall held upper and lower deep cabinets, creating more storage space.

Directly across the kitchen, on the opposite wall, housed the forty-eight inch built in Sub Zero refrigerator and freezer. Beautifully clad in custom-made cabinetry, flush to the wall, it took a minute to realize it was an appliance.

Julianne stood in the center of the kitchen. The rectangular island, dominated by a six burner Wolf commercial cooktop and crowned with a stainless steel restaurant grade hood, was the heart of the room. Julianne had made certain the island was built deep enough for the range and wide counters to prep and prepare food on. More doors and pull out shelves adequately stored the state-of-the art cookware and utensils that she loved to use.

"Let's go Mommy-o. Let the games begin."

With a laugh and a shake of her head, Julianne's mood escalated as she practiced mindful thinking. *What could be better than spending an evening cooking and eating with my daughter?* A child who never failed to fill her life with joy and love. From the first moment Julianne looked into those dark baby eyes, Natalie had given her nothing but pure happiness.

"Okay. The oil is hot. Let's add one diced carrot, one diced celery rib, and one small onion all chopped up."

Julianne held the oak cutting board over the sizzling pot and scraped off the vegetables with the sharp edge of her knife. Natalie, at the counter, scribbled down the ingredients as steam rose out of the heavy pan. Next, Julianne scooped out a small mound of sea salt from the wooden saltcellar. "I always add salt to sautéing vegetables."

Natalie looked up, a puzzled look on her face.

"Why?" Julianne smiled at her daughter. "Salt opens up the cells and lets the flavors escape and mingle. Plus, it aids in preserving our veggie's bright natural colors. Who wants a pile of gray mush in their pan?" Stirring constantly with the wooden spoon in her right hand, Julianne reached with her left hand for a glass ramekin holding four chopped garlic cloves. Before tipping them into the pot she teased, "Now, my dear, that would be a personal call on your part. Garlic? A date? Do spare me the details."

Natalie laughed. "But the sauce wouldn't be so good. Share the love, share the garlic. That's what I say."

The aroma was divine; garlic, onions, the oil, coming together. The sun was setting. The kitchen was warm. Julianne felt like she was caught in a cozy dream and wanted to stay right there. But she had to be practical, "Honey, jump up and turn on some lights. We're getting to the good stuff and this is important."

After turning on lights and adjusting the dimmer switches to create a tranquil atmosphere in the kitchen,

Natalie poured wine for herself and her mother. She carried the balloon glasses over to her mother and peered into the pot. "What is that? Chopped ham? I thought we were doing beef."

"Indeed we are, but this is beef's sidekick, pancetta. First I'll add the diced pancetta, just three or four ounces. Let's let it cook for a minute or two." Julianne took a long draw on the wine. "Now, my girl, I've got almost a pound of ground chuck, in he goes."

Natalie clicked her wine glass with her mother's, "Here's to boy bait."

"What?"

"Mother, all men love their meat. Beef sings out the call of the wild to any man. Not too sure about that pancetta stuff."

What fun to have a grown daughter. It's better than any girl-friend. Smiling, Julianne walked over to the refrigerator to bring back a quart of milk. "This will seem strange but I tell you, it is a secret to true Bolognese. Add about one cup of milk after the meat is no longer pink. Yes, write that down. See how the meat soaks up the liquid? We'll let that work for ten minutes or so. Hand me the wine bottle, please."

"Now wine, too?"

With a liberal hand, Julianne added over a cup of Chianti. All the while stirring, she leaned over the pot and inhaled deeply. "Isn't that magnificent?"

nice of you to include Shelby. I owe her an apology. There is no excuse, but my head hasn't been clear for weeks and I couldn't see my way to reaching out to her. But peek into the dining room on your way upstairs. I put together a few of Jock's favorite things that I think she'll like. I'll be giving her much more over time."

Natalie smiled slyly and shook her head. "And, you put this all out when?"

"Oh, now, you know I'm an early riser. Get moving girl or we'll be late."

Rushing out of the room, Natalie threw over her shoulder. "Hey. You're wearing those new shoes Aunt Addie made you buy. Right?"

A wave of happiness, long absent, washed over Julianne while standing at the sink rinsing the coffee cups and staring out the window. It had been the most wonderful twenty-four hours. With Natalie back in the house, she relaxed. Felt her spirits lift and was amazed at this present emotion. Indeed, she was feeling happy. *Oh, but what a silly idea. A cooking school right here in the house? Jock would have sixty fits and blow his stack!*

With a laugh and a throw of her head, Julianne said out loud. "But he's not here."

"NATALIE, are you staying for supper? I'll make something light. Shelby, I'll ask again, you know I would love to have you."

The three women arrived back at Julianne's house after brunch. The meal had gone fairly well. Natalie was effervescent with quirky tales of her fellow workers, living in a high rise in the big city, and the apparent lack of "quality" men. Shelby was quiet but pleasant, appearing happy to be invited. Julianne was proud to be with both the attractive, well turned out girls, who were stealing not-so-subtle glances of many of the men in the large dining room.

Shelby had a unique style, which reminded Julianne of the Bohemian look of the 60's. She wore leggings with a mismatched silk printed elongated blouse. A vest, scarf, and tight boots, huge earrings, and lots of dark eye make-up completed her outfit. With her long flowing caramel colored straight hair and pencil thin body, she pulled it off. Natalie wore the latest skinny black jeans and high heeled boots, set off with a red leather bomber jacket. All a perfect match with her toned athletic physique. Her dark hair, full of natural body, flowed around her shoulders. Nonchalantly, she often shook her head and threw back her wavy mane.

What Julianne didn't acknowledge was the fact a great many of those stares were for her. Dressed in a slim fitting St John knit dress, the new stilettoes, and her dark hair pulled back in a chignon highlighting high cheekbones and a long neck, she was the picture of elegance.

Shelby responded to the dinner invitation. "Thanks, Julie." Julianne's stepdaughter was the only one who called her this. Twelve ago, when the two first met, Shelby took an immediate dislike to the woman who would put a lot of time and space between her and her father. Shelby knew the first time she called Julianne, "Julie," it irritated the woman who would marry her father. Over the years, their relationship had softened but the name stuck. "I have a ton of stuff to do today. I'm freelancing with Delores the Monster Decorator first thing tomorrow morning. It's almost an hour's drive to the client's home. I want to have the drawings and fabric swatches ready and put together tonight."

"Oh, but that's such good news. Shelby, you have impeccable taste, a real eye. I've known Delores for ages. She might be a tough old bird but she knows her stuff. Honey, just look at it as a challenge and probably a good learning curve."

"Well, I do need the money. Not like the old days when . . ."

"You took care of that, right? Your father had a life insurance policy for you. Do you need me to follow up?" There was genuine concern in Julianne's voice.

Shelby shook her head, rolling her eyes. "It took almost two weeks to get the death certificate so it will be some time before I see a check." She knew what was coming next just by looking at Julianne. "Don't even ask." Shelby glared at Julianne. "I'll be fine." With a forced smile and clenched teeth, Shelby softened her tone. "But I do appreciate you parting with some of Daddy's stuff. I just wish I could sit at his desk, be in his office so I could feel him again, his presence I mean. What about his plaques and pictures? And that clipper ship, are you keeping that, *too?*"

Julianne's jaw dropped. The look of confusion and consternation on her face was evident, as she couldn't think of an appropriate reply.

In a flash Natalie stepped in. "I'll walk Shelby out and help carry the last of the books. Mom, I'm too stuffed from brunch to eat a thing. Plus, I want to get a run in before it gets too dark. The way I've pigged out the last two days, not good."

"Then I'll give you both a hug and kiss right here." Taking a deep breath, Julianne reached for Shelby, as the three women clustered in the foyer with the front door open. The hug between Julianne and Shelby was as genuine as both the women could manage and the kisses were a fleeting graze on the cheek. "Take care, dear. I'm so glad we all got together today. I'll call you next week. I promise."

Mother and daughter hung on for an extra few seconds. Little was said. It had been a good two days but they knew their lives were on different paths and it was time to get back to them.

Julianne watched with sad eyes as the girls got into their cars and drove off. She quietly closed and locked the door, walked through the house to the sun porch, plopped down in the rattan rocker, and closed her eyes. Willing herself not to cry, she forced herself to think positive. *Think of something productive*, she told herself. *Be thankful for all you have.*

She sank into a gloomy funk, aware that it was loneliness, plain and clear. A late Sunday afternoon on a bleak fall day. The house was dark, cold, dreary and so quiet. Julianne was a woman alone.

Maybe her marriage wasn't the very, very, best. Not that crazy soul mate, finish each other sentences, die within days of each other with a broken heart, stellar union. But it would be rated a good marriage containing companionship, mutual interests, laughter, lovemaking, kindness, and caring. Jock always treated Julianne with respect. She felt loved.

There were so many worthy qualities about Jock. He had immediately bonded with Natalie when Julianne and Jock first dated. An element absolutely necessary before Julianne could get serious. After they married, he took care of the bills, the cars, the taxes, the insurance, maintained the house. Julianne, a single mother for nine years, was more than happy to relinquish these duties to her new husband.

Jock Girard never met a holiday he didn't love to celebrate. Besides the usual Christmas, Thanksgiving, and Easter, he rallied and decorated the entire lawn for the Fourth of July with bunting and flags. He threw a backyard neighborhood barbeque for Memorial Day, planned a family get-away every Labor Day weekend, left a small wrapped jewelry box for each of the girls at the breakfast table and hid a good sized one under his wife's pillow on Valentine's Day. He was generous. Not only to his family, but to the community, his favorite charities and sometimes to a fellow human being who was down on his luck and needed a hand up.

There was another Jock. That man liked, and more than often, demanded his own way. Not in a cruel manner but with firmness, constant bargaining, lots of points to ponder, sometimes resorting to pouting and long silences. Finally, pontificating how his way would be the right way. The roadblock in his path would cave because it was so much easier to just give in. Her reward would be his good humor, adoring pats, sweet kisses, and peace-in-the-valley.

The other Jock had died in that hotel room on Michigan Avenue. Under strange circumstances no less. Someone else had been there with him, leaving several of her things behind. No clue to her identity but she didn't kill him.

The autopsy report was conclusive, a massive heart attack. He hadn't had sex before he died. But why? Why was he there? Who was the woman? Julianne thought she might never have the answers, leaving an open wound in her grieving process. How do you heal with no closure?

It was cold on the porch. Julianne thought about making a cup of tea, or fixing a drink. She wasn't hungry but there was no way she could make herself go into that kitchen, turn on the lights, and be inspired to cook something.

Another memory burned in her chest, but a nice one. Sunday evenings had been a good time, actually a special time, for the two of them. She and Jock would be in the kitchen, creating a great omelet, or a pot of soup, or grilling a wild cheese sandwich. They would scour the refrigerator and pantry pulling out the craziest ingredients. It was fun. Jock would open an inexpensive bottle of wine; they ate at the counter, and even cleaned up together. Then off to the family room, snuggle on the couch, to watch an old favorite movie. How many times had they watched *Funny Girl, The Great Gatsby*, or *Sound of Music*?

Julianne deliberated her choices for this Sunday night. Finally, she left the sun porch, locked the door, and without turning on any lights she got through the house, up the stairs, shed her clothes, and crawled into Jock's side of the California king size bed.

CHAPTER SEVEN

The name on the door said Maxwell H. Marconi. No other title. The directions the secretary gave were explicit which was a good thing or Julianne never would have found this unobtrusive colonial brick building on a narrow side street some twenty miles from her home.

She had been here shopping and to lunch on several occasions. New Colony, one of those lovely old river towns, dotted with quaint boutiques, upscale antique stores, trendy tea rooms, and canopied tree-lined streets where restored gingerbread Victorian homes nestled far back into the yards, never failed to charm. A perfect destination for shoppers, diners and residents looking to live outside of the big city and wanting to embrace a simpler lifestyle. It was a small town with pre-civil war history and post 20th century real estate and retail boom. Her brief visits had entailed walking up and down Main Street where the artsy shops were housed in a five-block stretch.

Julianne was more than surprised that Jock's personal attorney was located here in a small office on this obscure back alley lane. Surely, she thought, Jock's ego wouldn't permit anything but a big-wig firm in the Loop or North Shore.

It was Wednesday, the third day after her daughter and stepdaughter had a simple reunion at brunch and a rather uncomfortable encounter over her dead husband's personal belongings. Two days ago, about midday, the doorbell rang and there stood the FedEx man with a certified letter she had to sign for. Julianne wasn't surprised it was from this Maxwell H. Marconi person since his office had been deluging her with calls and other mail.

Sighing, Julianne tore open the heavy envelope, read the thinly disguised letter of veiled threats, called the man's office, and set up an appointment. There was no more to lose. She wanted all the cards on the table. She wanted the unanswered questions answered. And then, God help her, she was going to move forward.

So here she was. Fifteen minutes early, you could never guess the traffic. The name she was looking for was on the door. She parked in front of the brick square building, and in thirteen minutes, Julianne would walk through it.

"Mrs. Girard, my pleasure." Maxwell Marconi stood

behind his desk and reached across with an open hand. Julianne nodded a thank you to the young woman who escorted her in, walked toward the attorney, extended her hand, and gave the man a firm handshake. "Please sit. You found us just fine? Coffee, water?"

"No thank you. Yes, of course. New Colony is a pretty little town. Always a pleasure to visit."

"Well, good." The heavy-set man lunged back into his chair, folded his fingers in a pyramid across his chest, and gave Julianne a heartfelt look. "First, my condolences. I am deeply sorry for your loss. And, I feel some, also. I've known Jock for many years. I respected and liked your husband. We worked well together and I will miss him."

"Thank you." Julianne uncrossed her legs and leaned forward. "Jock and I had an attorney we both dealt with all our married life, Todd Kaplan. Jock met him when he was fresh out of law school, took an office in the same complex, close to Jock's. In fact, we did quite a bit of work with him. I don't want to be rude, but your name never came up. The calls, letters, from this office came as quite a surprise to me."

"Yes, I suppose they did. I apologize for that. But that was the arrangement. Your husband was a client and those would have been his choices." Marconi cleared his throat. "I have unfinished business to complete for him. Mrs. Girard, I have the will . . ."

"What will? No! Our attorney has Jock's will. He has my will. He's in Europe but I've contacted his office and will meet with him upon his return. There are no surprises. We drew up our wills together. I know what Jock wanted." Julianne started to rise out of her chair as if to leave.

"Please, Mrs. Girard, let me explain."

Two hours later Julianne couldn't remember a thing about the ride home. Her head was pounding with a jumble of details that made no sense. Her husband did what? Left her with just enough money to live a marginally comfortable life. Maybe hang on to the house. But for how long? No new car, trips, lavish presents for the girls, designer clothes.

The details were a blur. As soon as Todd Kaplan got back she would take this sheath of papers to him. Surely he would fix the problem. Then that arrogant Marconi would eat his words and she would have the four million plus. Julianne knew her husband had sold the business for almost five million. She was no dummy. Of course, a chunk went to taxes, brokerage, legal fees, accountants, and all the rest who got their share.

But, the memory, shortly after the closing of Jock's business, was as clear as if it happened yesterday, Jock sitting down and telling her they were set for the rest of their days. He invested the net proceeds in a Charles Schwab Life Management account. Damn it, why hadn't she paid more attention. Words like stocks, bonds, annuities, money market account played in her brain. A portfolio, to see them to the end, was what she had been told.

And now, as of this morning, she learns three fourths of it has somehow vanished. Okay, Marconi went into detail about back corporate taxes, two mortgages on the building, OSHA fines, delinquent payments on leased equipment, and several other issues she couldn't begin to remember. All liens that were cleared up with the final sale but items her husband never mentioned or deducted from the sales figure he showed Julianne.

Jock's estate left her with less than a million dollars. How could she make that last for the next thirty years or so? The mortgage on the house alone would eat up any reasonable monthly distribution. *For God's sake, I'm fifty-four years old. Get a job? Who hires a fifty-four year old woman with no current life skills?*

Working late into the night, Julianne battled the numbers. A dozen or so years ago, she had been an astute businesswoman. Letting her guard down, allowing her husband to manage all the finances, had been a mistake. Back into Jock's office she went. Digging through the file marked *Oak Grove Home,* pulling out property tax bills, homeowners' insurance policy, utility bills, gardeners, housecleaners, and much more, only darkened her spirits. Paperwork related to the sale of the business reflected none of the financial issues Marconi documented.

Julianne was dead tired. Probably more emotionally than physically but it was time to quit for the day. Deciding to leave the pile of household expenses until morning, when she would put a calculator to the numbers, Julianne firmly closed the double doors of Jock's office behind her. With a weary smile, she said out loud to no one, "Like that will help."

There was one last stop before bed. At the top of the curved staircase, instead of walking straight ahead and into the foyer that led to the master bedroom, Julianne turned left into the hall leading to the four guest rooms. She turned on the light in the smallest of the four. This was another favorite room in the house and the least used by anyone. When Natalie lived at home, she chose the largest one for her bedroom and outlandishly decorated it. It had long since been redecorated. Shelby often stayed with them in another room that remained a guest room.

But tucked under the eaves, in the corner of the house, was this sweet little room. Often times it had been her private retreat, even more so recently. When her mother died, Julianne used the things that defined Rose's gracious lifestyle to refurnish this bedroom. Running her fingers across the bedspread Rose had quilted by hand calmed Julianne and filled her heart.

Safely locked inside her mother's antique secretary's desk were Julianne's personal accounts. In the turmoil of the day, she hadn't given them a thought. The key to the desk was hidden under the bedside lamp and holding it in the palm of her hand gave Julianne a small measure of power. Something was still all hers; something was still in her complete control.

After seating herself at the desk and pulling down the shelf, Julianne's full attention was on the numbers in the checkbook and money market account. Rose passed away last January and with Jock closing the business, renting a condo in Florida for two months, and their usual busy summer schedule, Julianne had not found the time to make an appointment with their money man and invest her inheritance. No doubt the money would have been comingled with Jock's name and accounts had that happened.

Thank you, Momma. I need this right now. Julianne looked at the two balances. It wasn't a fortune but the low six figures on each statement was a tremendous comfort on a terribly uncomfortable day.

WINTER

CHAPTER EIGHT

Weather in the second week of January in the Midwest holds no surprises. It's always cold. More than likely, it is snowing, has snowed, or will snow. The days are short but gradually getting longer. Winter Solstice has passed but no one has hope for spring. It's better to acquiesce to another three months of miserable weather, stay busy, travel to a warm climate for at least two weeks, snuggle in, and wait.

In previous years, Julianne didn't mind winter much. She and Jock made the best of it. He ran his business for most of the years they were married so he was away during the weekdays and relished being home on Saturday and Sunday. Keeping up a house the size of theirs was Julianne's job and filled many hours overseeing the day-to-day routine of maintenance, cleaning, cooking, and entertaining.

With the death of Jock, the house lost its spirit, its life, its crackle. The rooms seemed dark even with the bright afternoon sun. The hallways were quiet now that a male's heavy footsteps ceased to tread on them. The high ceilings didn't bounce back the baritone voice of a man who always had something to say, usually quite loudly. There was no lingering aroma from the stews, roasts, and sauces of last night's dinner. The beautifully groomed stately two-story queen fell into herself, turning dour and sad.

If there was one thing Julianne was thankful for in this dreadful month was that the holidays were over and gone. The last two weeks of December were so terribly painful, it hurt even to think about them. Dear Natalie had done her best to bolster both their spirits. Even though it was the year for her to travel to California to be with her father and his family, she flatly refused, promising them a long weekend visit over Presidents' holiday in February.

It didn't take Shelby long to make plans. She drove to southern Illinois and spent ten days on the farm with her mother, Lenelle, and her maternal grandparents. Julianne had met Lenelle once, at Shelby's twenty-first birthday party. That was ten years ago. Jock and Julianne were newlyweds, hosting the elaborate event at a posh Chicago restaurant. The evening was terribly uncomfortable for everyone, especially Jock's ex-wife. The lesson was learned; two separate celebrations for the special occasions in Shelby's life.

Of course, Julianne only knew one side of the story. Jock told her Lenelle was one of those gals who thought they wanted the big city life, couldn't wait to leave their small town, come to Chicago, live large. Jock said he met Lenelle when she was a waitress at the diner where he ate breakfast practically every day. She was pretty, sweet, innocent, and had a big crush on him. They became friends, then lovers. Jock was her first. The pill made her queasy, headachy, so she skipped days. When the pregnancy could no longer be denied, Jock did what an honorable man needed to do and married the mother of his child. She never knew it wasn't his first.

The strained marriage lasted almost seven years. That was until Jock's business exploded and they were invited to the very best parties, membership into the right clubs, concerts, formal political fundraisers. Lenelle's country background was no match. Collapsing into herself she became a recluse as Jock grew successful, changed, drifted away, and Julianne suspected saw other women. Eventually Lenelle took Shelby and went home to the farm. Shelby couldn't wait to turn eighteen and leave.

For years, Lenelle and her aging parents begged for a visit as a grown up Shelby preferred the luxury of her father's big home and generous gifts from him and his new wife to the modest rural life of the other side of her family. This year, grieving for her father, the holidays

71

were not something Shelby wanted to share with Julianne and Natalie. Even though her stepsister and stepmother would be welcoming, there was no doubt she would be the fifth wheel.

Julianne's quest was to avoid all established traditions this holiday. So mother and daughter had Christmas Eve dinner at Chez Aimee in the village. The French bistro was surprisingly packed, noisy with merry making, and after the second glass of wine the two gave in and joined the Christmas carols, loud toasts, and camaraderie. The food, as always, was magnificent.

Christmas Day was spent with Adela and her boyfriend at Adela's condo. Adela, a childless, twice divorced real estate broker, collected friends and clients like some people collect rare coins or stamps and it seemed they all stopped by for a drink.

By midday it hit her. Julianne missed fixing a formal holiday dinner, setting the table with beautiful china and crystal, and being at home. Adela served platters of hors d'oeuvres and uncorked countless bottles of wine as her menagerie of comrades came and went all day. Julianne should have known this would be Adela's scene but once Julianne saw what fun her daughter was having she caved and enjoyed herself a little. Adela specialized in eclectic people from all walks of life. One couldn't help smiling at their eccentric comments and observations.

Now it was mid-January and the New Year loomed large and long in front of Julianne. Attorney Todd Kaplan assured Julianne that with carefully investing the principle from Jock's estate and her inheritance, she could live quite comfortably for many years off the dividends and interest. Julianne was not so easily convinced. Her reaction was to spend almost nothing. No clothes shopping, turning off the heat in the guest wing, dismissing the cleaning lady, bargain hunting the few groceries she needed, and limiting all Christmas gifts except for the two girls. At times, she knew she would be able to manage it all, other times panic set in and her world reeled out of control. Just yesterday, she called Adela and discussed putting her house on the market.

Adela went ballistic. "Are you crazy? You haven't thought this through. Where would you go? This time of year is no time to move unless you're transferred or desperate. You, honey, are neither."

ANOTHER Sunday morning. Julianne took her mug of coffee to the family room, thought about a fire, nixed that idea, curled up in one of the matching overstuffed chairs, and watched the lightly falling snow outside the partially frosted French doors. She hoped the Sunday edition of the Chicago Tribune was wrapped in plastic and contemplated venturing out to retrieve it off the long driveway.

Hearing noise from the back of the house, Julianne scurried to the kitchen and much to her surprise, Natalie walked in the door from the garage, dropped a bag in the mudroom, and smiled at her mother. "Surprise."

"What? What are you doing here?" Julianne couldn't keep the pleasure out of her voice as Natalie walked over, patting icy hands on her mother's cheeks, and hugging Julianne hard against her cold down jacket.

"Tomorrow is Martin Luther King's birthday. National holiday, the office is closed. I woke up this morning, thought to myself, can I fly to Miami today? Yeah right, probably not, or should I just go visit my mother. Bingo, you won."

"Silly girl. But I love it." Julianne helped Natalie peel off her scarf, jacket, Uggs, and purple stocking hat Grandma Rose knitted back when Natalie was in middle school. Julianne gave the hat a little hug before taking the entire pile to hang up in the big closet in the laundry room.

"Mom, let's go to a movie today. Then, can we make chili for supper? Like a really big batch? I could put some in freezer bags to take back."

BACK at the house after the show and shopping for the chili fixings, Natalie, perched on her favorite stool chopped onions, celery, and a jalapeno pepper for the pot simmering with the beef on the big gas range. Looking over at her mom stirring the meat she casually began, "Hey remember Blake? My college roommate's brother? Yeah, I liked him a lot more than I liked his sister, but I digress. I literally ran into him in the elevator last week. He works in my building. So we exchanged numbers and later he texted me. Like a bunch of the old group hangs out at this bar for happy hour every Friday. So, I went and wow, guess who shows?"

Julianne walked over to collect the chopped veggies and laughed. "Who shows?"

"Chelsea and Makenzie!"

"No way. You and Chels were best friends all though high school until her dad got transferred your senior year. Didn't they move to Denver? I always thought it was a shame you two lost track of each other."

"Oh, you know, college changes everything. So, she looks really fine and has this buyer job at Macy's downtown for wedding dresses. Anyway, she's loving being back in Chicago. It was like we never disconnected and knowing Blake was totally random . . . they meet at this bar and not really dating . . . just hang out together. Blake was blown away that we knew each other."

"Always a small world. What fun. But how does Makenzie fit in?"

Mak and Blake and me, all of us go back to our freshman year at the U. Blake had the fake I.D., got us booze. I've kept up with Makenzie and we go out once in a while. She does happy hour there, too. Best appetizers in town, which eliminates the need for another meal. So, anyway, this was just a hoot. They all asked about you, sorry about Jock, you know how that goes."

"I would love to see them all again. Especially Chelsea. Her mother and I were friends, too. I wonder how her folks are doing. I used to think you and Blake could have been a couple. He was one good looking guy."

"Still is, we're just buds."

"We took Makenzie with us to St. Barts one year on spring break. Remember? She was so pretty, really a smart young lady, but nice and polite. I never knew her parents but they certainly had done a wonderful job raising her. Jock adored that girl. Yes, it would be fun to see them again."

"Well, Mother, be careful what you ask for? Here's how it all went down. They all remembered you, liked you, and you know, sort of feel bad about Jock and all. Being lonely. I was like telling them how you still loved to cook, how you taught me to make that sauce, how I wanted you to do a cooking school. And well, one thing led to another and now don't lose it but . . ."

"Natalie, what did you do? So help me . . ."

"Ah, come on, it will be fun. We're all coming over Saturday night for a trial run cooking school. Honestly, they really, really want to do this. We all have places of our own and it's such a hassle all this ordering out, take in, and sometimes we need to cook. Like when it snows, everything is closed."

"What in the world would I cook? Three gals who probably eat like you most of the time, three celery sticks and coffee, with one big boy who wants a double burger and fries. Nattie, what have you done to me!"

Laughing, Natalie went to her mother at the stove and draped her arm around her shoulders. "Actually we have the menu all planned. Once we decided on our dish it made us so hungry we walked to Uno's for a deep dish pizza."

"Well, I am curious, but I do have veto power, young lady."

"Can you dig it? We all voted for a homemade chicken potpie."

NATALIE left late Monday afternoon to beat the after holiday traffic into the city. After hitting the toll road and settling into the middle lane, she turned to the Bluetooth and ordered, "Call Adela."

"Hey, kiddo, I saw it was you, how are you?" Adela picked up on the second ring. "Mission accomplished? I thought about you yesterday and I really gave some thought to our Sunday morning chat. Tell me."

"Well, I think I did it." Natalie knew she had crossed the line by interfering between her mother and her mother's best friend but Mother often said, *a person has got to do what a person has to do.* "We're all cooking in the kitchen Saturday night, and I think mom is excited. She was chatting up a storm this morning, planning this, arranging that; even changed the menu, added a salad."

"Oh good God. She thinks you young people live on beer and bagels and will succumb to scurvy or berry-berry or whatever the hell that was without fruit and vegetables."

"Aunt Addie," Natalie hesitated before adding, "I didn't mention you would be there, too."

"You didn't? Oh, boy. What do you think? I mean, we both know she'll smell a rat no matter what. I'm behind this cooking school idea one hundred percent but she's got to want to do it. And I can make it happen with the connections I've got in advertising, plus potential students, graphic designers for recipes, maybe a cookbook, commercial space when the project really takes off."

"Wow! You dream big." Natalie was taken aback. Had she created some kind of a monster by adding Adela into the equation? She had no intention of hurting her mother or putting her into a bad space. But she knew that Adela was the woman to launch this project, make it happen, make it work. "Aunt Addie, we better turn down the volume. First of all, let's get you in the door on Saturday."

"No worries. I'll handle it."

"Promise me you'll handle it with kid gloves? Please?"

CHAPTER NINE

In only four days, they will all be here. Julianne was at the kitchen table surrounded by half a dozen cookbooks, laptop, notebook, pen, and a yellow highlighter. The variations for chicken potpie were countless. If she were to do this right that would mean exactly measuring every ingredient, recording it, noting the order in which it was added, and what action to take with it. For years she cooked like a free spirit at Woodstock. Add a little of this, try this new spice, take a shortcut here, sauté instead of bake, marinate overnight, and then add another clove of garlic. But this was the real deal. These kids would take home her recipe, follow it exactly, and expect a perfect outcome, as well they should.

In spite of these anxious moments, Julianne put down her pen and looked out the window to the snow covered back lawn. She smiled. By tomorrow morning, she would have a rough draft of the recipe done by combining hers with several of these famous chefs.

Okay, that would be Wednesday, Thursday I will shop, Friday take a trial run and make one, and then Saturday is show time. Oh, my, I'm busy. I'm busy all week.

Closing the laptop, Julianne could tell by how hungry she was that it was noon. Meals alone were quick, meager, and usually eaten standing up over the sink staring at nothing out the window. But today she would take the time to prepare a sandwich, maybe grilled with Gruyere cheese, a slice of ham, and cranberry relish. She would bring it here, to the table, sit down, have a glass of milk, read over her notes, and nourish her body. *Is this what recovery feels like?*

The phone rang as Julianne rinsed out the milk glass and stacked it on the drain pad next to the flowered plate she chose to serve her sandwich.

"Oh, hi. I was thinking of you, thought I might give you a call later this afternoon."

"Well, you sound good." Adela sang out. "Might I even venture to say, chipper? What's up?"

"Are you out and about today? Stop over this afternoon for a cup of tea. I think I'll make up a batch of macaroons."

"That, my dear, is precisely why I called. Not about

cookies, but I was hoping to get together. I'm showing some 'tire kickers' two houses at one-thirty, see you four-ish."

The afternoon flew by. A little before four Julianne built a fire in the fieldstone fireplace in the great room, laid out a fresh plate of cookies on the cocktail table in front of the u-shaped burgundy leather couch that faced the cozy blaze, and flicked on the burner under the kettle. Then hurried upstairs to brush her hair, change into a pale blue cashmere sweater, and apply matching eye shadow and soft coral lipstick.

She didn't know how she could have managed these last five months without her friend. Julianne never cultivated a lot of close personal friends. Sure, she and Jock had a wide network of all the "right" acquaintances. Wasn't it strange how few bothered to call after the first couple of weeks following the funeral? Oh, they all sent Christmas cards with sorry little notes but she could bet how many would arrive next year. There hadn't been a holiday invitation in one of them.

But Adela, she was like a rubber band, snapping back faithfully. When Julianne stopped to count the years they had known each other, she was amazed. They'd met at one of those popular nineties' Power Women seminars. A three-day retreat that regaled the emerging female business woman to *think like a man, work like a dog but act like a lady.* And, remembering correctly, they had met in the bar after a laboriously long day, skipped the homework assignment, and sat and drank and talked the night away. Both were single at the time, good looking, and hungry to make money in a man's world. Especially Julianne, she had a young daughter to support.

Adela was funny, smart, brutally ambitious, and wanted you to believe she was tough as nails. Julianne might be one of the few people that knew her sad story, alcoholic parents who drank themselves to death when Adela was seventeen and left on her own. She escaped state custody, rented a room, waitressed at night, slipped in and out of a big Chicago high school and finally graduated. One dead end job after another followed. At age twenty-one, she bought a book all about cocktails, memorized each concoction, then talked her way into a bartending job at a mediocre local lounge. She was brassy, broady, and the guys loved her. One of the "regulars" was a real estate developer who saw her potential. He convinced his girl-friend, who owned a small time real estate agency, to take Adela under her wing. Show a hungry woman the amount of money to be made on a six percent commission on a hundred thousand dollar house and she'll work. So the rest, as they say, is history.

Over the years, their life stories changed. Both became successful. Together they celebrated marriages, suffered through divorces, shared important occasions, cried together at funerals and as strange a partnership that it was, they stayed best friends.

Julianne hurried to answer the doorbell. Adela liked to come to the front door.

"Look at you, girlfriend! All prettied up. Thanks for coming back to us." Adela stomped the snow off her high-heeled boots in the foyer, plopped down on the walnut bench to unzip and pull them off as Julianne held out her arms to receive her best friend's full length mink coat. "You. Look. Wonderful. And it smells wonderful in here. You did make cookies. Wish I could get my clients to understand the remarkable selling feature of smell. And I ain't talking about the damn litter box they can't remember to clean."

Laughing, Julianne took Adela's arm. "Come in, the tea is just about ready, I've laid a fire, we'll snuggle in, and then I'll tell you what my crazy, and somewhat naughty daughter, has cooked up and I mean that quite literally."

There was a Cheshire cat grin on Adela's face as she was ushered into the family room.

CHAPTER TEN

They burst through the door from the garage into the mudroom practically glued together. One minute Julianne stood in her quiet kitchen reading over the recipe for chicken potpie, rechecking the prep dishes, coating the twelve inch skillet with olive oil and the next minute she was surrounded by four beautiful young adults all babbling at once.

Blake was the first to reach her. Tall, surprisingly still tan, and very handsome, he extended his right hand. Julianne grasped it with both of her hands, looked into his clear blue eyes, and greeted him warmly. He responded with a genuine greeting of his own and a thank you for the evening. Much to Julianne's surprise, he pulled his left arm from behind his back and presented her with a bottle of Italian Prosecio. "Mrs. Girard, for the chef, hostess, and mother of one awesome Natalie."

With that, the three girls surrounded Julianne. Kisses and long hugs were exchanged. After Natalie organized coats, scarfs, hats, and gloves over the back of the big sofa in the family room, she went back into the mudroom and carried in the twelve pack of beer. "Mom, don't look so surprised. It's Saturday night."

"Honey," Julianne cut in, "Of course, go over to the bar and bring back the beer mugs. I should have iced them. Then pour away."

"No way." All four seemed to say at once. "We do bottles."

Adela, arriving through the front door, caused pandemonium all over again. It took almost a half hour before all the greetings, catching up, and reminiscing finished. Finally everyone was seated at the counter. Natalie sat in the middle, flanked on either side by Makenzie and Chelsea, in the very seat where the original idea was born. Blake pulled his end stool a little off to the side to see Julianne better and Adela, on the far left, had a Nikon D610 camera ready.

"Okay." Julianne stood behind the Wolf range in the center island, took a deep breath, and continued, "You each have a recipe in front of you to keep. Feel free to follow along or just watch and enjoy the show." Her students smiled and turned to the paper in front of them. "First, we need chicken because after all this is a chicken potpie. By popular request, I might add." Blake let out a cheer and they all laughed, breaking the tension.

With that Julianne relaxed, fell into a groove, and did what she did so well. She cooked.

First they sautéed a large chicken breast in the skillet she had earlier coated with two tablespoons of olive oil before adding a half cup of chicken broth from a box she pulled from the refrigerator. While the breast cooked in the covered pan, Julianne talked about the ingredients that were lined up in front of the cooktop in identical glass bowls.

Within ten minutes, she removed the chicken to a platter next to the range and added another tablespoon of oil to the same skillet. "Now, I'm not sure if the meat is totally done, and I don't really care. After it cools, I will dice it into bite size pieces and remember, it will cook further when the pie goes into the oven."

The pan sizzled as Julianne added a half-cup each of chopped celery and onions, and a teaspoon of salt. "The salt is to make them sweat." Her students liked that phrase. After two or three minutes, the onions were translucent, and the aroma spread up from the stove and over to the audience. They visibly inhaled.

"Time for the other veggies to join the party." Julianne emptied three more glass bowls. "A cup of cut carrots, a cup of frozen peas, and a cup of crisp white cubes."

Julianne laughed as she watched all five look down at the recipe to find out what that was.

"Mom, did you know you left that out?" Natalie asked as she and the others looked at Julianne for the answer.

"It's a surprise." Julianne continued to stir the vegetables with a large wooden spoon. "After we eat our potpie, I have a prize for the one that gives me the correct name of our mystery vegetable."

Adela moved off her stool to snap another picture. Julianne turned to her and through the rising steam said, "Sorry, Addie, you don't get to enter the contest. Just my young students." Adela stuck out her tongue and snapped a close up of her friend's busy face with a tiny line of sweat above her upper lip.

Minutes later the veggies were on another platter. Julianne diced the chicken breast and let it rest on the cutting board before turning her attention to the same skillet. "Now we are going to make a Roux. I heard that." She smiled at Chelsea's remark. "A Roux is the base of any sauce. It thickens and holds it all together, and it is so simple to make." Looking over her row of students she asked, "Makenzie, do you know how to make a Roux? No? Well, you will soon, come over here. You are going to make our gravy, if you want to call it that, and that will be the thick creaminess that binds the pie and gives it the velvety texture."

Makenzie surprised herself and everyone with how easy it was. She put two tablespoons of butter into the empty pan and added two tablespoons of fine flour called Wondra. Just as Julianne instructed, she stirred until it combined as one, then added the cup of chicken broth Julianne poured into a measuring cup for her. Continuing to stir, it was fun to watch it come together and form a thick shiny golden sauce.

"Perfection." Julianne affirmed as Makenzie returned to her seat. Julianne took charge of the skillet again. "Show time. Everybody in," she said, scraping into the skillet the vegetables and chicken, blending it all together with her big wooden spoon.

"Not quite there, is it?" She looked up at the students sitting at the counter. "Everyone here like the smell and taste of Thanksgiving? Yes? Let's put a bit of that into our dinner tonight. I'm adding a teaspoon of sage and a teaspoon of poultry seasoning." Julianne blended the spices into the mixture. The rich bouquet filled the kitchen.

"Lucky me, I'm going to sample." With that, she walked to the silver ware drawer and counted out six spoons. "We can't cook without tasting. But never double dip. Oh, almost forgot, a good dash of salt and a nice grind of pepper, a little stir." Taking a half spoonful she murmured, "Just right. Are you ready?" Holding up a handful of spoons, she signaled for them to come over to the stove.

One by one they dipped into the richness, licked off the goodness, and uttered exclamations of yummy praise.

"The oven is set at 400. Let's find a dish to bake this in, and let's put a lid on it, like a pie crust maybe?"

Earlier in the week, Julianne had decided it would be too much to make a pie crust from scratch. Certainly not for a lot of people but she felt that could turn this project into a major production and she didn't want her young students overwhelmed the first time out.

"Well, thank heavens." Adela exclaimed as Julianne pulled a box of ready-made pastry from the refrigerator. "Rolling out pie dough is not my forte. I've been known to throw the whole mess in the garbage and head to the bakery."

After scooping the potpie filling into an oval La Creuset casserole, Julianne unrolled the pie crust, laid it over the dish, adjusted the size to cover tightly, and demonstrated crimping the edge. Next she sliced through the crust with a paring knife making small slits to vent the steam.

"I've got one more trick up my sleeve." Julianne put a small rubber spatula into a bowl of softened butter and spread it over the crust. "The butter makes it flakey and golden. And to keep with the rich savory flavors, I'm going to shake a bit of thyme and parsley on the butter. Oh, you will see how that adds another layer of flavor to our masterpiece. Into the oven we go."

The class applauded.

"Hey, Blake," Chelsea called as the group left their stools for a break. "I pass on another beer. You guys drink up. I'll drive. I have to get up early tomorrow and drive up to Racine."

"Nothing in Racine but Great America." Blake joked, as he snapped off the caps on three fresh brews. "That's going to be one cold roller coaster ride! I'm pretty sure it's closed for the season."

"Actually, funny man, there is something very special in Racine, my Grandma and her ninetieth birthday party."

"Hey, Addie," Julianne signaled to her friend as she walked to the refrigerator. "Help me put the salad together. I thought we might make it as a class project but I think they need a break." She turned her head to the young adults as they mingled in the family room, watching as Natalie went to the entertainment center to tune in some music.

"Love to, Hon. Yeah, let them be." Adela and Julianne huddled together at the back counter emptying the baggies of sliced red onions, cubed cucumbers, and seeded tomato wedges on top of the torn crisp romaine lettuce that filled the bottom of the big wooden salad bowl. "Beautiful bowl! You have the most gorgeous stuff."

"I love this bowl. It's handmade from bamboo. I bought it at an open market in Los Cabos one year. Jock had a fit.

I had to carry it on the plane and it was too wide to fit in the overhead compartment so I held it on my lap all the way home. He teased me every time I used it."

"Good memory, huh?"

"Yes. There are a lot of good memories. I just don't know what to do with the ones that aren't." Julianne shook her head as if to clear it. "But, right now I've got to throw a quick dressing together. I plan to do a honey mustard combo. Addie, throw those pine nuts on the salad and get ready to toss. The pie will be done in about ten minutes."

Julianne took a plain-Jane pint jar, filled the bottom with two inches of honey, added four tablespoons of coarse ground mustard, a fourth of a cup of extra virgin olive oil, a fourth of a cup of champagne vinegar, a teaspoon of dill weed, salt and pepper. Screwing the top on tightly, she vigorously shook it for several minutes. "Here we go." Julianne poured the thick dressing over the vegetables and Adela tossed it all together.

Adela carried the salad to the oversized round table in the kitchen. Julianne followed with the steaming potpie. The table had been set with care since morning. "Let's eat. Anyone hungry?" Julianne called to her students before she returned to the kitchen to get another pie out of the warming drawer under the cooktop. "Here's my trial run. But let's all have a piece of our creation first and seconds from this one."

After all the ooohs and aaahs the table settled down to enjoy the food. Checking to make sure each of the students had eaten at least two bites, Julianne made the announcement. "The prize, going to the winner of *Name the Mystery Vegetable*, is that wonderful bottle of Italian Olive Oil all wrapped up over on the buffet. I'll start with you, Blake, name that veggie."

"Mrs. Girard, you're a real nice lady and all but you're just trying to fool us." Blake picked a small white square off his plate and held it up on the tip of his fork. "This ain't nothing but a potato." The crowd booed.

"Cute, but oh so wrong. Makenzie?"

"I win. I know it. My mother loves Mexican, we have it all the time. It's a jicama."

"Sorry sweetie. Chelsea?"

"I won't complain because it really tastes okay but I usually can't stand any kind of squash. Right? It's a squash piece." Chelsea said, looking closely at her plate.

"Oh dear. No. One last chance. Natalie? Surely you will know."

"I know. I know a parsnip when I see one. Good try Mom, to fool me."

"But I did!"

Adela couldn't keep quiet. "The prize is mine. After all I wasn't allowed to play."

"And, in about a million years you wouldn't know a

turnip if it bit you, girlfriend." Julianne laughed. "Yes, it's a delicious turnip. Taste it again. The baking process has turned it sweet. It adds such a richness to our dish."

A good hour passed and still no one wanted to end the evening. Everyone was enjoying the food and each other too much. Natalie, seated next to Julianne, reached over, took her mother's hand, and squeezed it tight. "It was a great success."

Adela winked at her from across the table. "We told you so."

CHAPTER ELEVEN

It seemed to happen all at once. Or, if she thought about it, maybe it was timing. Jock always said timing was everything. There was no doubt the weather played a huge part in it all. Day after day of dark skies, sleet turning to snow, temperatures below zero for weeks at a time, it all made for a lonely depressing month.

"Will January ever end?" Julianne lamented to Adela. They were having lunch at McDonalds of all places. Adela had only forty minutes between appointments and Julianne said she didn't care, she had to get out of the house before she went crazy.

"And, then what? February. Like that's an improvement?" Adela said as she picked up the hamburger patty and discarded the bun. Noticing the queer look Julianne gave her, she chanted, "Carbs, carbs are the enemy."

Picking at her salad, Julianne said, "I've got to get back to the gym. I'm starting to go flabby. I'm bored. I should have learned how to play bridge. Those women always have something to do. Books. I've read a zillion books. Movies. I figured out how to do Netflix." With a sad look on her face, she peered out the window at the brown dirty snow in the parking lot. "Natalie wants me to come into the city Friday. Do dinner. Spend the night. I guess I might as well."

"Do it. And, hold on a minute." Adela picked up the briefcase she used as a purse and rifled through it. Finding what she was looking for, she handed a manila envelope across the table to Julianne. "Might want to take a look at these and then give them to Nattie. She and I are working on this project together. These are my preliminary ideas for a small ad in the Oak Grove Voice."

"What project?"

"Open it up. Take a look. I think you'll get the gist of it." Adela ate three French fries before she threw the carton into the sack with the other garbage. Wiping her mouth and reaching for lipstick, she studied her friend's face as Julianne unsealed the envelope and took out several papers with rough sketches of a woman cooking and verbiage explaining the benefits of a small private cooking class.

Dumbfounded, Julianne shook her head no and stared

across the table at Adela with her mouth open but unable to speak.

Adela sighed, "Oh, come on. Don't be like that."

DRIVING home, Julianne fumed and ranted in her head. *How dare they? Who do they think they are? Who do they think I am? Some fool. Some down in the dumps old lady with no life.*

Walking into the kitchen, she threw the packet toward the kitchen desk and smirked when it slid off onto the desk chair. "Next stop will be the trash can, Buddy."

Unable to quit pacing, she walked into Jock's office where her anger exploded. "You son of a bitch. You up and die on me. Leave me holding the bag." Julianne walked around his desk, plopped down in his chair, and yanked open the right top drawer. She pulled out a file, flung it open. "Where is that damn paragraph?"

Flipping through the pages of The Last Will and Testament of Jock S. Girard, she found what she was looking for and preceded to read out loud. "As soon as practical after my death, my Executor shall set aside from the assets of my estate the sum of $750,000. Said sum will be delivered to People's Place Bank and deposited into the previously established Blind Trust account. The appointed trustee will manage the fund in a manner appropriate to the trust fund's specifications."

Julianne pounded her fist on the desktop. "That's a lot of damn money, Jock. Who the hell is getting it?" Round and round she had gone with her attorney. Todd Kaplan had investigated all possible paths to assure Julianne that there wasn't anything to do about this last will created by Jock's other lawyer two years ago. It superseded the work Kaplan had done for the Girards when they were first married.

"Will I never know?" In disgust, Julianne jammed the document back into the drawer.

She turned to the stack of mail that sat neglected on the other side of the wide desk. Some days she found dealing with all this paperwork overwhelming so she would throw it on Jock's desk and bury her head in a book or rent a movie. Today's foul mood gave her the impetus to rip through the pile and deal with the trash she was forced to face. One by one Julianne slit open the envelopes, putting the unfolded bills with their return envelopes to the side.

"Oh, shit, a property tax bill that's due. Oh my. This is due in ten days and it's way more than last year. Welcome to Illinois."

Two hours later, she ran a tab on the outstanding bills. Not only did she calculate the usual household expenses, mortgage payment, car lease, utility bills, and insurance but also a statement from the IRS regarding a first quarter

payment now due. That statement blind-sided her equi-
librium. "I cannot keep this up. I'll be out of money. I
have to sell this house. I have to get a job."

Too stunned, numb, and heartbroken to go on, Julianne
folded her arms on the desk, laid her head down and
sobbed, howled and cursed her dead husband.

"I don't see how five strangers sitting in my kitchen one
night a week for a month solves any of my financial problems," Julianne lamented over the telephone to Adela the
next day. "Yes, I could use extra income, and I won't put
the house on the market until spring, just like you advised,
but . . ."

"It's a start, honey. That's what this is. You're too young
to not get out and do something. Being at home and married, that's a horse of a different color. Jock was retired and
the two of you were on the go, out and about. But single?
Let me tell you, those walls will close in pretty darn soon."

"So you and my daughter think what?" Julianne asked,
trying her best to be civil.

"Gourmet is back. Cooking is in. Designer kitchens are
the selling hot button. But most people don't have a clue
what to do with those big red knobs and convection settings. Listen, I can line up, by this time tomorrow, five

ready and able students for your first class. I promise
not one of them will be a serial killer. Let me make an
announcement at Rotary tomorrow morning. We're all
business people with all kinds of contacts." With that sales
pitch, Adela quit talking, knowing the first one to speak
again concedes.

The pause was long and painful.

"Okay. I'll try one session," Julianne responded with a
rueful laugh. "Then I'll probably not only have to sell my
house but leave town, too."

THE next morning Julianne awoke with a renewed sense of
purpose. At first, she was confused. *Why do I feel like this?*

"Oh, yeah, now I remember."

It took those first minutes of waking for Julianne to
grasp it all. Indeed, she had said yes to the ongoing bad-
gering from her daughter and best friend. And now, she
mused, there was nothing to do but do it.

What happened next surprised her even more. She
bounded out of bed, grabbed her favorite chenille robe,
headed down stairs, ground the coffee beans, flipped the
switch, dove into her desk, found a new legal pad, a roller-
ball pen, and a seat at the counter. "All right. This is where
one of my students will sit. Let me get the perspective."

Draining her first cup of coffee, feeling the morning sun creep through the kitchen windows to warm her back, Julianne took charge of her cooking class. The old business muscle memory kicked in. Her inborn commitment to succeed, to do a job and do it right, be the best or one of them, surged through her once again.

Without hesitation, at the top of the yellow page, she named her school. Simple, clean, clear and to the point. *The Kitchen.*

Next, she wrote a mission statement.

> Cooking is an art. It can be as unassuming as stick people or as complicated as a Monet. The artist chooses his paint and brushes. The cook chooses his ingredients and utensils. With careful strokes and prudent blending, each creates their own masterpiece. *The Kitchen* will aid the novice and the advanced with tips, techniques, recipes, and fun. The results will be deep flavors, delicious food, all of which makes a meal satisfying and pleasing for family and friends.

On the second page of the legal pad, she outlined the school's curriculum. She knew immediately how she would conduct the classes. *Keep it simple, stupid. Words to live by when one is starting out.* Yes, it became clear that limiting the class to beginners, at least for now, would simplify matters, not only for the students but for her. Granted, she didn't want somebody who couldn't boil water. What she visualized were five students, probably women, who had cooked the basics but were unsatisfied with the results.

That's it. I've got it. Julianne scribbled her thoughts as fast as she could get them down. *Four week's session, one night a week, Thursday, three hours, one complete meal, three courses. I can do this!*

Julianne flipped to the next page. Menus, meal planning, she loved it all. An idea came to her in a flash. The first class would be a complete dinner, start to finish, and each item consisting of only three ingredients. A meal fit to serve to a family or even a small dinner party. *Appetizer, main course with a protein, starch, vegetable, (maybe a salad), and, of course, dessert.* Ideas flew on the page. Food she had been cooking for years. Fast fun food that never failed and always amazed her guests as to how easy it was to put together.

Week two and three could be classes with more technique, different spices, and advanced recipes. The fourth week might be fun to call *the student's choice*, with each student requesting a recipe, one they wanted to master. Class participation would be essential and fun. Julianne visualized one or two women prepping at the long back counter, another sautéing at the range, others by the big farm sink rinsing and trimming vegetables for a salad or soup.

"This could work. I could do this." She smiled. "I'm excited. Oh, my, I'm actually excited!" Julianne flipped through the pages filled with ideas, foods, and notes. It was then she realized she needed to call Kaplan. Surely, additional insurance would be needed. Probably some sort of disclaimer form for everyone to sign. A business license? She added his name and Adela's on the 'To Do' page. Wondering if Adela had found any students, another random idea flew into her head. Ah, what to charge? I'm a ninny. I'm not doing this for my health."

After calculating figures on another page, Julianne decided to charge fifty dollars per student, per session, but they would have to commit to all four weeks. February, yes, she would start her class the first Thursday in February and since this was mid-January she might as well kick it all in gear in the next two weeks. Next she called and made appointments with her attorney and with her friend for later that morning.

Quite pleased with herself, Julianne ran upstairs to shower and dress. Carefully, she applied makeup, brushed her dark shoulder length hair back off her face, and sprayed a conservative spritz of Chanel cologne. Next she chose a calf length camel colored wool pencil skirt, black cashmere turtleneck, knee high black leather boots with a three inch heel, wrapped a Hermes scarf twice around her neck, added thick gold hoop earrings, and decided she looked like a woman who means business.

"REALLY? McDonald's again?" Julianne exclaimed as she and Adela exchanged a quick hug in the parking lot. "Next time you move your office will you try to have a nice restaurant next to it."

"I know it's too close, too handy. Thanks for under-standing."

Minutes later, seated in a quiet booth, prying open the lids of their southwest chicken salads, Adela looked over at her friend. "You are fired up. When you called this morn-ing, I could hear it in your voice. And now. Look at you. Tell me everything. Then, I have some neat news for you."

The meeting with Todd Kaplan had gone well. Julianne filled in and hit the high spots for Adela. The attorney was excited for Julianne's prospect for a new adventure. His advice was to get through the first school and imply it was a group of friends doing dinner one night a week. If she proceeded and turned this into a full time, professional endeavor, then the need for business licenses, food handler license, additional liability insurance, and probably setting up an LLC would all have to be considered.

Adela knew all this but moved her head up and down as she steadily ate bite after bite of salad. Every so often, she would grunt or raise an eyebrow to signal her surprise and approval. It was great fun to see Julianne so animated and excited. When Julianne laid the yellow legal pad in the center of the table and paged through her notes, Adela was more than impressed. "Look at this. You've been busy. Wow. Menus, shopping lists and a mission statement! Girlfriend, you are good to go. And your first student will fit in perfectly. Listen."

"That's why I'm here. Any leads? Did you make an announcement at Rotary?" Julianne asked, taking her first bite.

"Yes. And it's never the people you might think would be interested. Do you know Carolyn Deaver? Probably heard of her? Well, she is the principal of Oak Grove Elementary. Has been for decades and has been a Rotarian as long. Great gal. Single for years. Has a beautiful home on Oliver Court. Loves people, loves to entertain, well-traveled. But, as she told me after the meeting, she plans to retire and has never been a cook. For a dinner party she calls a caterer and most days does deli foods."

"Like someone sitting at this table?" Julianne interrupted.

"Yeah, well, I'm busy. But, this is too perfect. As she said, now she'll have time to cook but needs easy recipes.

'Starting simple but good enough to serve as a small dinner party' . . . right here, in your notes, says it all. Carolyn would fit right in. I'll give her a call. February is right around the corner. Shall I tell her to save the dates?"

"Oh, Addie dear. I have four other stools to fill."

"No worries. Build it and they will come."

The rest of the noon meal was filled with plans and laughter. Julianne beamed with excitement as the momentum for the cooking class grew. Adela assured her over and over that a little advertisement in the community newspaper and word of mouth would fill those other stools in no time.

The women were in the parking lot saying good-bye when Adela called out after Julianne. "Price? What is the cost? Four weeks, one night a week? Right?"

Instead of getting into her car, Julianne closed the door of the silver Mercedes and walked back to Adela. "I've been struggling with that. I think I've decided on forty dollars a session. At first I wanted fifty but now I'm down to forty."

"No way. That's too cheap. Take it from me." Thinking it through, Adela looked skyward. "Seventy-five sounds better. People want to think this will be an exclusive experience."

"Do you really think so?"

"Honey, this is Oak Grove. Nobody moved here because it was cheap. We like to pay more," Adela said, laughing."

Just as Julianne fastened her seat belt, her cell phone buzzed. Grabbing it from the center console, she saw it was an email from Natalie. Keeping the car in park, Julianne opened the message.

> Hey Mom, got a student for you. Blake's aunt.
> LOL, Blake made the potpie for his mom & aunt.
> He said they were like so impressed. His mom is a
> good cook but not Aunt Libby. She's totally stoked
> about your class. Blake will get me her # or email
> Hold a seat at the counter!

All the way home Julianne smiled. At a rather long stop light, she laughed out loud. This wasn't how she envisioned her life but maybe it wasn't too bad.

CHAPTER TWELVE

Four days later, Julianne's enthusiasm waned. Only one student had made a solid commitment to *The Kitchen*. Carolyn Deaver called the same day Adela and Julianne met. She was just as pleasant and charming as Adela described. If all the students were as amiable, the cooking classes would be a success.

Surprisingly, Blake's Aunt Libby called, wanting to know if the schedule were flexible. Wednesdays would work better. Would the food be gluten free? If she couldn't find a sitter for her ten-year-old son, because her husband just wasn't dependable, could she bring little Timmy along? Being as diplomatic as possible, Julianne said a polite no to all of her questions and hung up.

Hopefully, things would turn around. Adela planned to put a small tasteful ad in the Oak Grove Voice. She had been too busy to let Julianne proof it but what else was new. An ad could generate some response.

Yesterday, while shopping at Angelo's market, the small high-end neighborhood gourmet store she frequented often, she ran into Angelo who kindly asked how she was doing. Julianne shared her hopes for a culinary class in her home, admitting she needed to fill the lonely days and the big house. The Italian grocer was very fond of Julianne. On more than one occasion, he had whispered seductively into her ear. "If I were twenty years younger I would give that Jock of yours a run for his money and his wife."

After listening intently to his favorite customer, he gazed into her sad brown eyes, moved closer to her, put a big wrinkled hand on her arm, and said he knew a guy. This man, he said, needed to learn to do a little cooking. Maybe he would have him call.

As touched as Julianne was by Angelo's compassion, she had no intention of her class being a "boys' night out." But Angelo knew everyone in the Village who was a foodie or wanted to be. Maybe he'd produce a good student or two. She'd like her kitchen filled with housewives, young mothers or retired women like Carolyn.

There was nothing to do now but wait, keep busy planning the lessons, and think positive about what might come along. Julianne tried not to give in to dark thoughts about the whole business.

What the hell have I gotten myself into!

THE afternoon wore on. By dusk Julianne realized she needed to turn on some lights to continue paging through cookbooks and taking notes on recipes.

As she headed for the bank of light switches, the telephone rang. Startled, she grabbed the receiver and barked. "Hello."

"My realtor gave me this number. Are you Julianne Girard?"

"Oh yes, I am. And you're probably calling about the culinary classes."

"That's right. Well, my name is Willow LeClair. I certainly don't know a lot about cooking but Adela, you know her, right? She said, well, she just went on and on about you and how great . . ."

"That would be Adela," Julianne interrupted. "Willow, what a lovely name, are you interested in learning more about food preparation?"

"I was transferred here from Minneapolis, bought a condo from Adela, closed last month, and I don't know anyone too well. I'm single. I don't do a lot of cooking. But I thought if I could fix a nice dinner, I could invite people over which would be a good way to get to know people. Sharing a meal is enjoyable. I'm sorry, I don't mean to be rude, but is this complicated stuff?"

"Let me explain the four classes. First, the classes are scheduled for Thursday nights, six to nine. Does that work for you?"

After Julianne described the basic outline of the four-week course, she not only had sold Willow LeClair on the school but had reinvigorated herself.

"Please count me in. That is if I'm not too late and you are already full."

"No, Willow, there is room for you. Now please give me your email address and I will be in touch with all the information and directions you need."

"I am thrilled. Thank you, Mrs. Girard."

"Just Julianne, please."

JULIANNE dozed on the couch in a nest of throw pillows, wrapped in a cozy afghan her mother had made years ago as the ten o'clock news was ending. When the phone rang, the answering machine was about to kick in before Julianne made it to her desk to pick up on the sixth ring.

The voice on the other end jumped right in babbling as Julianne attempted a normal hello. "Libby Ellis here again. I know it's late. We talked earlier today. Well, to make a long story short, I'm going to enroll in the cooking school after all. My husband will help out with Timmy and my nephew, Blake, said he'd babysit if I needed him. So, when again, do we start?"

Shaking her head, attempting to clear out the cobwebs, Julianne said slowly. "Well, Libby. Thank you for calling back. I remember us talking this afternoon. But what about the gluten issue? And the Thursday night conflicts?"

"No problem. All worked out and a little gluten never hurt anyone. Well, only three percent of the population or so I've read."

The two women talked for another fifteen minutes while Julianne took Libby's pertinent information and continued to answer a string of silly questions.

Turning out all but one small kitchen light, Julianne made her way through the house and up the stairs to bed. Climbing the back staircase, she grinned. *I guess I can sleep tonight. Three students. Not quite what I hoped for but I'm over half full. Two more to go. Twelve days to show time. It's all good . . . I think.*

It wasn't like Angelo to make house calls anymore. Back in the day, decades ago, when he opened his grocery store, he delivered groceries several times a week. People called in their order during store hours. When he found the time during the day, he gathered and bagged the food. At six o'clock he closed the store, loaded his old Chevy station wagon, and made the deliveries until every order was filled. Personable, he spent a few extra minutes with each customer. Now that his nephews ran the business, and much to Angelo's chagrin, they pared down the inventory to elite gourmet shelf goods, copious choices of hot and cold deli items, fine wines and craft beers, a state-of-the-art meat and seafood counter, and installed those inane computers everywhere.

Fortunately, the eighty-year old bachelor still had his name on the deed and the door. Sitting home was not an option. Angelo went to his store every day to mingle with the customers, keep a bead on quality control, and never failed to give plenty of business advice to his whipper-snapper nephews, now almost into their fifties.

But today he was ringing a doorbell again.

"Angelo, what in the world are you doing here? Come in out of the cold wind."

"Please, Mrs. Julianne, I am so sorry to bother you." Angelo quickly stepped inside so Julianne could close the frost-covered door behind him. Before he said another word, he snatched his wool plaid Yukon cap off his head and held it nervously in his hands. "I call. But, you see, I didn't know the phone number and there are no more phone books in my own store anymore. Everybody say I should Google it. Not for me. But I know where you live."

"Yes, you do indeed. All the special deliveries you made at the holidays, those wonderful fruit baskets for your favorite customers. Jock and I loved that."

"I miss your Jock every day. But I have come on a mission."

"Angelo, a cup of coffee, tea? Oh yes," Julianne teased, "I remember, you and Jock sneaking into his office for a shot of his special bourbon."

"Indeed! Christmas cheer. But I need for you to take this paper." Angelo pulled a crumpled yellow sheet from his coat pocket. "This man. He is so nice. So sad. He lost his wife to cancer, now there is more trouble, his daughter divorced. She works lots of nights as a nurse and Rob, his name, takes care of the children. They grow like a weed, these grandchildren. Rob, he needs to feed them. All the time he is shopping in the store. Frozen pizza. Lunchmeat. Broasted chickens. It's all good at my store, but I tell him, cook, you need to learn to cook and that's even better."

Julianne unfolded the note. The name Rob Murphy and seven numbers, all run together with no hyphen, were carefully printed out in heavy block letters. "You want me to call him?"

"Yes. Yes. He knows all about you. I told him. Please do this for my friend who needs to come to your cooking school." Angelo sheepishly looked down at his boots. "Besides, he should meet a pretty lady like you."

Closing the door behind her unexpected visitor, Julianne sighed then groaned as she watched the old grocer shuffling down the front walk. "Oh shoot. I don't know what to do. Angelo!"

Knowing she could never face her old friend again if she didn't at least pick up the phone and try, Julianne went to the kitchen and stared at the telephone. *I'll bet he has railroaded that poor guy and badgered him until he can't say no. And made it sound like a blind date! That old fool.*

Get it over with. Quickly she dialed the number.

"Robert Murphy here."

No hello! Julianne forced a calm greeting. "Yes, hello. This is Julianne Girard. Angelo, at the market, gave me your number and asked me to give you a call."

Silence.

"So I am. And, well, I couldn't disappoint my old friend so I am, well, I am calling and thought if you wanted any further information on *The Kitchen* I would be more than happy to answer any questions."

Silence.

"Hello. Are you still there?'

"Yes, but I'm trying to place you. Do I know you? And that Angelo you mentioned. Is he the guy at the grocery store over on Cardinal and 5th?"

"No. You don't know me. And I am referring to that Angelo. You know what? This is all a big misunderstanding. I am so sorry to bother you. And quite frankly, I'm more than a little embarrassed."

"Oh, please, don't be. You have a nice voice. I'm not busy right now so tell me all about what you do. I gather you design kitchens? Angelo thinks I need a new kitchen?"

Julianne surprised herself. She was a bit taken aback by Robert Murphy's deep voice and the whispery edge of his words. She found she had to swallow before she could go on. "No, I'm starting a cooking school in my home. Just a few students. My friends and daughter think I'm a lonely widow withering away. It's a small evening class, starting the first Thursday in February, and, oh, well." Julianne couldn't figure out what was wrong with her. "I guess it's not turning out like I thought. So sorry to bother you." Julianne was appalled. What more was she going to rattle on about? "I'll let you go, have a nice day."

"No. Don't hang up. I get it and I sort of remember. That old geezer at the store bent my ear all about your cooking school but I really didn't pay attention. Except, as I recall, he did say you were good looking. So, you called me because the old man thinks I should go to cooking school? And you need students? Wow. Will I get a degree, a diploma?"

Not in any mood to be teased or humiliated and now quite uncomfortable, Julianne just wanted to end this conversation and find a hole or a book or a movie to crawl into. "Thank you. Bye . . ."

"Wait. Tell me about this *Kitchen*. Really, I do a lot of cooking for a guy who supposedly lives all alone. It's for my grandkids. I love them to pieces but I'm doing a whole lot more lookin' after them than I ever thought I would."

Most of this information Angelo had given Julianne but she didn't want to interrupt or let on.

So, go ahead. Should a guy like me go to this?"

"Mr. Murphy . . ."

"Sweet Jesus, don't call me that. Rob, I'm Rob. You're Julie?"

"Julianne. And if a guy like you wanted to learn a few basics, learn to cook simple foods, put together a nice meal, then maybe, a guy like you, might want to come to these classes." Good Grief! Now was she flirting?

"Well now, when you put it like that. How do I enroll?"

Switching gears again, Julianne smiled, turned on her business voice, and explained the particulars of the classes. Several minutes later Rob Murphy said, "What the hell. I'll be there. Julianne. I don't have the kids on Thursdays."

Numb was the word that came to Julianne when she finally hung up. Her hand was stiff from clenching the phone and her right ear lobe burned. As she rose to get a glass of water, the phone rang again.

"Rob Murphy here. Quick question, Teach. Do I bring my own apron?"

Julianne giggled. "No, Rob Murphy. You do not need an apron."

"Okay, then." With a sexy twinge in his voice, he joked, "How about a bottle of wine?"

CHAPTER THIRTEEN

"It's show time. Today's the day." Adela burst through the front door. "Julianne, where are you?"

"In the kitchen, where else!"

"Hi, honey." Adela walked over to Julianne as she worked behind the big Wolf range positioning skillets and fussing with utensils. Adela gave her friend a big hug. "Nervous?"

"Of course not. I always invite total strangers into my home, perch them on a stool, cook for them, boss them about, and charge money for the pleasure of it all."

"Now, now. Just opening night nerves. Look at these." Adela pointed to a bulging folder on the counter. "I had my P.R. girl do these. I think they look great. Really professional." As Julianne had planned, the first class would feature simple classics, each item only three key ingredients. Adela pulled out a tri-folded menu with the recipes, complete with clever illustrations, and the back page featuring a shopping list.

"Really? This is great." Julianne scanned the brochure, a smile spreading across her face. "I'm feeling better already. Keep track of your expenses and I'll pay you later."

"No. I feel bad we couldn't fill the class. I still can't believe that ad in our little rag, Village Voice, didn't pull anyone. Well, at least anyone worthwhile. The crack-pots that called you! Who knew?"

"Actually, it was just a couple of strange calls. But, you know, Adela, there was someone who still has me perturbed. This woman sounded okay, a little off maybe, but she asked the strangest questions. Didn't commit but wanted the address, times, and now that I think about it, seemed more interested in me than the cooking part of the classes."

"Listen, I've been selling real estate longer than I want to remember and people never cease to amaze me. Some days I feel like I'm on another planet working with aliens." Adela smiled, adding with encouragement. "So, four students?"

"Doesn't that seem lame? Should I take a stool away from the counter?" Julianne walked over to the island and stood behind the end stool. "But then, what if that woman does show up? I wouldn't want anyone to feel . . ."

"Leave it. Life is full of no-shows. The others won't give it a thought." Adela buttoned up her navy pea coat, kissed

Julianne on the cheek, and headed for the door. "Call me the minute everyone leaves. I'll be waiting for the big success story."

An hour later Julianne headed upstairs to change. She chose gray wool flannel slacks, a Ralph Lauren white cotton oxford shirt, Kate Spade black ballet flats, and pulled a narrow black belt through the loops on her pants. Standing in front of her well-lit make-up mirror, she decided to keep the cosmetics and jewelry to a minimum and her hair pulled up in a high ponytail. She put on her mother's pearl stud earrings for luck. Standing back and surveying the results, she managed a half smile in the mirror.

As Julianne was about to turn off the lights to head back downstairs, the flash of diamonds on her left hand caught her eye. The decision was instant. Walking over to the vanity table on the far wall, she flipped open the jewelry box and tossed in the double wedding bands. "Jock, God knows you always did what you wanted. Well, now it's my turn."

THE doorbell rang at 5:40. Two women stood chatting on the wide front porch.

"Hello. Welcome and come in. I'm Julianne Girard."

After stepping across the threshold, the older of the two

gently grasped Julianne's hand. "Oh what a pleasure. I'm Carolyn Deaver." Looking down the foyer and off into the lit spacious rooms she exclaimed. "Lovely home. Won't this be fun."

Julianne felt the genuine warmth in Carolyn's voice. *This is a very nice lady.*

"Willow LeClair." The tall thin woman firmly shook Julianne's hand. "We spoke on the phone and now it is my pleasure to meet you."

"And my pleasure, also." Julianne didn't want to stare but what a provocative, stylish, person this was. Jet-black hair, razor cut in the ultra short trendy punk style, one side amazingly shorter than the other and bangs covering her eyebrows. Her heavily blackened eyes were set off by the almost white lipstick. She was stunning in a way that wasn't beautiful but exotic and striking.

The two women followed Julianne into the formal living room to leave their coats and bags. Carolyn continued to chat about the weather and whatever else as Willow took off her full length black leather coat, laid it smartly over the back of a club chair, along with a Gucci handbag. Fussing with her black turtleneck sweater and black designer jeans, she said nothing while taking in the furnishings and artwork.

Conversely, everything about Carolyn was shop-worn but neat, tidy, and well taken care of. As a sixty-five-year-old woman who had spent a lifetime in the education field, this was a person who knew the value of setting a good example. From her tight curled salt and pepper hair, tweed jacket and skirt, chunky leather pumps, and softly wrinkled face, Carolyn's personality was evident. What you saw was what you got.

Julianne pointed the women in the direction of the kitchen as the doorbell chimed again. She rushed to open the wide glass door. "Libby?"

"Oh, I tell you. Getting out of that house tonight was a chore. My Timmy wouldn't eat a thing and my nephew Blake was supposed to be there to babysit at five-thirty. He was late . . ."

Of course this is Libby. She dressed like she talked. Her faded black yoga pants had a small rip in the knee and an oversized Cubs sweatshirt hung out of her unzipped puffy hot pink down jacket.

"Please come in." Julianne closed the door behind the chatting Libby but not before noticing a new and very big silver pick-up truck pull in along the curb across the street. *I bet that's the guy.*

"You don't mind if I take these off?" Libby grunted, blocking the doorway, squatting and pulling off well-worn dirty UGG boots, revealing a man's pair of gray thermal socks.

"No, just be comfortable," grimaced Julianne. Once again she escorted her student to the living room and then

127

to the kitchen where Carolyn and Willow were politely standing. Julianne introduced the women to each other. "Please, have a seat. Tonight's menu and recipes are in front of you. And there's the bell again. I'll be right back."

It was exactly six o'clock.

"Oh!" Julianne jumped back. A six-foot tall man had one arm resting on the door frame and the other holding a bouquet of wooden spoons of various sizes and tied with butcher's string. Rob Murphy grinned down at her.

Caught off guard by how close he was standing didn't deter Julianne from assessing his appearance. He was good looking in that way an aging fifty plus ex-athlete looks, tight body gone a bit soft, rounded full shoulders, a few facial scars, and a short spiked haircut.

"Okay, let me take a guess, you are Rob Murphy?"

"Yes. And you would be Jul-lee-ann." Rob handed her the bouquet, his hazel eyes twinkling. "For the chef." He made no attempt to move back into a more comfortable zone. The expression on his face conveyed his appreciation for the woman he was looking at. Julianne laughed and grabbed the arrangement with two hands before it fell apart.

Smiling, she stood aside to allow Rob to step into the foyer. "Nice digs. But this is the high rent district. Not my usual classroom situation. So, what's next, Teach?" Rob asked, looking around playfully.

"Let me take your jacket. Just follow the hallway to the kitchen where the other students are. I'll be right along."

Rob pulled himself out of a well-aged navy blue leather letter jacket embossed with the bright orange letter "I" on the left shoulder.

"Handle with care. She's been everywhere and knows all my life secrets." Rob joked, turning to toward the chatter of women's voices. Julianne smiled watching his back, noticing that his sport shirt and jeans were neatly pressed and his brown loafers highly polished.

The letter jacket was warm, heavy, and smelled like winter, expensive aftershave, and cigars. Julianne laid it over the back of the couch before hurrying to the kitchen, shaking off a peculiar feeling of excitement she hadn't felt in a long time.

Taking her position behind the cooktop, Julianne began. "It's 6:05. I think we should start as I'm not sure of the fifth student." Julianne looked at the Elgin clock on the far wall.

"I hope you've had a chance to look over tonight's menu, our simply made cuisine. You will be surprised to see what delicious food we can craft out of just three ingredients." Julianne was pleased watching her students nod approvingly while reading the menus.

"But first, let's take a minute to get to know one another." One by one, Julianne looked into each face. "After all we're going to spend the next four Thursday evenings together. I'll start to break the ice. I'm Julianne. No, not a professional chef but I do love to cook. I won't bore you with a list of the culinary classes and cooking schools I've enjoyed over the years at some pretty wonderful locations with remarkable foods. I've never taught before, but . . ."

The doorbell rang. Once, then once again. The fifth student had arrived.

WITHOUT giving Julianne a chance to say hello, the woman on the other side of Julianne's front door blurted out, "I'm late. It's this new car or truck or whatever they call these big things." The woman pointed to the end of the driveway and shook her finger at a Range Rover. "The GPS. I can't figure it out."

"Not to worry. We just started. You're definitely at the right address. I'm Julianne Girard."

"The Kitchen, the cooking classes?"

"Yes, come in." Julianne invited the woman into the foyer and closed and locked the door behind her. "You called? Several times? I don't think I got your name?"

"Oh, sorry. I'm Marta."

"Marta . . .?"

When it was clear that Marta had nothing more to add to her first name, Julianne continued. "Let's get to the kitchen. May I take your coat, I mean cloak? What a beautiful garment." Marta untied the neck of her calf length deep burgundy wool cloak to reveal the entire cape was lined with mink. "It was my Busia's. My mother brought it to America."

"I would like to hear that whole story. But for now, let's go cook."

"Here's Marta." Julianne announced, pulling out the end empty stool for the last student and watched as Marta lifted herself up and settled a brocade paisley ankle length skirt around her legs. It was difficult for Julianne to pin an age on Marta. Her blonde shoulder length thick hair was threaded with grey. She was slender, fine boned, with a lovely complexion. Her neck and the wrinkles around her eyes spoke to a fortyish woman.

"Marta, this is Carolyn next to you, then Libby, that would be Willow, and how lucky for us to have a man among us. He's Rob."

They greeted the fifth student by nodding and saying, "Hello."

Julianne again moved to the range and stretching either arm along its side took charge. "We know each other's names. Instead of re-introducing ourselves, how about each of us giving a brief reason or two as to why you chose to be here and what you need from *The Kitchen*. As I mentioned, I'm here because I love to cook, entertain, and try new foods and recipes. And, because it's cold dark February, I'm sick of winter and we all need an adventure." Her students laughingly agreed.

"Rob, you're at the end. Go first. Then we'll move down the row."

"It's pretty simple I can't believe I'm here!" Rob chuckled, then looked over to Julianne wistfully. "Seriously, I'm alone and I do a lot of caregiving to my ten and eight year old grandkids, mostly in the evening. They need to eat dinner."

As Julianne studied Rob, she felt a twinge of empathy, making a mental note to make sure her future recipes were "kid friendly."

Willow spoke next. "I recently transferred here with a promotion to chief administrative officer at Bates-Morgan. Dinner parties would enhance my personal resume and achieve a cohesive atmosphere with my peers."

With effort, Julianne took her eyes off Willow's extraordinary hammered silver cuff bracelet with matching wide band on her index finger. Fascinated with Willow's jewelry, she didn't pay attention to her speaking. *What did she say?*

"My turn?" Libby turned to her left and shouted toward Willow. "Okay then. My Timmy is such a fussy eater. At first, we thought food allergies, then lactose intolerant, maybe a touch of IBS. My husband says it's my cooking. He's allergic to my cooking. So here I am!"

Carolyn suppressed a laugh before she began. "I'm now a new retiree. And I'm going to do all sorts of things I never had time for before. I heard about these classes and said, let's do it. Let's cook."

Marta's cobalt blue eyes were orbs of glacier ice. She stared directly at Julianne as she spoke. "I saw the ad in the paper. I was curious."

CHAPTER FOURTEEN

The appetizer was a huge success. The Swiss Baked Onion Dip surprised everyone with the easy and simple steps. Julianne filled a one-cup measuring cup with a chopped sweet onion, then emptied it into an ovenproof dish. Opening a package of pre-shredded Swiss cheese, she used the same one-cup measuring cup, filled it with the cheese, and added it to the casserole dish. From the refrigerator, she brought back a jar of mayonnaise, explaining to her rapt audience that this was the emulsifier that would hold it all together. With a rubber spatula, Julianne spooned the mayo into the measuring cup, leveled off the top, and scraped it into the bowl. Folding it together carefully, and explaining that it needed to bake at 350 degrees for fifteen minutes, Julianne walked to the double ovens to slide the dish into the pre-heated bottom one.

As with all the recipes tonight, Julianne had prepared one in advance and it was resting in the warming drawer ready to demonstrate the finished product. Smiling, she looked at her students, "Why should we wait? I've always liked instant gratification." With that, Julianne retrieved a tray from the back counter filled with small plates, a basket of water crackers, and cocktail size napkins. Placing the baked dip on a trivet in the center of the counter, she told everyone to help themselves. Soon oh's and ah's of her students filled the kitchen.

"On to our main course. First, let me explain that yes, we are cooking with only three ingredients. Our dip was a true three item recipe. But we have three other, shall we say, standard items that don't count. These are 'essential' ingredients that every kitchen has and we use every day. Olive oil, salt, pepper. They are exempt from the three ingredient rule."

"Next, Lemon Chicken with Rosemary and Garlic for four," Julianne removed a Pyrex glass pan from the refrigerator and sat it on the corner of the island. Four chicken breasts were in the pan.

"Let's put a little oil under our birdies." Julianne took a metal tong, lifted each piece with her left hand, and poured in a dash of oil. "Now, we all know how terribly boring a skinless, boneless, chicken breast is. But they are everywhere and it's healthy eating. So thanks to three very diverse but outspoken simple ingredients we can awaken this zero flavored meat and liven up our palates. Simple, simple."

Julianne took a glass ramekin, added three-tablespoons of olive oil, four crushed garlic cloves, two tablespoons of crushed dried rosemary leaves, and the juice of a half lemon to the small bowl. "Next week we'll practice the technique of cleaning garlic, using fresh spices and zesting citrus but tonight we keep it simple. All of the items I am using are available at your local grocery or possibly in your cupboards right now."

After each piece of chicken was liberally coated with the pungent mixture, Julianne dusted them with a sprinkling of salt and pepper, popped the pan into the top oven to bake uncovered for thirty-five minutes. Turning to her students, she said, "This is baked on a 325 convection roast setting or at 350 on a standard oven.

"We will dine on that chicken later." Julianne pointed to the oven. "It will take about thirty minutes to prepare our two side dishes and one amazing desert. I think you will all love them." She smiled at her students. "I hope." Four friendly faces smiled back.

Only Marta's face was blank. She either stared at Julianne or twisted in her seat to look around the house. Marta didn't seem interested in the food preparation or the recipes, just Julianne and Julianne's home.

"Let's prepare a vegetable. Brussels sprouts are very much in season. I know, I can see by the expressions on your faces you probably are not a friend of the little green cabbage. Yes, it is one of the most maligned vegetables in the plant world. But, if you're tuned in to foodie news, you may have noticed this guy is making a comeback." Julianne pulled a basket full of the vegetable from a shelf on the island.

"We're going to make this tart, bitter, bad boy into an appealing sweet but savory accompaniment to our poultry."

As with the other dishes, Julianne had prepped the brussels sprouts by trimming off the ends and slicing them lengthwise in half. Next, she oiled a large non-stick skillet and laid each sprout cut side down in the hot pan. "Using our 'essential' ingredients of salt and pepper, I'll season them now. First the salt. Salt will help 'sweat' out some of the bitter cabbage flavor, open the tissues, allowing the flavors to enhance and soften. Pepper adds spice."

Julianne mixed together equal parts honey and ground mustard in a small glass bowl explaining this would change everyone's minds and they would want to welcome this tangy but sweet vegetable into their meal-planning repertoire. "To speed up the cooking process I'm going to add a fourth of a cup of water and cover the pan with the lid." The water hissed when it hit the hot skillet and steam billowed out as Julianne clamped the glass lid in place.

"I don't want to interrupt," Carolyn all but raised her hand, saying, "I just have to say this kitchen smells divine. That chicken has my mouth watering! Can anyone else smell the combination of garlic and rosemary?"

They all agreed the aromas were wonderful and even Marta nodded with a small approval.

"A well rounded dinner calls for a starch." Julianne set a three-quart pan on a burner, produced a package of mushrooms from the refrigerator, and started to chop a scallion.

Every so often she shook the pan of brussels sprouts, loosening them from the bottom as she continued to instruct, "Potatoes, pasta, couscous, and many varieties of rice round out most evening meals. Rice is simple, popular, and goes well with poultry but please, plain white rice is so so boring. It is on the menu tonight. Let's jazz it up."

After coating the pan with olive oil, Julianne added two tablespoons of chopped scallion and a cup of washed small sliced portabella mushrooms. She let them sauté for several minutes before adding a cup of rice. "How does that smell now? Shallots are a cross between garlic and an onion. It's used in small amounts because it adds that extra kick of flavor without being obtrusive. The mushrooms give the rice texture and an earthy flavor to an otherwise bland dish. Okay, I have one more ingredient to add. The liquid. The instructions call for two and one fourth cups of water but I will add one and one fourth cup water." Julianne added water from a glass measuring cup, walked to the refrigerator and brought back a container of chicken stock. "Let's keep with the flavors of the evening. By adding some stock, instead of all water, we intensify and enhance the rice. In goes one cup. That completes this dish. Back to the veggie."

After using a wire whisk to combine the mustard and honey, Julianne lifted the lid, turned off the heat, and drizzled the mixture over the sprouts. "I like to use a silicone or heat resistant rubber spatula to mix this. The reason is harsh metal might break them apart and it could scratch my pan." Julianne covered the pan, stirred the boiling rice, reduced it to a simmer, and then turned to her students. "Let's take a fifteen minute break, powder room is back there off the mud room. Please help yourself to a water or soda out of the iced bowl over by the sink."

"Me, me, first." Libby cried out rushing in the direction of the bathroom. "Since I got *the change* it's no telling when my bladder will burst."

Willow rolled her eyes and went to retrieve a bottle of water with Carolyn right behind her. "Are you enjoying this, Willow? I certainly am. And, welcome to your new home. How do you like our fair little village?"

Overhearing Carolyn's remarks made Julianne smile. *She is a born peace-maker.*

As Julianne was tidying up the cooktop, Rob walked

over to her. "You're good. I mean you've got us in the palm of your hand, Lady." Rob leaned in. With a faked stage whisper very close to her ear, he said, "Glad you twisted my arm and made me come here."

"Rob Murphy, I did no such thing!" Julianne felt goose bumps creeping up her arms as his warm breath tickled her ear.

"That's okay. I'm not holding it against you." Rob laughed and walked over to the refreshments.

Minutes later, Julianne cleared her throat to get everyone's attention and asked they return to their seats. All but Marta had gathered by the refreshments chatting amicably. Julianne almost hated to interrupt them. "I'll look for Marta," she said, leaving her students sitting at the counter.

"Marta." Julianne looked through the kitchen, into the great room, noticed the half bath door was wide open, obviously empty, before starting down the main hall. "Marta, can I help you?" There she was. It looked as if she was about to enter or was coming out of Jock's office.

Caught by surprise, Marta swung around and did something that startled Julianne. She took her left hand up to her hair and tucked a thick bunch of it nervously behind her ear over and over. *Shelby has done that since she was a little girl. I always knew she was upset or guilty or nervous when she started with the hair. Good God, who is this woman!*

"Your house. It is so exquisite. It must be divine to live like this." Marta spit out bitterly then quickly brushed past Julianne to hurry back to her seat.

This is not the time. Julianne regained her composure and returned to her place in the kitchen.

"Once again, we are going to repeat a taste of the night. Remember our chicken? Yes, I pulled the birds out during the break and they are perfect. The internal temperature was 165°F, they are tented and in the warming drawer."

"Lemon. We basted the breasts with lemon and now we make a lemon cream pie."

Julianne moved to the edge of her island. She held up a pre-made, store bought, graham cracker crust in an aluminum pie pan. "Into this we will put three ingredients. I need a mixing bowl, a hand electric mixer, and an eight ounce tub of ready whipping cream, and a fourteen ounce can of sweetened condensed milk, and a cup of fresh squeezed lemon juice. We could make a pie crust from scratch and I think that is much better, but tonight we go simple. And, these are just fine."

Once the creamy batter was blended, Julianne scooped and spread it artfully into high peaks over the crust. "Into the fridge. We'll see this beauty again soon."

Julianne walked over to the counter, stood in front of her students and said. "But for now, find a place at the table and I'll serve a taste of our first night in *The Kitchen*."

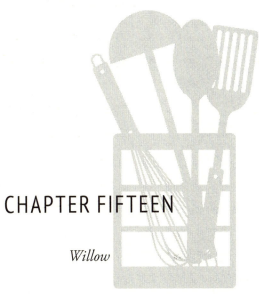

CHAPTER FIFTEEN

Willow

The cold winter air was a blast of fresh oxygen as Willow raced to her car. The glow of Julianne's big home shone like a castle looming behind. Every light in the house appeared to be lit and the snow shimmered silver white from the glow. Sliding into the frigid black Lexus, Willow turned on the ignition, pressed on the seat heat, cranked the heater to maximum, laid her head back, and sighed in relief.

Wondering if it was too late to call her therapist, Willow decided to savor this victory herself. Eight months had passed. Relocated in a small, presumably safe community, a 9mm Glock in the side pocket of her handbag, all car doors locked, Willow felt almost secure. She had not ventured out at night, alone, since last June. The short dark days of winter with long black nights made life problematic. Shopping was an issue. After work, she wanted to get home before dark which made stopping at a grocery store impossible. Willow learned the Internet was a source of everything one needed. Groceries, clothes, furniture, make-up, wine, and Christmas gifts were a click of the mouse to confirm the purchase and add a delivery address.

The settlement was generous. No one wanted to go to court to tell those awful sordid details over and over. Not her. She didn't press charges even though she had done nothing to provoke the attack. Unless being smart, attractive, young, naive, and ambitious made her guilty. She didn't even work in his department. He was a senior vice president. She worked four floors down in marketing.

The payment was discreetly wired into three separate bank accounts. Her transfer out of that office was swift with a liberal moving allowance. The promotion and salary increase were nice but the nightmares continued. Radically cutting her long chestnut hair and dying it black didn't help either.

Since no one knew her in Oak Grove, Willow was comfortable seeking the help of a psychologist. Every Thursday at noon she took a longer lunch break, drove to the new strip mall on the edge of town and parked in back. An obscure walkway led to an elevator and a set of offices on the second story. The other renters were quite an assortment. Beside her psychologist, there was a private detective, a collection agency, and an IRS agent.

The sessions helped. Talking about the incident felt good. Willow hadn't disclosed any of the details, only that she was attacked at night, in the company parking deck after a late night of finishing second quarter reports. Finding out her reactions to the aftermath were normal comforted her. Her therapist assured her that with time her fears could diminish.

When Willow casually mentioned the cooking classes, her psychologist encouraged her to attend. She pointed out the safety of the posh neighborhood, the small class size, and the importance of breaking the spell of the fear of night.

Willow put the car in drive. *I did it. I feel okay.*

Libby

Oh! I hate myself! Why did I dress like a slob? That Willow lady was impeccable. Everything on Carolyn matched perfectly. And Julianne is beautiful and chic, so chic. How do you get to be like her?

Shivering in the cold car, Libby fought the urge to have a cigarette. She kept a pack hidden under the seat and often comforted herself with a leisurely smoke. But it might be too risky tonight. If her husband were home, he would be angry if he smelled smoke on her breath. Not like his breath wouldn't reek of cheap booze.

Surely Blake would have Timmy in bed by now. It would be nice if Blake would stay for a while so she could tell him about the cooking school. It had been fun. She had really enjoyed herself and looked forward to next week. Blake was a good friend of Julianne's daughter, Natalie, and he was the one who told his mother and Libby about the cooking classes. *He is such a nice guy.* Libby hoped her Timmy would grow up to be like her nephew. Blake and his mother, Libby's only sister, were her best friends.

Next week she would dress better. She would go to Macy's and look at the mannequins, copy what they wore. It was hard to remember how the rest of the world acted when you were a stay-at-home mom with little or no social life. Her husband's drinking had alienated most of their friends.

God forbid her son would turn out like his father. Oh, once he had been an honorable, hardworking, and devoted husband. That all changed when he was fired from a job he loved, another victim of a sluggish economy. She thought they called it downsizing. Finally, he found another job with less pay, long hours, and little prestige.

Then there were the miscarriages, three of them. Libby fell into a dark hole and he fell into a bottle. Five years later, when Libby did get pregnant, her husband rallied for several months. Seemed like his old self. Unfortunately, Libby only had time and attention for her baby boy. When her husband felt she had forgotten about him, he emotionally left again.

Everyone at the cooking school has been so nice except for that foreign woman. She is strange. But the others? Maybe, I can have friends again.

Carolyn

STILL cold from the ride home, Carolyn hastily hung up her coat, kicked off her shoes, and poured a small glass of sherry. Curled up in Ira's old lounge chair with the afghan a former student crocheted, Carolyn wanted to relax and review the evening.

Yes, keeping busy, keep going, that was a good antidote to loneliness. Ira had been gone for years now but still the house was too empty. Especially since she retired, mourning the end of another era. So many times in the last years, Carolyn regretted her decision not to have children. Ira was eleven years older and set in rigid bachelor ways when they married, making it clear that children were not to be in the picture. Carolyn was thirty-seven and assured her new husband all the children she needed were with her every day at school.

So they traveled, enjoyed the theatre, did the restaurant

tours, and lived well together. Even after Ira left, Carolyn managed nicely on her own, holding her head up high. She was a well-respected school principal and a community figure. She knew that people whispered behind her back wondering how anyone could live with a man all those years and not know he was gay.

Now life was different. It had been one thing to come home after a long day at the school, or evening meetings, or weekend conferences. Then the quiet and solitude were welcomed. Spending almost every day, 24/7, in the house by herself was a different situation.

So this was the plan. Join groups, travel more, learn new things, and perhaps write her memoirs. All those years in public education with all those boys and girls would give her many stories to tell.

Carolyn drained the last of the amber liquor and smiled. *Tonight was a good start. And, oh, I can't forget, tomorrow afternoon I have my first Mah Jongg lesson.*

Rob

HE wanted to hang around after they ate. He thought about volunteering to do dishes, sweep the floor, wipe off the counters, anything to spend more time next to this fascinating woman. The feelings started with their first phone conversation. It was like *a vibe* came through cyber-space. When Julianne opened her front door tonight, Rob took a long look at her and felt his heart pound and his breath shortened.

For the last two years, Rob retreated from the world. Sara broke his heart. Long before she succumbed to cancer his world fell apart. Sara was gone two years ago next month. Maybe he was ready to start living again.

They were college sweethearts. She was a pom-pom girl and he was the star on both the basketball court and the baseball diamond. Everyone said Sara and Rob were the quintessential couple. Good looking, popular, smart, and destined to big things in any career they chose. They married two months after graduation and moved to Dallas, Texas. Sara immediately became pregnant. Rob had a head coaching job at a small community college. The world seemed theirs for the taking. And for the first twenty years it was.

Rob guessed Sara's affairs started after their daughter left for college. Sara was a stay-at-home mother who was active in the community, church, and an elite country club Rob had very little time or patience for. Sara reinvented herself into an excellent tennis player and an avid golfer. She was one of the youngest members at the club.

The same year Rob and Sara became empty nesters, Rob was appointed Director of Athletics at SMU. The new job took him away from their quiet home for long days and most weekends.

All the attention Sara missed from her husband she got from the tennis pro, the head of the golf committee, and a certain captain of industry who sold his business for many millions at the young age of fifty. He was bored with his wife and had a lot of time on his hands. Rob never suspected a thing. For several years, they lived parallel lives.

Even now he blamed himself for being caught up and consumed with the plum of a job he'd dreamed of all his life. He assumed Sara would always be waiting for him.

When Sara was first diagnosed with colon cancer, they knew she could beat it. They were golden, undefeatable, physically strong, and beautiful. But the news the cancer had spread to her liver shook Sara to the core. Was she being punished? Was this karma? She went back to church. Did God not believe she was truly sorry for her infidelities?

When that didn't work, Sara confessed to Rob, begging his forgiveness. She pleaded with her husband to move out of Texas so they could get away from it all. When the term, terminal, was used, all Sara wanted to do was go home to Illinois. They did. Three years later, surrounded by her daughter, aging mother, two sisters, and Rob, Sara died.

Sara had broken Rob's heart and her dying didn't fix it.

Marta

So this is where he lived. So that is his wife. Marta drove away from Julianne Girard's house and pushed all the feelings of anger and betrayal down deep into herself.

CHAPTER SIXTEEN

Julianne rolled over half asleep, smiling. In a second, it occurred to her that this was the first time in many months that her first thoughts of the day were not of Jock. Nor the other will, or the mysterious box she discovered in his office, or the photos hidden inside of women and babies she never knew about.

Julianne laughed. *It's about me. I'm thinking about me and last night. I loved it. I love my little school. The Kitchen.*

Still grinning and feeling more alive than she had in months, Julianne leaped out of bed. "Good grief, it's cold!" Pulling back the silk brocade drapes revealed another over-cast monochromatic winter day in the month of February. "This is sweatpants and sweatshirt weather."

It didn't take Julianne long to tie back her hair into a

messy ponytail, add thick wool socks to her outfit, splash water on her face, and head downstairs for coffee.

The kitchen was dreary in the thin gray light. Julianne flicked on lights as she made her way to the back counter and the coffee station. Remnants of last night were scattered through the kitchen but Julianne didn't care. The tell-tale signs made her smile wider and added another bounce to her steps.

Minutes later, she wondered why she was sitting on the stool Rob sat on last night? She merely wanted to drink her steaming coffee and collect her thoughts. Again she grinned. *What? So what? He's handsome, sort of, and nice but ... Julianne, stop it right now.*

By midmorning the kitchen was back in perfect order. A brief text, as promised, went out to Natalie assuring her the first class was a success and asked her to phone when she could and to come to dinner Sunday evening. She added that Shelby would also be invited. A longer email was sent to Adela inviting her to stop over for a glass of wine after she finished at the real estate office.

Julianne was about to retreat back upstairs to shower and dress when the phone rang.

"Good morning to you, too." *Keep neutral, not surprised, or pleased, and good god don't giggle.*

"Really, Rob? You need help tweaking the recipes from last night for dinner tonight? Remember, each course was only three ingredients. Yes, Angelo's will have everything you need or the new Publics out by the mall."

The next request made Julianne's head spin. "Coffee? You think we should meet to go over the menu, make sure your first dinner is perfect, help preserve the repetition of *The Kitchen?* And you feel you need extra tutoring.*"

"Or lunch?" Julianne chuckled. "Okay, coffee. Say, ten-ish?"

"Yes, of course, I'm fine with the Java Hut. I don't need directions. See you there."

Before Julianne could put the phone down the computer beeped with a new email. Adela confirmed she would be over by five o'clock with a bottle of bold red wine and all ears to hear every detail from last night. Well, there might be more to hear about, Julianne thought to herself as she sent off a brief reply.

What a day! But what to wear for coffee? My hair! Julianne nearly tripped rushing upstairs only to pull herself up laughing.

"I'm here." Adela let herself in. "Jul, where are you?"

"Laundry room." Julianne yelled, lowered her voice, continuing to talk to herself. "I'm such a nitwit. I was going to order coffee, but I'd already had too much, so I decided on a hot chocolate and clumsily spilled it down the front of my sweater. It's cashmere and I've been soaking it all afternoon and I'm afraid it's ruined and of course I made an absolute fool of myself. So what else is new."

"What In The World Are You Talking About?" Adela walked into the laundry room.

Julianne turned. "I need a glass of wine. I'm just beside myself."

Adela followed her friend through the back hall, into the kitchen, finally catching up with her at the wet bar in the great room. Adela watched Julianne take two stemmed bubble glasses off the shelf. Very patiently, Adela fairly asked, "Are you all right?"

"Where's the wine? Here, hand me that bottle. I'll open it. Go take off your coat and boots. Come sit on the sofa. I'll bring the wine over."

Julianne collapsed into the deep cushions of the sectional that ran almost around the room. "I'm beat, Addie. I mean I was wired for days before last night. And then this morning." Julianne sipped her wine, looked coyly at Adela, and said timidly, "Never thought I'd be needing advice from a loose, notorious, girlfriend of mine. That would be you!"

"Spill it. Spill it. What is going on? I came to hear about last night but I can clearly see we are in much deeper than that!" Adela parked herself next to Julianne.

Julianne sat up straight. "Yes, let's start from the beginning. Last night went well. It was perfect. Carolyn, your Rotary friend, is lovely. I'm so glad she's in the class. Willow, your real estate client, is a bit of a mystery. But all in all, I do like her. I sense an inner conflict though. We'll see."

"Good." Adela nodded. "I was a bit concerned about Willow. A strange woman. A realtor and her clients usually spend hours and hours together. I get close to my people. But never her. She was very closed. I think sad." Adela hastily added. "Of course, Carolyn, the best of the best. Brave woman. Life has thrown her a curve or two."

"What do you mean?"

"Another time, honey. Refresh my memory. Who else? Five participants total. Right?

"Yes. Oh, Blake's aunt Libby. And as Natalie would say, she's a *hot mess*. But I liked her. Maybe I can help her. You know, with a little tenderness you might make a difference in someone's life. Then there is Marta, the fifth student. Remember all the bizarre phone calls I had from her? Well, she was different. In an almost spooky way."

"How so?"

"Can't really say. Wandered around the house, kinda looking at stuff. Didn't reveal a thing about herself. Eccentric, but beautiful clothes. I'll keep you posted. She's a 'wait and see' kind of study."

"There was a guy? Right?" Adela looked over at her friend, burst out laughing, sat her wine down on the edge of the massive cocktail table, clapped her hands, and shouted. "Look at you. You are blushing. It's the guy. Oh my god tell me everything."

"There isn't much to tell. Rob Murphy showed up at exactly six o'clock with a bouquet. Yeah. It was made up of wooden spoons. He hands it to me, stands and grins, kind of sexy-like. He's an ex-athlete, coach, widower, father, involved grandfather, and cute. Like in funny cute. You know, one of those guys that's in your space but you like it."

"Okay, I got is so far. He showed up last night. You were flattered, flirted with, and . . ."

"And he called me this morning. I met him for coffee. I like him. But it's craziness. I'd never be attracted to a man like him. He wears a letter jacket! And his hair is mostly blonde but cut in that stand up longish butch deal. He has one of those scruffy unshaven beard things like all the supposedly sexy guys on TV have. My husband was always impeccable. The best dresser. Every hair on Jock's head was groomed."

Adela drank her wine and just kept nodding, all the while suppressing laughter.

"I can tell he's a really good person. He came to the cooking school to learn to cook for his grandchildren.

Apparently, they are with him several nights a week as their single mother, Rob's daughter, works nights. She's a nurse. Rob wants to feed the kids tasty, nutritious, home cooked meals. How wonderful. But now I have this stupid eighth grade type crush on the man. I'm an idiot. Like today, he was doing this insane imitation of me. He thought I took brussels sprouts way too seriously last night. Well, I was giggling like a dope and ended up dumping half my cocoa down my front."

"Poor baby!"

"It's not funny, Adela. I have to get over this. Really? A guy like this? What could it possibly lead to?"

"Good times. Great sex!" Adela tried not to cough as she swallowed and giggled at the same time. "Just saying."

"Adela!"

CHAPTER SEVENTEEN

Early Sunday morning, February unleashed her fury as only she can in the Midwest. A powerful wind howled down from Canada churning up the atmosphere over Lake Michigan and dumping a winter's worth of snow in ten hours on the entire Chicagoland area. The subzero temperatures kept the flakes light and fluffy. But the prevailing gusts of the north wind packed the snow into high hard drifts.

The flashing lights and scraping grind of a snowplow attempting to keep one lane open on the street outside Julianne's home woke her up. Snow had been predicted but Julianne instantly surmised this was a good old-fashioned blizzard. One didn't need to look outside to determine the sound of the wind howling and wailing.

After checking with WGN local weather, it became clear the plans for a nice Sunday supper with Natalie and Shelby would be cancelled. Julianne was disappointed but there was no way she wanted the girls to risk driving out from the city in this weather. So off went a text to both of them. Deciding not to share the menu was a wise decision. They loved the spinach and ricotta cheese stuffed shells with red sauce that Julianne had prepared on Saturday. The casserole was waiting to be heated up in the refrigerator along with other favorites; garlic crostini's with Parmesan, and a chocolate cheesecake. And, as was her usual habit, Julianne made extra. To go care packages were fun and handy for the busy career girls' lunches and dinners.

"What a disappointment," said the returned texts, "maybe next week?"

SUNDAY, alone in a blizzard, the sky a steel gray, the house felt cold no matter how high Julianne cranked the furnace. The wind rattling the windows, eaves and downspouts was depressing. Curled up in one of the deep wingback chairs in Jock's office, Julianne stared into the unlit fireplace and cried. Salty tears crept into the corners of her mouth and her nose started to run but she didn't care. All she felt was sorry. Sorry for herself and the way this had turned out. What happened to growing old with her husband? What happened to sharing retirement, traveling, waiting for their daughters to marry, bounce grandchildren on their knees?

"What happened?" Julianne whispered over and over.

This is crazy. One day I'm as high as a kite, the next I a lonely sad sack. Finally all the tears there were to cry were cried.

It is a new life now. Pulling herself together, Julianne went to the powder room, blew her nose, washed her face, and brushed her hair. Next, Julianne heated up a can of soup, sat at the kitchen table, and looked out over her deep white back yard. By now, the snow was letting up and the wind had died down. Suddenly a thought occurred to her. *I'll bet I'm not the only lonely one sequestered away on this miserable Sunday afternoon wondering how life got so far off track.*

Another voice came to her as it often did since Jock died. "Yes, dear Mom, I hear you, you always said, "Life is for the Living." And you did, right up until the end. Okay, I'll do it."

There was his number plain as day on her phone from his call two days ago. Hitting redial was simple. Waiting for the phone to be answered was hard.

"Hi. Nice day? Hey, you've got that big truck that probably has four wheel drive or a plow or something. I was thinking, I have a refrigerator full of food for a Sunday supper that got cancelled and if you could, would you like to come over and help me eat some of it? Got to warn you, it's girlie food, not a bit of meat."

Two hours later the doorbell rang. A cold and snowy man wearing a letter jacket and frayed stocking cap was grinning from ear to ear. Julianne giggled as the frigid air bit her face. "Get in here quick. Look. Your 'I' letter has snow all over it."

She reached up to brush off the wooly letter as Rob Murphy bent down to softly and quickly kiss her.

THE ten o'clock Sunday night news was over when Rob got home. Certainly in no mood to go to bed and not wanting a thing to eat or drink, he wandered around the dark house not inclined to turn on a light. Instead, he found himself standing in front of the French doors leading out to his wide snow-filled deck. The moon illuminated the snow and the bare tree branches cast sinister shadow figures on the whiteness that filled the yard. It was eerie but beautiful. Mother Nature apologized with a dead silent winter night after her temper tantrum of the blizzard.

Standing with his arms tightly crossed over his chest, Rob tried to savor the feeling of Julianne in his arms. The evening had been wonderful. His total surprise to Julianne's impromptu call changed his miserable snowbound Sunday into an enchanted evening. Thank heavens he hadn't been out shoveling when the phone rang. That was a call not to be missed.

It had been a long time since he'd held a woman in his arms. At least a woman whom he cared for or could grow to care for. Sure, there had been a liaison once or twice. They ended almost before they began. Rob always got the feeling that he was being sized up for "the catch." Would he be a good prize? Lately, it was easier to be with his daughter and the kids, do a pick-up basketball game down at the YMCA, go for a run in the park when the weather was reasonable, and enjoy a good book usually related to military history.

Once upon a time, the true love of his life had been Sara. Sara was the one. Never thought there would be another. God, he had loved her. The first time he saw her she was shaking those silly pom-poms on the sideline of the crowded basketball court and he was headed right toward her at breakneck speed trying to stop the ball from going out-of-bounds. One more step to the right and it would have been an ugly collision. After the game, he sought her out, apologized, and asked to buy her a beer. Sara was impressed with his false I.D. and they got drunk together at the Ratskeller that night. But she was a good girl, he never kissed her until the third date, and they finally made love the night he put an engagement ring on her finger. It was the Christmas of their senior year at the U of I. Another snowy night filled with raw emotions and promise.

Even now, when he occasionally woke from a sound sleep in the middle of the night, he could not fathom the awful truth of her infidelities. He wondered every so often, if the marriage would have survived. Of course, her dying took that option off the table. Rob is sorry she suffered at the end, it was extremely difficult for their daughter and him. It's just been in the last year he hasn't felt so empty. Time was healing. Having those crazy busy grandkids around helped. He loved them even though there were days he considered them a real pain.

But this Julianne Girard was amazing. From the very first, the first night of the cooking class, Rob found himself intrigued. Every man alive likes to look at a pretty woman with a nice shape. Now it was different. Twice they'd been together, just the two of them. Not only did he find her beautiful, charming, and smart, but Rob felt deep feelings stirring.

Tonight, at her home in the aftermath of the storm, being together was cozy, intimate, safe, a time to share their stories, a little of themselves. Sitting side by side in front of the roaring fire after dinner, each carefully crafted a 'Cliff Notes' version of their former lives, as much as they felt ready to divulge.

He shocked himself when he impulsively kissed her upon his arrival. He should have apologized, and would have, except she didn't seem to mind. So for the rest of the evening he played it cool. It was enough to be in her company, two people having dinner and good conversation.

Their good night kiss lingered longer than the hello kiss, making him want more.

Leaving her tonight was difficult.

CHAPTER EIGHTEEN

By Monday night, the day following Illinois's big storm, all the major roads were cleared and sanded. Disappointed children knew Tuesday would not be another snow day and Tom Skilling promised warmer weather for the week ahead with a bit of a thaw.

Natalie and Julianne were meeting for dinner at a trendy chain restaurant located on a well-traveled highway half way between the City and Oak Grove. Natalie's office declared Monday an optional workday depending on peoples' location and ability to get into the office. Natalie chose to take advantage of the situation. By midafternoon she was bored, called her mother, and talked her into putting aside her work on Thursday night's menu to join Natalie for an early dinner.

There was more to Natalie's motives than dinner. The memory of her stepfather with another woman haunted her. The early days after Jock's death and the way her mother acted, isolating everyone from Jock's office, and barely speaking of her grief bothered her, too.

There didn't seem to be a right time to broach the subject. When the time seemed right, the holidays arrived which was not a good time to bring up unpleasant issues. Holidays were difficult enough. January brought on the hoopla of the cooking school. Natalie couldn't bring herself to say a thing to dampen her mother's enthusiasm.

The mystery of the fifth student was the tipping point. Julianne told her daughter about the unusual phone calls from a woman inquiring about the classes. Because of the past crazy weekend, Julianne hadn't said much, barely had a chance to tell her anything about last Thursday night. The only thing Natalie knew from their short conversations was an eccentric foreign woman by the name of Marta showed up. She acted strange and left as soon as she could.

Natalie had a nagging suspicion this was all connected.

Settling into the wide booth and placing their food order with a disgruntled waitress, Julianne and Natalie knew the food would be mediocre at best. Sipping a glass of inexpensive red wine, they snickered.

"So tell me everything about the first class." Natalie leaned in toward her mother.

"It was good. I was nervous. Didn't have a clue what to expect as far as the people were concerned. But I knew the menu and recipes like the back of my hand. I like to be organized and I was." Julianne giggled. "You'll get a kick out of this. All my seasonings were lined up on the island in little clear glass bowls like on the cooking shows."

"Good job, Mom."

"This Thursday is coming quickly. I should be home right now doing some test baking. But, my beautiful daughter, she needed a mommy fix." Julianne smiled across the table.

"I did. Not too old or proud to admit it." Natalie smiled back. "Tell me, I want to know about the students. Each and every one, except Blake's aunt. I know Libby. A space cadet, for sure. Who showed up?"

Julianne did a brief bio on Willow, Carolyn, defended Libby, hurried over Rob, and barely mentioned Marta.

"So . . . this Marta woman. Tell me more."

"She is the least amount of story I have. Elaborate old world type clothes. Wandered around the house . . ."

"Whoa! Why would she be snooping around our house?"

"It was rather strange," Julianne muttered.

"Mom, what *exactly* does she look like?"

"Natalie, what's going on here? You're giving me the creeps."

Burned into Natalie's memory was the picture of Jock

and a woman sitting very close together at a fashionable bar in Logan Square, a neighborhood Natalie didn't visit often. Jock probably knew that. But that night was a fluke because she had a random last minute invite from an old college boyfriend. Two things happened. The guy was more narcissistic than ever, now a total jerk, and the sight of her stepfather inches away from this woman, hugging her, sickened Natalie. She had no trouble leaving ten minutes after she arrived, sure that Jock never knew she had been there.

"Just curious. Lots of kooks out there. If anything should go missing or happen, then we both have an idea of who to look for, you know, being careful."

Julianne didn't buy that. Natalie was fishing. For what? "Well, I remember her being almost as tall as I am. Blonde, long curly, kinda wild hair. A little gray in it. Generally fair complexion and eyes, I'd guess. Somewhat attractive. Probably quite pretty as a young woman." Julianne watched her daughter's face change ever so slightly and knew something was up.

Natalie flinched. Lots of women are tall and blonde but still. She knew that was all she would get for now from her mother. Thursday was four days away and plenty of time to launch a plan. Julianne's home was her home. Not like she didn't belong there. Quietly she ate her dinner while the wheels were turning.

CHAPTER NINETEEN

Julianne looked at her watch as the doorbell rang twenty minutes before six on Thursday evening. She hurried to the door. There was Carolyn standing in the cold, doing a little dance to keep warm. "Quick, come in. Aren't you freezing in this weather?" Julianne greeted her student as she hustled her into the foyer, hurriedly closing the front door behind her.

"I'm sorry to be this early." Carolyn took off her gloves and scarf. "But the roads, you just don't know. At my age, I'm a little timid about driving in winter. So I thought I would start out with plenty of time and really the streets were all clear."

"Good to hear. Of course. Safety first. All is good. Carolyn, drop your coat and stuff in the living room, meet me in the kitchen and you can watch me finish puttering."

Julianne glanced out the beveled glass front door and saw a big pick-up truck and a small foreign car pull into her driveway. Rob and probably Willow arriving together. *Good. This is no time to give myself away. I can't be alone with him and pull off this class.*

"Carolyn, would do me a favor? Grab the door for Rob and Willow? I'll be in the kitchen." *Okay. Safety in numbers, they'll all come in together.*

"Mrs. Deaver, are you the official greeter tonight? Hurry, Willow, I'm holding the door. It's not summer out here. Just saying, but maybe those spike high heel boots aren't the greatest choice in winter." Julianne heard Rob's deep voice all the way in the kitchen followed by a schoolgirl giggle. *Good grief that was Willow!*

Libby and Marta arrived a little before six. Julianne ushered both of the women into the living room where they left their coats and purses. "Libby, look at you. That sweater is gorgeous. Oh but purple is your color. New hair cut?"

"Do I look okay? My Timmy even gave me a wolf whistle when he saw me tonight."

"Very nice. We all need to treat ourselves now and then. Especially in the dead of winter. Keeps our spirits up." Julianne didn't go on as Libby was blushing and looked uncomfortable.

Marta carefully laid her black full-length wool coat, beaded leather handbag, and fur Cossack hat across the back of a chair before leaving the room, without saying another word. She had curtly greeted Julianne at the door while ignoring Libby.

Minutes later, Julianne was stationed behind the center island with all five students seated on the same stools as last week. She cleared her throat to get their attention. Rob gave her a big grin and little wave but Julianne ignored him and shuffled her notes. "Well, it's winter! Hope everyone survived the weekend nestled in with family and friends and, most importantly, had something wonderful to eat. Which brings me to tonight's dishes. Let's call them what they are . . . comfort foods. This is the time of year we crank up the oven, pull out the soup pot, and think about something chocolate for dessert."

"Amen. I need to cook all that." Libby was the first to speak.

"Libby, the first recipe I chose for your family, and Rob, your grandchildren. Yes, it is good ole macaroni and cheese. And really? Who doesn't love it? My daughter, Natalie, now twenty-five, orders it in all of the upscale Chicago restaurants. It's an appropriate side dish for a dinner party, just kick it up a notch or two. That's what we do tonight, big people's mac and cheese. I've also included a simpler recipe and we'll talk about that one. It's kid friendly." Up until this point Julianne had looked directly at everyone but Rob.

"Comfort food entrée number two. Is there anything more consoling than a meatloaf baking in the oven? The aroma of hearty beef, onions, spices, tomatoes, all baking nice and slow in your warm kitchen. What a way to greet your family or friends as they come in from the cold."

Carolyn was nodding and smiling. Libby was scanning both recipes intently, appearing more than ready to get started. Even Willow had a pleasant look on her face. But Marta stared straight at Julianne as if to study her every feature and movement, making Julianne nervous. Julianne could feel her steely glare. Turning to avoid looking toward Marta, she accidently made eye contact with Rob. He gave her a small smile and a wink. Julianne felt her heart flutter as she sent a little smile back and felt both warm and happy.

They had not been together since Sunday. Rob had the kids Monday, Tuesday, and Wednesday after school until his daughter picked them up at eight. She worked three twelve-hour shifts every week so her weekends were free to be a mom. The dad lived in Omaha and his visits were as sporadic as his child support payments. It was a significant financial help that Rob could do the babysitting.

Rob phoned Monday night but Julianne was out with Natalie. On Tuesday, he tried again and they connected. "Maybe I'm a day late and a dollar short here but I want to thank you for dinner on Sunday night. You sure are a good cook and all . . ."

At first, the conversation was awkward. But Rob, being a direct sort of guy, finally blurted out. "Hey, Lady, I'm an old ball player with not a lot of fancy manners so I'm telling you like it is. I like you. You're amazing and beautiful and I want to see you again and more often. I guess that's the same thing, so there, I did it, I spilled my guts and look like the fool I know I am and . . ."

"Yes," Julianne said quietly.

"I'm sorry. .did you say something?" Rob stumbled.

"Rob, I said yes. I would like to see you again and not only on Thursday nights."

Julianne wasn't quite sure what followed but it might have been a Texas cheer reserved for the end of the game when victory was near.

ON Thursday night, *The Kitchen* was in full swing, session number two. Thirty minutes later a casserole of creamy pasta and cheese was on its way into the preheated oven. Julianne had turned up the volume on this tried and true old friend using three distinct cheeses; sharp white Vermont cheddar, Swiss Gruyere, and an aged Italian Pecorino Romano, all blended in the béchamel sauce. Six drops of Tabasco, a pinch of nutmeg, a teaspoon of dried mustard, fresh ground pepper, and kosher salt finished the dish. The crowning glory would be the lightly browned crust made with melted butter and panko and sprinkled over the top of the macaroni mixture before popping it into the oven.

"I think almost everyone has their favorite concoction for a meatloaf, even the most naive of cooks. We'll talk about a couple of standard ingredients and then we'll put together the recipe that's in front of you."

Julianne took a large tray off the back counter and brought it to the center island. "Yes, I assembled all the necessary ingredients beforehand to make the prep quicker, cleaner, and more fun. Try it at home. Bring everything in the recipe you're making to one location. Just like now."

Next Julianne plugged in the Cuisinart. In seconds, she had perfectly chopped one medium onion, three garlic cloves, and one-half of a green pepper. After scraping out the work bowl and putting the vegetables aside on a glass plate, Julianne added seventeen saltine crackers and one third cup whole milk back into the Cuisinart. When the mixture was smooth, she surprised the students by putting all three meats into the processor. In about ten one-second pulses, the mixture was a cohesive structure.

"I'm using three meats. One pound lean ground beef. One half pound each ground pork and ground turkey. Be adventuresome. Tempt the taste buds. Try ground veal or lamb. Might want to add more garlic or rosemary. At this point, I'll put all this together, our meat, chopped veggies, and the rest of the ingredients into this big mixing bowl."

With a teaspoon, Julianne measured into the bowl Dijon mustard, Worcestershire sauce, dried thyme, salt and pepper. "Now it gets fun. After I break these two eggs and add one half of an eight ounce can of tomato sauce, I go to work."

At the sink, Julianne talked over her shoulder to the class as she washed and scrubbed her hands. "The best two tools in your kitchen are your two clean hands."

Several minutes later, the loaf shaped meat was transferred to a rectangular baking dish. Julianne washed her hands again and popped the heavy dish into a 350 degree oven.

"Break time. I'll clean up a bit. Water and soda in the same place as last week. Meet me back here in fifteen minutes."

Rob headed toward Julianne at the island but Carolyn made it there first with the recipes in hand, along with a pen and a questioning look. Rob's face fell. Julianne sent him a half smile before turning her full attention to Carolyn.

Julianne was about to get everyone back in place and start the dessert course when the doorbell rang. Rob saw the perturbed look on Julianne's face and quickly jumped in. "Finish what you're doing. Let me get it." Heading toward the front of the house and joking, he said, "Pretty darn cold for a couple of Mormon boys to be out. Plus we're all saved in here."

Everyone chuckled and Julianne smiled to herself. *A man that makes me laugh.*

"Well hello. You look cold." Rob opened the door to a shivering pretty girl in a long down coat. She scooted past him and pushed the door closed with her hip.

"With cars parked in the drive and in front I walked from the corner. Hey, I'm Natalie." Natalie pulled off a fluffy mitten and stuck out her right hand toward Rob.

"I'm Rob." Rob wrapped his warm beefy hand around her slender fingers. "Are you . . ."

"Yes, I am. Julianne's daughter. This is a last minute thing. She might actually be surprised. Uh . . . would you mind asking her to meet me in the front room?"

In the kitchen doorway, Rob caught Julianne's eye and motioned her to follow him.

"What's up?" Rob told her she had a guest in the living room. Julianne didn't like to get off track with the schedule.

"Natalie! What in the world are you doing here? Tonight, of all nights!"

"Just listen a second. Monday night at dinner you seemed so happy. Like your old self. And you said the cooking school was great, you wanted to keep it up, do one four session class every month." Natalie was talking as fast as she could to keep her foot in the door. "So, I got talking to Ernie, my web guy. Long story short, you need a website, some brochures, business cards. I thought I would pop in, take some pics, and get a feel for what you're doing. Have you up and running, advertising for March, by next week."

"Really? I'm flabbergasted. But that's typical you. However, my dear, you will publish NOTHING unless I okay it. Savvy?"

"Of course!" Natalie reached toward her mother with a quick hug.

"Now, come on." Julianne gave a gentle push toward the kitchen. "I have to get back. I will introduce you to the class. But please don't be too obtrusive."

Standing off to the side, Natalie waited for her mother to introduce her and explain a bit about her visit. Julianne named each student starting with Rob. Each said hello, or you look like your Mom, or how fun to be on a website. Libby already knew her, Willow was polite, Rob was charming, and Carolyn was warm. Marta only gave a quick nod in her direction, then kept her eyes downcast.

NATALIE knew she had scored big. She hadn't arrived at break time by accident. She'd been circling the house, peeking in the back patio French doors, and waited for her mom to break off from cooking. This entire scheme was gutsy enough without upsetting her mother by disturbing her class.

The cute guy that answered the door had no idea how cold she was. *Funny, Mom never elaborated about him.* She'd been outside for over thirty minutes. Jock had only been dead about five months but don't overlook a four-leaf clover, as Grandma Rose use to say. Natalie made a mental note to ask her mom about student Rob.

The webpage wasn't entirely her idea. But when Ernie sent out a random email looking for clients and offering a winter special on new websites, the wheels turned and Natalie thought she'd found a way into the Thursday night session. She needed a good look at the mysterious woman who attended, the one who made her mother nervous, and who might have ulterior motives.

So far so good. Julianne didn't seem to suspect a thing and Natalie was enjoying the warmth of the kitchen filled with the smell of something delicious coming from the double ovens. While watching her wonderful mother whipping up a batch of red velvet cupcakes, she thought how nice it was to be here. *Mom is really cool . . . she's having a ball . . . wow!*

After everyone got tuned back to cooking Natalie snapped a few pictures, walked stocking-footed around the room, took note of the food, presentation, and techniques. Marta would be in many of the photos. Maybe in a corner, maybe from behind, maybe almost a shadow, but Natalie would know this woman from every angle. She would find out exactly who she was and what she was doing in their home.

BACK at the center island, Julianne was about to make a dessert to compliment the night of comfort food. "We are just days away from Valentine's Day. I love the holiday. It brings back so many fond memories of my dear mother. On Valentine's Day, my sister and I would rush down to the breakfast table. We knew a small present was waiting by our plate. Then off to school we went with a brown paper bag filled with those crazy little store bought cards all made out to our good friends. At school the cards were exchanged, candy hearts passed around, girls dressed in something red . . . great fun."

Carolyn and Libby were visibly touched by the memories. Willow wasn't hearing these traditions for the first time but they were ones she certainly had never enjoyed. From K through eighth grade, Willow had attended a strict Catholic academy. She wore a plaid skirt and navy sweater everyday for nine years. The nuns were old-fashioned and tomfoolery wasn't tolerated. Valentine's Day was looked upon as a pagan holiday, somehow connected with gratuitous sex. For Willow and her classmates it was just another day.

Marta half listened to the syrupy story and blankly stared at Julianne.

Meanwhile, Rob watched Natalie watching Marta.

Julianne continued, "Coming home after school was the best! The kitchen smelled of cake baking. And the finished product would sit in the center of the table. A two layered red velvet cake in the shape of a heart all covered with cream cheese frosting. Mother baked that cake every year. So moist and delicious. She kept those two heart shaped cake pans long after we left home."

"Are we using the pans tonight?" Libby asked.

"Don't I wish. Years after Daddy died, Mom was thinking about selling the house and moving to a condo. I asked for a few keepsakes. Like the heart shaped pans but she'd sold them in a garage sale the year before."

Natalie whispered loudly, "And mom's never gotten over it. Poor Grandma Rose."

Four out of five of the class laughed. It was a nice tension breaker. Rob said he guessed Natalie had heard the story before.

Even Julianne had to grin. "So it is the year-of-the-cup-cake. Cupcakes are all the rage. Red Velvet cupcakes for Valentine's Day? I think that's perfect. Let's get started."

This was the session Julianne planned to ask for class participation. Not wanting to put anyone on the spot, she asked for volunteers to run the mixer and cream the sugar and shortening. Libby immediately jumped up and seemed to know how to slowly add the two eggs and vanilla. Julianne was taken by surprise when Willow said she would mix the dry ingredients together and dissolve the baking soda in the vinegar. Carolyn lined the cupcake pan with pink papers and had an ice cream scoop ready to fill them. Julianne took charge of the final batter adding the sour cream and milk. The two ounces of red food coloring was the crowning glory.

While this was going on, Natalie tiptoed around the island snapping pictures of the students working while her mother peered over their shoulders. Many of the shots were sure to have Marta in the background.

The more Julianne realized the class was running smoothly, the more she realized how happy she was. She felt useful, alive, and proud of her endeavor. Her beautiful daughter was sharing the moment and that man sitting over there, well, that story was waiting to be written.

CHAPTER TWENTY

Class number two was over. The evening seemed to be a success. Julianne walked Carolyn, Willow, and Libby to the front door. She held the three to-go square boxes, each containing two red velvet cupcakes, while the women slipped into boots, coats, gloves, and fumbled for car keys.

"I had so much fun." Libby practically squealed. "Thank you. Thank you." Impulsively she grabbed Julianne and wrapped her in a big bear hug.

"Whoa. Don't make me drop the cupcakes." Julianne freed herself, passed out the cartons, held the door open, and called after the three women. "Don't forget to think about your recipe-wish-list for the last class."

Carolyn turned back to say. "Can't wait to see what we all pick. Neat idea. Student's choice. See you next week."

With a deep sigh and tired smile, Julianne closed the

door. It had been a long day. She kicked off her shoes on the corner of the front mat, headed back to the kitchen, and anticipated a few special moments with Natalie. Hopefully, Natalie would head back to the city soon and Rob might stay for a glass of wine.

The sight of Marta's coat and hat draped over the club chair in the living room stopped Julianne short. She remembered her leaving the kitchen first. She had assumed she'd left.

Julianne headed to the back of the house. Rob and Natalie were seated side by side at the table with remnants of the evening meal around them. Natalie was intent on explaining the pros of an established website. Rob seemed interested in Natalie's camera and was flicking through the photos from the evening. After a cursory glance around the kitchen, great room and noticing the powder room door open and empty, Julianne retraced her steps to the front hall.

There it was. One of the double heavy wood doors of Jock's office was slightly ajar but it was dark inside. Julianne slowly pushed open the door and as soon as her eyes adjusted, she saw her. There, seated in Jock's leather desk chair, sat Marta. She watched as Marta ran her hands over the rich wood of the desktop, fingered the Mont Blanc pen set, closed her eyes, and gripped the arms of the chair.

"Who are you?" Julianne took one step into the room.

Marta slowly rose and walked toward Julianne. "Who do you think YOU are?"

"What are you doing in my husband's office?" Julianne blocked the doorway. "What do you want?"

Marta stared deep into Julianne's face. Julianne had to look away. The hatred in the other woman's eyes was tangible. In one sudden motion, Marta reached around Julianne, grabbed the door handle, and flung open the door, almost knocking Julianne over. With her face inches from Julianne's, Marta spit out the bitter words. "The last twenty years! That's what I want!"

With that, Marta hurried into the front room, grabbed her stuff, and raced out of the house.

Shaken, it took Julianne several minutes to compose herself. She stood in the dark room, staring at her deceased husband's desk, the trophies of his life that lined the walls and bookcases. She could almost feel his presence. A million thoughts raced through her head. A hundred different scenarios played out in seconds. With her stomach tied in knots, her fists clenched, she screamed in silence, *Secrets, lies, I don't even know you anymore. Why . . .*

"Mom, oh Mother, where are you?"

"Coming." Her voice cracked.

Nearly colliding in the hall, Natalie was startled by the look on her mother's face. "You okay?"

"Tired. It's been a long day. Well, actually a long week. The snow and all. You spending the night?" Julianne had to ask even though she was hoping the answer would be no.

"No. I'm leaving now. I was going to get my things. Need to be in the office early tomorrow." Natalie headed toward the mudroom off the garage. Her mother followed. "Big meeting and performance reviews coming up." Natalie pattered on as they passed through the kitchen. Natalie paused to exchange farewells and happy to meet you with Rob. Graciously, Rob returned the compliments.

Once out of Rob's hearing, Natalie grabbed her mother's arm. "He is one cool dude. You know that, don't you? Did you know he was single? And I sure hope you noticed he's hot. Nice bod. Nice guy, too."

"Darling, drive carefully. Text me when you get home." Julianne was all but pushing Natalie out the door. *Enough, enough for one night.*

Before she knew it, Rob was standing in the foyer just feet away from her. She fell into his arms. His arms felt so good, so strong. For a brief moment, she laid her head on his shoulder. "I was going to suggest a nightcap but you look beat." Rob gently caressed her back.

Pulling away, Julianne smiled weakly. "Nightcap. I haven't heard that word for ages. My father would send me and my sister off to bed and then fix a nightcap for mother."

"Oh, yeah. The old nightcap ploy."

"I'm exhausted. Not tonight. Here's another idiom, rain check."

"I'm cashing it in right now. Dinner. Saturday night."

As exhausted as Julianne was after such a long day, sleep would not come. Thoughts of Marta swirled in her head. Plus the memories of the papers Julianne found hidden above the mantle last fall and the old photos of people she didn't know. Then there was that attorney, Marconi, in New Colony, who said he had the last valid will and testament of Jock Girard. A great deal of money was left to someone else. What a shock that was. It ended with a pitiful amount of money she finally received after probate. There was no recourse.

Everything had to be connected, and this Marta woman figured into the mix somewhere.

It wasn't like Julianne to be an ostrich and hide her head in the sand but the situation was too painful, too complicated, too much of a betrayal. She took the whole collection of unanswered questions, compartmented it, and buried it deep inside. She stayed busy with the cooking classes, her daughter, and her friends. The money situation was thin but doable, really, what did she need? For now, it was all working out.

Her mantra soon became *I'll think about it tomorrow*.

Julianne also locked the other stuff away. The mystery surrounding Jock's death in an upscale hotel room, the unanswered questions concerning his past, the strange inheritance he left to an unidentified person. She had spent twelve years assuming she had a great marriage. Her husband was dedicated if not infatuated with her. He told her how beautiful she was, how smart, how fortunate he was to have her. Yes, he could be difficult at times, insisting he get his way, a bit arrogant. But then he would turn on the charm and all was well. Plus, he adored Natalie. Jock treated her as well as he treated his own daughter. The girls got along. When Shelby came to visit, they acted like any happy family.

Long before dawn, Julianne gave up hope of more sleep. She got out of bed and went directly to her kitchen desk. Only four student information sheets fell out of *The Kitchen* folder. That's right, the fifth student had been a mystery, uncommitted, arriving late, saying only she was Marta. Julianne hadn't gotten around to processing any paperwork for her. For a prior businesswoman, as successful as she had been, this was careless.

Damn, no phone number, no email. Julianne had planned to call Marta or at least fire off a strong email. She wasn't sure how the confrontation would go, but the overwhelming need to take action had Julianne wired. *Yes, Marta, even at five a.m.!*

JULIANNE wasn't the only one up early that morning

Thirty-five miles away, Natalie popped out the blue memory card from the digital camera and plugged it into her computer. Most of the shots turned out quite well and she downloaded them. Before she started to click on each one, enlarge, or edit the frame, she took a moment to turn her back on iPhoto.

Pulling a legal pad off her desk, she methodically wrote down every detail of the night she saw Jock with that strange woman. Being careful to list every aspect of the woman's face, hair, possible weight, composure, and expressions, Natalie wanted to be sure. Didn't want to transpose a memory into a photo. Last night Natalie was careful not to stare at Marta or aim the camera directly at her or engage her in conversation.

An hour later, she felt she had her answer. Natalie was a savvy young woman confident enough to trust her gut instincts. She now wanted much more information.

"Hey Mom. Hate to call so early. But you sound wide-awake. Me, too. I know, early bird I'm not usually. So your class was awesome. I loved it. Quick question. Shout out the names of your students. Yes, I do want them. I'll list them under that group pic I took. Good advertisement. Be nice in the brochure."

Moments later, Natalie held the phone away from her ear, too upset to speak. *You're flippin' kidding me.*

"You have everyone's name but that foreign woman. Really? You have a person in your house and you don't know her last name? Or her phone number, or address, or email? Mom!" Natalie knew she needed to tone it down. "Yes, you're right. No need for me to be upset, it's your little business."

After some forced niceness, Natalie said good-bye and all but threw her cell phone across the room. "I'm at a dead end! No further along than I was. With a last name, phone number, or address, I could track that broad down in a heartbeat. Now what! Damn it all!"

CHAPTER TWENTY-ONE

Saturday night was cold and blustery. Julianne didn't have a clue how to dress. Thinking about spending the next hours with Robert Murphy took her mind off Marta. For the last two days, she wrestled with different options, each one making her angry and agitated. This woman was the fly in the ointment of her wonderful cooking class.

Early this morning, she'd received a quick text from Rob saying he'd be over to pick her up at six. Wasn't that a typical man? Not a hint about the dinner destination. When she and Jock dined out she always knew it would be a special place and often for a special occasion. Jock would note her dress, go to the safe, and bring out her Miyamota pearls or sapphire brooch. Or maybe the three-carat stud diamond earrings that got so heavy by the end of the night. He loved to decorate his wife with the lavish jewels he bought.

Her favorite piece of jewelry was the rose gold Tiffany key that hung between her breasts from a matching box chain. It hadn't been a gift from Jock. Julianne bought it for herself with money she inherited from her mother. She loved to finger it and think of the wonderful life gift she'd been given when she was born, her splendid mother.

Tonight, what a quandary, what to wear with a guy who wears a letter jacket? Keeping it simple, she chose slacks, a long cashmere sweater, high-heeled boots, and her key.

"You climb up into a pick-up truck like an old hand." Rob fastened his seat belt and reached across the wide console to give Julianne's hand a quick squeeze. "Warm enough? I had your seat heater on when I drove over. Of course those dead animals you're wrapped up in should do the trick."

"Oh! Did I goof? I thought a letter-jacket-guy wouldn't mind a mink-jacket-girl?"

"Just kidding. You look good. I didn't spend most of my life in Texas with bunny huggers. When the big alumni boys with the big checks for the athletic department invited us coaches and administrators to their hunting lodges, we loaded our guns and went."

"You know what, Rob? I'm looking forward to hearing about your life."

"And me, yours. Here's the game plan for tonight. We're headed to my place for a cocktail and then out highway 27 to Round Prairie. Got a hole-in-the-wall tavern that makes a prime rib on Saturday night that will blow you away. You get a wedge of iceberg lettuce with the bartender's homemade blue cheese dressing and Grandma's scallop potatoes. Four star food in a one star joint. You in?"

Laughing and nodding Julianne said, "You bet, Tex. Bring on the beef."

Rob's house was a modest size ranch style tastefully furnished. Evidence of a woman's touch was present but it did look like a single man had been in charge the last several years. In the corner of the family room a neat pile of toys proved that two children spent time here.

After Rob seated Julianne on a stool at his built-in wet bar on the opposite wall, he proceeded to set out a silver martini shaker, a bottle of Bombay Sapphire, olives and two chilled martini glasses from the ice bin. "I saw that bottle of gin half hidden on your back counter last week and I took a chance you were a kindred spirit. We gin drinkers are a dying breed."

"Good call. And, being physic, you knew I liked it dirty with extra olives?" Julianne challenged.

"Seriously? I scored!"

After the shaker was shaken and the glasses filled, Rob looked at Julianne with his glass raised and proposed a toast. "Going out on another limb here." Clinking his glass against Julianne's, he looked into her eyes and said. "But, here's to us. Getting to know us. Us spending time together. You, me, becoming us."

Julianne put her glass down, reached across the bar, took Rob's face between her two hands, and leaned in to kiss him long and tender. With that, Rob set his glass down, wrapped his arms around Julianne's neck, and returned the kiss.

Breaking the moment, Rob took a sip of his drink and said, "Well, got to say. Necking over a bar isn't the best situation."

"No, not really. But the bartender is cute and he sure can make a mean martini."

Dinner was just as promised. They took a wintry drive out in the country on crunchy snow-crusted roads to a small rural farm community boasting a feed store, gas station, and bar. The food was excellent. The only drink of choice was draft beer. Thick prime rib a perfect medium rare, rich cheesy dressing on the lettuce and the most amazing potato casserole. Julianne wanted to hustle right into the kitchen and nab the recipe but of course she didn't dare. Some things are made with so much care and love the actual ingredients never really stack up. Grandma's au gratin potatoes were probably a good example.

Driving back to town, Rob rested his big leather gloved

hand on Julianne's slender knee. "I can fix us an after din-ner drink. Or shall we head to your house?"

"I think my home."

"Can I come in?"

"Rob, I don't know what to say, I . . ."

"I know, me, too."

"My house is still so full of Jock. And then there is Thursday nights. We have to act neutral."

"I get it. Not my place either. Sara, you know, you know it was the end there."

Julianne took Rob's hand, pulled off his glove, raised his hand to her mouth, and gently kissed it.

They drove along quietly until Rob turned his head to look over at Julianne. "Jul, I got it. Two more weeks and cooking school is out. I graduate. We'll go on spring break. Just the two of us . . . maybe up to Wisconsin. A weekend?"

"I've always wanted to go to Kohler."

"I played golf there last summer. The American Club is fantastic. The rooms are all about the fixtures. Oh my, the spa, right in the bathroom. It was wasted on me, all by myself. You will love the food. Lots of local fare. Yes, Lady, you got it. We'll drive up to Kohler and snuggle in."

The good-byes in the foyer of Julianne's home were long and sweet. The caresses were filled with anticipation and a promise of much more to come.

CHAPTER TWENTY-TWO

Looks like the gang's all here.

It was Thursday night. The third session of *The Kitchen* and Natalie was there, also. Only she was outside, in her car, waiting. It hadn't taken Natalie long to come up with a solution. Okay, so this Marta left no trail of her identity. *More ways than one to skin this cat.* And her plan wasn't dangerous. All she would do was wait until Marta left her mom's class and trail her home. Natalie decided not to confront her. Not yet. Tonight was a fact-finding mission. Her plans were to get an address, maybe a last name off a mailbox, for sure her license plate number and car description. The mission sounded simple enough.

After that, she would find a people search network through Google. For a fee, you enter a first and last name, or a phone number, or address with town or state. Any one of them will pull up a response. You pay more for photographs, social media accounts, police records, aliases, previous addresses, and people related to your search.

By this time tomorrow, Natalie believed she would have a bead on Ms. Marta Whoever-You-Are.

THE third cooking class started late. Everyone arrived by six but now that the camaraderie of the group had increased, so did the chitchatting. Except, of course, with Marta. As usual, she came in, dropped her coat and bag, took her stool at the counter, busied herself with the itinerary and recipes, and barely acknowledged the others. Carolyn tried to engage her in conversation but after Marta's one-word replies, Carolyn gave up.

Julianne was surprised that Marta showed up. If she had found an email address or phone number, Julianne might have contacted her to ask her to leave the group. But once Julianne gave the situation some thought, she realized the best way to find Marta's identity would be to see her again.

The cooking class registration paperwork was on the kitchen desk and Julianne was determined that Marta would fill it out tonight. She planned to approach her at the break and stand there until the pertinent information was down on paper. Not sure what to do about this woman, at least she would know her name.

How did someone check out another person's background? Hire a private detective, she supposed.

The mystery was getting out of hand. Julianne felt it was time to confide in someone. Maybe Adela, not Rob, definitely not Natalie, and least of all, Shelby. She didn't know Rob well enough to judge his response and no way did she want her daughter or stepdaughter involved in something that could adversely affect them. Tomorrow she would call Adela. Julianne felt bad that she'd not found time for her friend these last two weeks. Adela would be a good sounding board. She'd know what to do.

Time to cook. "Let's get started." Julianne finally got everyone's attention. Except for Libby who was busy telling Carolyn another long story about "her Timmy's" new achievement in school. "Libby, are you excited about tonight's menu?"

Poor Libby hadn't glanced at any of the pages at her place setting. "Of course, what's not to like?" In the next instance, she ducked her face to hide the blush. As her confidence was growing with each class, Julianne didn't mean to embarrass her. Tonight she was especially well groomed.

Taking a moment to pull it together, Libby added, "Everything we make is wonderful. I try each recipe at home. My husband now makes it in time for dinner almost every night."

"Wonderful news and thank you." Julianne expanded to the class. "Cooking is a form of love. I like to make food for my family and friends. I know they appreciate a good meal. On some level, they feel the affection and care that went into the preparations. And, Libby, your husband and son now feel that, too. Good for you."

As Julianne was about to continue, Willow stated, ever so softly. "My mother came to town to visit me and to see my new place. We always eat out. But I surprised her and made dinner. I did all the recipes from the first class." Willow actually giggled. "All the extra easy ones. They were really good and we had a nice evening. One of the first in a long while."

When she finished, everyone in the room clapped. Julianne wanted to give her a hug but didn't. Willow had been cold as ice and now she was warming around the edges. *That girl has a story and I fear it's not pretty.*

"Willow, thank you for sharing. What a nice thing to do for your mother. How happy you made her with a simple but delicious dinner. That's a great lead into tonight's agenda."

For the next ninety minutes, the pots and pans cluttered

most of the six burners on the Wolf range. The double ovens were heated and filled with meat searing and a French tart baking. Tonight's theme was a formal dinner party. Julianne explained how every cook, regardless of skill level, should have a dinner plan in their repertoire. A menu they could put together with confidence, time and time again, explaining, "It helps the stress meter go way down when we have to entertain. And there are times in our lives when we do have to do that."

Everyone participated. They cooked in a fury. Julianne brought cutting boards and knives to the counter and assigned them prepping a veggie or spice. Others she called up to stir a pan or start the Roux for a sauce. The kitchen hummed with the noise of cooking and the muttering of the students as they worked.

Once everything was in the ovens or resting on the stove people returned to their seats.

"Let's take a minute to review what we've accomplished." Julianne leaned with her back to the island. "Our stuffed pork tenderloin is seared and now slowly roasting. The root vegetables are boiling on the stove and we'll be mashing them shortly. Our dark cherry tart is baking in the bottom oven and soon we'll start sautéing the pears in the brandy butter for our warm pear and blue cheese salad."

Julianne walked over to the row of students and stood at the end next to Rob. "Can everyone smell the sage seasoning from the stuffing in the pork? How about the buttery tart crust starting to brown? Ah, that sweet aroma is the cherries releasing their sugar and cooking down."

All five students took in the amazing scents and nodded in agreement. Carolyn wiped a tear from the corner of her eye. "I'm sorry, but I can't help it. Yes, it is the smells. I'm remembering Grandma's kitchen. Out on the farm. I stayed with her most of the summer when I was growing up. Always a fruit pie in the oven and lots of pork. They raised pigs."

Libby put her arm around Carolyn and gave her a brief hug. Rob looked up at Julianne, smiled and winked, as if to say "good job teacher."

"Cooking is going home or back to a favorite friend's house after school." Julianne was touched by Carolyn's reaction. "We forget how powerful our sense of smell can be. Now let's take a break. Back in fifteen."

Julianne intercepted Marta as she slid off her stool. "Can I see you for a minute? I have a form I'd like you to fill out. Okay?"

"Actually, no. I have a headache. I'm leaving." Marta brushed by Julianne and headed to the living room to get her coat and pashmina.

"Will I see you next week?" Julianne followed and forced herself to casually ask as she watched Marta bundle up.

The words were hard and nasty as Marta stormed out,

"You won't see me here next week. But you will see me again. That I promise."

"Wow! Good thing I got here early. Why is she leaving forty-five minutes before the class is up?" Natalie hastily put her IPhone down in the empty cup holder and started her car. She was parked on the other side of the street, which enabled her to have a clear view of the four cars lining the curb in front of her mother's house but she didn't know which one belonged to Marta. The silver pick-up was parked in the driveway. Natalie assumed it belonged to Rob. If she wasn't so consumed with this Marta woman, she would give him a little more attention for her mother's best interests.

The range rover was wedged in between two vehicles. Marta lost no time rocking it back and forth, straightened the wheels, and took off down the street at top speed. Natalie jerked her car into the nearest driveway, threw it in reverse, and headed down the street after Marta.

Natalie gripped the steering wheel in the ten and two position. The BMW slipped a little on the icy road. Natalie clenched her teeth. "Hold on! I didn't expect a chase. But I'm on it!"

CHAPTER TWENTY-THREE

"**W**hat the hell?" Marta glanced in the rear view mirror and then looked again.

The BMW behind her blew through the yellow light, spun out ninety degrees, quickly righted itself, and now was directly behind Marta's Range Rover.

Marta was in no mood. She'd stormed out of that stupid cooking class when she couldn't abide another minute in the same room with that Julianne woman. *Now really? Someone is following me? We'll see about that?* Holding the steering wheel with one hand Marta reached across the console, flipped open the glove box, removed the Smith & Wesson 38 Special from its leather holster, and laid it on the passenger seat.

For most of her life Marta had lived "on guard," so being hyper-alert was a natural state. Even more so since she'd left his dead body in the hotel room. He'd died a natural death but she should have called an ambulance, or the police, or at least the front desk. But the authorities weren't a choice. Not with the political atmosphere concerning immigration. Not with her past police record and probation.

It had been their third visit and it felt like they were bonding. Over morning coffee, they talked amicably about their lives. He seemed genuinely interested, displayed remorse, concerned for her well-being, even affectionate. At lunch he complained about being short of breath. He hardly ate a thing, said his stomach was upset. Marta encouraged him to come back to her room to rest before he drove back to Oak Grove. The room was in his name, put on his credit card. As usual, he'd made all the arrangements when she came to Chicago.

"WHAT the hell?" Miles later the BMW followed the Ranger Rover through the busy intersection and maneuvered the tight turn onto a little traveled side street. "I'm being followed! My God, it looks like a woman driving!"

Marta slammed on her brakes. The fifty-five hundred pounds of SUV sat in the middle of the street like a brick wall. The BMW plowed into it at forty-five miles an hour.

Marta cranked her head to the right to look between the front seats and back toward the car. "Lots of white in that front seat. Oh well. Looks like the air bag worked." She pulled the Range Rover slowly forward. The vehicles were not hooked together. Working quickly she put the gun back into the holster, laid it carefully in the glove box, and nudged the door closed.

"Good!" Marta laughed and sped off.

THE third cooking class ended on a strained note. Julianne had to tell them something as they heard the front door slam. Julianne saw the questioning looks when she returned to the kitchen. Her first thought was to say that Marta had a sudden onset of a migraine. That sounded okay. But why? Julianne asked the remaining four to be seated. Told them that for whatever reason Marta chose not to stay for the entire class. Would she be back next week? Julianne answered with a shrug of her shoulders, saying, "I don't know."

The pace picked back up. The warm pear and blue cheese salad was simple and fun to make. Everyone loved the idea of cooking with brandy and marveled at the deep flavor it added. Dinner was served in Julianne's beautiful dining room. The theme of a dinner party and the formal setting made for a perfect mood. Only the empty chair and untouched place setting cast a shadow over the night.

After oohing and aahing over the culinary delights they created tonight, there was much discussion about the recipes the class was to make the next week. Julianne had asked each student to submit a dish they particularly liked but didn't know how to prepare. "Leave me a note tonight or send me an email by Saturday. I will need time to research and shop." Laughing, she added, "I retain the right to veto your choice. Who knows, maybe I won't have a clue how to fix it. If that's the case, I'll ask you for plan B."

Carolyn had to ask, "If you don't hear from Marta, what about her choice?"

"I'll try to contact Marta. But the show goes on. I'll throw something of mine into the mix and it'll all be good. We'll call it an old-fashioned smorgasbord."

"I haven't heard that term for a million years. My mother called those potluck church suppers smorgasbords." Carolyn smiled. Libby said "Yes," her grandma had used the term.

Julianne pursued the group to leave the dishes and start for home before the weather turned nasty again. Really, she was the one with a headache. This business with Marta was upsetting and she thought it had a hint of danger. *Tomorrow, tomorrow I share this story with Adela. I need some good, sane, practical advice.*

Five minutes after everyone left the doorbell rang.

Julianne hastily wiped her wet hands before hurrying to the foyer thinking scatterbrained Libby probably forgot something. "Rob?" Julianne opened the door in surprise. Before she could say another word, Rob stepped inside, closed the door behind him, took Julianne in his arms, and just held her. "I drove around the block. Then drove right back. You looked like you needed a hug."

With a chuckle, Julianne pulled back and said, "This would be quite lovely if the front of your goofy letter jacket wasn't freezing cold."

"I'm sorry. It's warm on the other side." He unzipped the jacket, pulled it apart, and hugged Julianne into his warm chest.

What was it about this man that made Julianne smile? It felt so good to rest her head against him, breathe in his manly scent, and not think about a thing for the moment.

"You looked upset after Marta left. Now don't get me wrong, you carried on like a real trooper. Couldn't have expected anymore from one of my guys after they'd get their bell rung and I'd push them back out into the game." Rob kissed her forehead. "But I suspect there's more to this story." Rob held her back at arm's length and looked into her eyes. "Going to give it up?"

"I need to tell someone. But I don't know what to tell. Or if there is anything to tell." Julianne took Rob by the hand and lead him into the dimly lit living room. Seated side by side on the brocade couch Julianne relaxed into the deep cushions, curled her feet up under her, and sighed.

"Hey." Rob smoothed the loose hair off her forehead. "Start at the beginning. The day she enrolled in your cooking classes. How did you meet her? Where did she come from?"

Thirty minutes later Rob was as miffed as Julianne. Marta's cold demure, hatefulness toward Julianne, the wandering through the house, the snooping in Jock's office, looking here and there, not revealing her full name, address, phone, were random bits and pieces. Yes, it all warranted concern but not enough information to figure out why.

If it occurred to Julianne that her husband's hidden secrets and a previous life pertained to this stranger, she wasn't ready to admit it. Or she wasn't ready to reveal Jock's sketchy life to Rob. Was it standard allegiance to a family member, especially a dead one?

When it seemed there was nothing more to hash over, Rob suggested a snifter of brandy. Julianne agreed to just one. "Thank you for coming back. I liked that." When Rob offered to help clean up, Julianne shook her head, "Really, don't help me clean up tonight. I'll sip this. Then I just want to sleep."

"Tell you what. If you want, I'll come over tomorrow

and do all your pots and pans. I'm a mean man with scrub brush and . . ."

The phones rang throughout the house. Julianne rolled her eyes and thought about ignoring it but something told her a call this time of night might be important.

She made her way to the phone on her desk. There it was. The caller I.D. read Mercy Hospital.

"Hello?"

"Is this Julianne Girard? Are you the mother of Natalie Bennett?"

CHAPTER TWENTY-FOUR

For the rest of her life, Julianne Girard would not remember the next thirty minutes. Once she hung up the phone, she turned to Rob and said she had to leave *Right Now.*

Rob Murphy took over. He found her shoes under the coffee table by the couch where they had been sitting. Told her to find her purse and cell phone. Rob knew there was a closet in the laundry room where he found a white down woman's parka, gloves stuffed in the pockets, and somehow got Julianne into it while she kept yelling they had to leave *right this minute.*

Together they rushed out the front door to Rob's pickup. Later, upon returning home, Julianne would find the door unlocked.

Rob knew exactly how to get to Mercy Hospital. More times than he wanted to remember, he'd made the trip with Sara for countless tests, consultations, and emergencies.

His daughter worked in the smaller, private hospital on the other side of town. Mercy Hospital was home to the best trauma center outside of the city.

The minute Rob stopped in front of the emergency room's double doors, Julianne bolted from the truck, not taking the time to reply to Rob's statement about parking the vehicle and then finding her inside.

Julianne cornered the sleepy woman at the registration window, got the information she needed and rushed to the cubicle assigned to her daughter. Natalie was sitting up on a gurney holding an ice pack to her nose. A doctor and assistant bent studiously over her left knee.

"Mom." Natalie mumbled. "They got ahold of you. I couldn't call. Lost my phone."

Julianne wanted to barge in and hug her daughter but there wasn't room to reach the head of the bed. Julianne saw in an instant that her child was not seriously injured. Julianne's legs started to buckle under her as the adrenalin spike dissipated. She caught the edge of the bed, took several deep breaths, and tried to speak. "Oh, Natalie," was all she managed.

"Mom!"

Another nurse, carrying a small computer, pulled back the drapes surrounding the bed, noticed the failing woman, pulled a chair over, and helped Julianne sit down.

"That's better." The kind nurse patted her shoulder. "Are you Mrs. Girard? I'm the one that called. Just relax while I ask our patient a few questions."

"Mom, are you alright? Please calm down. I'm going to be okay. Really."

"Ms. Bennett, do you have your insurance card? No? Purse still with the car?"

"Natalie, between 1 and 10, what is the pain level of the knee?" The doctor asked, as he carefully manipulated her knee.

Natalie winced and breathed out. "I'd say a 5, border-line 6."

"Nurse, we need to start an I.V. as soon as you're done there." He took Natalie's hand. "Young lady I think you owe a big thank you to your air bag. We'll see what the damage is in this leg but my guess is it's not something we can't handle and you will completely recover. We'll take you up to X-ray next."

Sirens blared in the distance. Everyone left the room but the nurse. Julianne moved to Natalie's side. All she wanted to know was what happened. But Natalie's nose started to bleed again so Julianne reached for a fresh towel and gently laid it over her daughter's mouth to catch the blood.

Rob wasn't allowed into the emergency area. He paced the length of the waiting room, asked twice for an update, and was told HIPAA laws forbid it. Of course, he knew that.

Before the aide arrived to wheel the gurney to X-ray, Natalie and Julianne had a couple of minutes alone together. Julianne held Natalie's free hand and looked into her bruised face. "Are you sure you're all right? What happened, honey?"

"I think so. My nose hurts but they said it isn't broken." Natalie grimaced at the taste of blood in the back of her throat. "My leg is killing me. But the ambulance driver didn't think it was broken either. But something is wrong with the knee." Natalie swallowed. "I rear ended a car. I promise, I will tell you all about it. Just not now."

"Of course, honey." Julianne arranged the thin blanket around her daughter. "Are you still in a lot of pain?"

"They gave me a shot. I'm not too bad now." Natalie closed her eyes and succumbed to a light sleep.

"Excuse me, ma'am. I'm going to take the patient upstairs." A burly man with a buzz cut and purple scrubs walked in and unplugged the connections to the bed.

Julianne quickly kissed Natalie's cheek as she was wheeled out. Natalie weakly smiled and gave a little wave with her hand.

As Julianne stood alone in the center of the empty cubicle, she looked at her watch and realized it was only a little after ten. This had all happened in the last hour. It felt like two days. She knew Rob still had to be somewhere out there. Probably waiting, worried, with no information.

It was well after midnight before Natalie was assigned a room.

Rob had long gone home as Julianne had insisted. She was staying the night and would call her girlfriend in the morning for a ride. But he did not leave until he made Julianne promise to call him if she needed him. And not before he set her up with a large coffee and a chair off by herself in the crowded waiting room away from all the other luckless sick, injured folks and their families and until Julianne could rejoin Natalie.

The pleasant woman at the admittance desk tried to keep Julianne informed. But it was a busy night filled with children with bad colds, the flu virus, complaints about chest pains and other ailments. A lot of people needed help.

Finally Natalie's tests were over and she was moved up to the hospital wing. Room 214 was a private room. Julianne saw to that. The night nurse settled Natalie in, explaining how to adjust the bed and use the call button. Lightly patting Natalie's shoulder and speaking in an efficient voice, she assured her new patient she'd be comfortable, as a pain management drug had been added to her I.V.

Before Julianne could get close to her daughter, a young woman arrived with a tray filled with tall vials and explained she was to take blood for the lab work the doctor had ordered. After she left, the nurse returned with the blood pressure machine and also took Natalie's temperature. "Natalie, I just took a call from Dr. Willis, he's the Hospitalist who will be handling your case. He may not be in to see you until early morning. He'll have all the test results then. The police will also be here in the morning to question you. Apparently, the other driver left the scene."

Julianne leaned against the windowsill and shook her head feeling totally helpless and totally flabbergasted. *I'd like to talk to the doctor now. But I'll wait. What choice do I have? What the hell went on with this accident? Who cares? That is not important right now! Thank you, God. My baby girl is going to be okay.*

The night was long and fitful for both mother and daughter. Julianne wanted to climb into the narrow hospital bed with Natalie and hold her close.

When Natalie was five, her father left them, moving to California to find himself and a music career. Julianne, single and alone, would put Natalie in her toddler bed, check to make sure she was asleep, and then crawl into the big empty bed down the hall. Somehow, little Natalie wound up with her mother, snuggled into the curve of her back and breathing softly. Julianne never minded. It made them feel safe and secure. They had each other.

An overstuffed vinyl chair was Julianne's bed. She pushed it next to Natalie and held her daughter's hand. The nurse was quiet but she woke them every couple of hours as she checked Natalie's vital sign.

Finally morning came. An aide that spoke little English brought them fresh towels, soap, toothpaste, and brushes. Julianne thought she could smell herself and was grateful to freshen up.

The knock on the partially open door startled them. "Good morning. I'm Dr. Willis." A man in his mid-thirties strode into the room carrying a metal clipboard. He walked over to Natalie, shook her hand, and explained his position in her care and recovery. He nodded toward Julianne who quickly explained she was Natalie's mother.

His report was concise. "The X-ray showed the knee sustained a patella dislocation. Which means, when the air bag inflated it jammed your left leg forcefully into the driver's door. This caused the kneecap to be pushed off the knee. It appears there are no torn ligaments." Dr. Willis looked up from his notes and asked, "Natalie, what kind of a car were you driving."

"A BMW, not new, and not a big one."

"And that is the good news. Heavy frame. Side air bags.

Saved that leg from serious injury." The doctor lifted up the sheet and uncovered Natalie's leg. "Last night we put this immobilizer on and that's it. The kneecap is back in place. I want you to wear it for three, four weeks. Along with crutches that should do it. You look in good shape. Work out?"

"I do. And run. What's the prognosis for running again?"

"Not any time too soon." Dr. Willis smiled regretfully.

Next the doctor explained the facial trauma. Natalie's nose was not broken but the cartilage of the nasal septum was bruised. "Keep ice on that. I'll order the nurse to see you have a continuous supply. I think there will be ecchymosis. Maybe both eyes. We all know that as a black eye. Ice, time, your pretty face will be back." Dr. Willis took Natalie's hand. "It could have been much worse."

Turning to Julianne he added, "Mom, you can take your daughter home this afternoon. I'll release her after lunch."

After Dr. Willis left, Natalie raised the head of her bed, swung the tray over her lap, and declared. "Bring it on. I'm ready for breakfast."

They both laughed. The tension was released now that they knew she would be fine.

"Mom, go home. Take a shower, eat something, and bring me some clothes for me to wear home. I'll call you when they release me."

"You sure? You'll be coming home with me. I want you to stay with me for a while. What about work? What about your car?" All of a sudden all the details of real life bubbled up. "What about the police?"

"Mom, go home. I can handle a few cop questions. This afternoon we'll work out the logistics of my convalescence." Natalie was getting impatient. The last thing she wanted was the police and her mother in the same room. She hadn't decided how much of the actual details of the accident she would reveal to the police. "Mom, please, I want to eat, then sleep. You need to go home."

CHAPTER TWENTY-FIVE

Julianne was in the hospital lobby when a terrible thought occurred to her. There was no car waiting to drive home sitting out in the parking lot. It took her about five seconds to remember what she told Rob she would do.

"Adela, I need a ride." Julianne was dead tired. "Don't be alarmed. I'm at Mercy Hospital. Please don't shout. It's Natalie, she was in a car accident. Will be okay. Please, I'll tell you everything, but I just need to get home right now. Thank you. Yes, I'll be outside waiting, just pull up, I'll jump in, nobody will see you in pajamas. Wear a coat for God's sake, it's cold."

On the short ride back to Julianne's house, Adela asked a million questions. It didn't take her long to figure out Julianne wasn't going to elaborate about Rob Murphy and her ride to the hospital last night with him. Anyway,

Adela cared much more about Natalie, her injuries, and recovery.

Adela was very fond of Natalie. Not having any children of her own, she'd developed a special closeness with her best friend's daughter. Back as two single women, before Julianne married Jock, little Natalie had been included in many of their outings. Julianne jokingly accused Adela of turning Natalie into a shopaholic before she was age ten.

An hour later, they were seated at Julianne's kitchen table. When they got home, the first thing Julianne did was run upstairs for a quick shower. There is something immediate about getting that hospital smell off one's skin and hair. Meanwhile, Adela made a pot of coffee and scrambled three eggs with scallions, mushrooms, and Swiss cheese. When it was finished, she nestled the omelet pan and a plate into the warming drawer and turned on the heat. Next she cleared off the dining room table, unloaded the dishwashers, wiped off counters, the big island, and decided to ignore the floor. "That's what cleaning ladies are for." Adela said to no one in the empty kitchen. She was still opening cupboards, looking for a toaster, when Julianne came down the back stairs with her hair wrapped in a bath towel, wearing sweat pants, and a sweatshirt.

"You cooked! Addie, a woman of many talents! Who knew?" Julianne walked over to her friend, put her arms around her, and hugged her tight. "Thank you, I needed that."

More than a little surprised, Julianne wasn't a huggie touchie kind of woman, Adela hugged her back before pushing her toward a place setting at the counter. "Sit, let me get your plate. Eat while the eggs are warm. And the toaster is where?"

"No, don't bother. This is perfect. I need gallons of that coffee. Did you know the hospitals only serve caffeine free? I mean, really? We're not there to sleep!"

Adela served her friend a warm plate piled high with fluffy eggs. She brought two steaming mugs to the table. She sat across from Julianne and watched her eat. When Julianne's plate was clean, she looked her directly in the eye. "Now, start from the beginning."

It took Julianne a minute to contemplate where exactly the beginning began. And she still didn't know any of the details of Natalie's accident. Later this afternoon, or this evening, when her daughter was settled in here, in her home, they would talk it all out.

"It all started with the fifth student . . ." Julianne began and then unloaded it all. She described the mysterious and sullen woman who walked into the house the evening of the first cooking class. The times she found this woman, named Marta, snooping in Jock's office. How this woman refused to give Julianne her name, phone number, address.

Julianne, tired and wary, told Adela how there had been, at times, gestures, expressions, a strange feeling in her gut that this Marta reminded her of Shelby, Jock's daughter by his first marriage. She told Adela she'd suppressed this crazy intuition because she didn't want to believe Marta could in anyway be connected to her family.

"But last night, oh my goodness, was it only last night, in the middle of class, she, yes Marta, stormed out of here." Julianne anticipated Adela's next question. "I have no idea why. Well maybe, a little. I asked her to fill out one of the information cards. She bolted."

"Okay. I get all that. And you are right. It is imperative that we find out her last name. Where she came from." Adela looked out the kitchen windows, deep in thought, before she continued. "But then Natalie has an accident. Way out here. On a Thursday night. Did you know she was coming?"

"No. She's being a real pill about talking about what happened. I'll find out this afternoon. I wanted to stay and be with her when the police came to question her but she balked. I was too tired to fight her."

Adela rested her hand on top of Julianne's. "She's a grown woman. It's her life. For all we know she has a guy out here." Adela squeezed gently and looked at the big clock on the back wall. "Honey, it's only nine, you go upstairs and lie down for an hour or so. I'll wait here in case Natalie or anyone calls. I've got my laptop in the car. I can work from here this morning."

"Oh, I don't think so." Julianne rose and cleared her plate.

"You are dead on your feet. An hour's nap could do you a world of good. Give me that dish. Off you go. Hand me your cell. I promise I'll wake you if anything important happens."

Julianne smiled weakly and muttered, "Thank you," as she slowly climbed the stairs.

After quickly cleaning up the breakfast mess, Adela pulled on her boots and ran through the cold. She grabbed her laptop out of the rear seat. Once back inside, she set it up on the kitchen counter. Then she quietly walked to the bottom of the stairs and listened. Hearing nothing from the direction of Julianne's bedroom, she made her decision. *Those old photos, the birth certificate, the name change, there's a link there some place, and I just know it! One of us has to try to figure this out. Poor Julianne, her plate is full. Let me see what I can do.*

In her stocking feet, Adela tiptoed down the front hall and stood in front of the closed double doors of Jock's office. Very quietly, she turned the handle and let herself in.

THE young policeman cleared his throat several times. He stood in the back of Natalie' hospital room nervously twirling a pen and a balancing a yellow notepad. The rookie cop couldn't help but notice the patient's nice figure under the thin blanket and her long dark hair splayed across the pillow. "Excuse me ma'am." He coughed to get her attention. "Ma'am, sorry to intrude. But I do have to ask you a few questions."

Natalie stirred, opened her eyes, and woke up. She had been busy concocting her story when she must have fallen asleep. "Oh, yes. Sorry, I nodded off. I was expecting you." Natalie pushed the button to raise the head of the bed. She modestly pulled the blanket up to her chin and looked into the uncomfortable and naive green eyes of the rookie police officer.

This will be a cinch. Almost fun.

IT didn't take Adela long. Julianne had obviously sat at Jock's desk with the pile of documents, old photos, and opened the most convenient drawer. And because she is right handed and Adela is right handed the logical first choice was the top right hand drawer. *Bingo.* It was all there.

First things first. Get the last name. Adela found a notepad and pen. But wait. Tucked away on the bottom shelf of the back credenza Adela saw the printer. *Good job, Jock, you bought the expensive one with the copier on top.* Adela made short work of gleaning the information she wanted.

As silently as Adela entered the office, she left.

In the kitchen, she reached for her cell phone and scrolled through her contacts. "Damn it all. Why don't I have his number on here? Oh, there it is."

Buck Milbank was a private detective Adela knew from a long time ago. Back when Bucky was a cop and Adela a new real estate agent who liked to party, she and Buck seemed to drink at the same bars and had hooked up more than once. They got along well together, in and out of bed. They were good friends. Both eventually married but as the years wore on so did their relationships. They knew the difference between love and lust, the big difference between commitment and convenience. On some lonely nights or boring afternoons, being together for a few hours soothed the restlessness.

Middle age found Bucky divorced and retired early. He always liked snooping around so when he became bored, he opened a one-man detective agency. Adela, divorced for years, continued to be one of the top realtors in town, and lived with a guy she was quite fond of. But Buck was always a phone call away. Like he was right now.

After the usual banter, Adela got down to business,

explained Julianne Girard's position as a new widow, how Julianne found disconcerting history regarding her dead husband and then meeting a strange woman while teaching a cooking class. "All I know is this woman's first name might be Marta. And I'm thinking her last name might be Kochevar. I'd really appreciate it if you'd run a background check on her. No license plate number. Yeah, I might be able to get you a fingerprint. I'd have to come clean with Julianne and tell her what I'm doing."

It came as no surprise what Buck asked next.

Amused, Adela snickered, "Uh, hum, I remember that house. No, sweetie, I don't have a listing out in the country that's vacant and furnished. Don't worry, we'll work something out. I'd like to see you, too."

"Did I oversleep? Has Natalie called?" Julianne stumbled down the back stairs not completely awake.

"Got to go. Bye." Quickly hanging up, Adela covered her tracks by stuffing the copies she'd made in Jock's office into the side pocket of her computer case. "I was finishing up my calls and on my way upstairs to wake you. No, Natalie hasn't called. Here's your phone. Maybe you should give her a ring?"

"She has no cell phone. It's in her car. Along with her purse, I hope. The policeman who's visiting her today should be giving her the details. Like where is her car!"

Julianne's home phone rang. The caller I.D. showed Robert Murphy. "Addie, take this." Julianne brought the receiver over to Adela. "Tell him Natalie's okay, banged up knee, black eyes. I'm going to get dressed, get back to the hospital, and take care of my girl."

CHAPTER TWENTY-SIX

D r. Willis was standing next to Natalie's bed when Julianne arrived. They were deep in conversation and Natalie didn't look pleased. Julianne stood back, trying to catch the drift of the conversation, reminding herself that her daughter was a grown woman in charge of her own health care.

"Oh, Mom. I'm glad you're here." Natalie said as the doctor left the room. "I was about to call you. My room has a phone somewhere. Change of plans." Mother and daughter held hands as Natalie continued. "I might have a slight concussion. After boy-cop left, I went back to sleep and the nurse came in and woke me. I was a little confused, and I had double vision. Not serious, didn't last long, but I'm still a little blurry."

"Oh! And now what? What did the doctor say?"

"Well, he said he didn't think I had a severe concussion. But to be sure, he ordered an MRI and wants to keep me another day. When the airbag deployed, it snapped my head back. Thank you, headrest! Saved my neck. But it's like a whiplash. He said it's very common in car accidents and since I never lost consciousness, vomited, or have a terrible headache, I probably will be fine with rest."

"Thank God! Oh, honey, how did this happen? The car accident, I mean."

"Well, it's pretty straightforward. I rear-ended the car in front of me." Natalie turned her head away. "Not much to tell."

Julianne studied her daughter's face. A mother knows a lot of things and for sure she knows when her child, no matter what age, is lying or avoiding the truth.

"Scoot over. There's room for me to sit here on the edge." Natalie made room for her mother on the bed.

Several minutes passed in silence as both women were making a hard decision. Julianne spoke first. "There is too much going on. Your behavior regarding my cooking class has been strange. One Thursday you show up, take pictures, tell me it's for a webpage I've yet to see. A week later you're back in Oak Grove, on a Thursday, and involved in an accident. And why didn't the other car stop? I mean it was your fault. You were following too closely."

"I was trying to get her license plate number."

"What? Whose?"

"The crazy woman from your class. You think her name is Marta."

"What do you know about her?" Julianne raised her voice.

Natalie looked directly at her mother and said slowly. "I've seen her before. Over a year ago. Now, what do you know about her?"

Secrets are a terrible taskmaster. They are hard to hide, work around, and keep the cover on the details. There is an old axiom: you are either the keeper of the secret or the secret keeps you. Both women shared the burden.

"I think she knew Jock." Julianne decided it was time to share the truth about the man she married and the stepfather of her daughter.

"I know she knew Jock." Natalie stated. "I don't want to hurt you but this is what I saw." Natalie proceeded to describe being in an out-of-the way bar in Chicago where she saw Jock and Marta in an intimate conversation, and leaving without his noticing.

With a neutral face and steady voice, Julianne told her daughter that Jock had been someone else. Years ago, he had another name. He was Polish. He lied about his education. Maybe he had another marriage and may have had a child besides Shelby. He left a big amount of money to an unnamed person.

"How long have you known all this?" Natalie was dismayed.

Julianne shared it all. The hidden key, loose brick above the mantel, old lockbox filled with Jock's birth certificate, legal documents changing his name, and the faded family pictures.

"You still have all this, right? Will you show me all this stuff when I get home?"

"Yes, of course. But you, no more detective work." Julianne felt lighter. Her daughter was a grown woman. It was okay to tell her everything. With a loving touch, she brushed Natalie's hair off her forehead, bent and kissed her bruised cheek, and smiled. "Well, that was something!"

Natalie smiled back. "Mom, how about we make a little deal? I give up my spy career and we have no more secrets."

The door to room 214 burst open. "Ms. Bennett? I'm here to give you a ride to the big machine we like to call the Magnet, so we can look inside that head of yours. Easy does it. Let me help you into the wheelchair."

After they left Julianne, collapsed into the recliner by the window. The sun had peaked out from the thick gray winter clouds and covered the chair. Julianne closed her eyes and basked in the warmth. *It's all out. My daughter is back to me. Adela knows all about Marta. I'm no longer alone in this mess. I see three scenarios: Jock had a lover, Marta is his sister, or maybe she's the baby in his arms in that old photo. But what does she want with me? And why?*

Soon she fell asleep, too exhausted to keep thinking and guessing.

THE defunct strip mall that housed Buck Milbank's office was a deserted, rundown, unplowed old place. Adela shook her head as she parked in front of his sign and waded through the snow.

"Hey, lady, come on in. Welcome to my office." Buck greeted her at the door. "I've been here almost two years. Where have you been?"

"Buck, honey, this is not an office per say, this is a hole in the wall." Adela carefully stepped inside and looked around in dismay. The furniture was beyond second hand. Most of the drawers in the rusty file cabinets didn't close. The carpet had holes. The walls were gray or maybe just covered with years of dust and grime.

Bucky was as handsome as ever with his chiseled chin, rumpled Ralph Lauren, two-day-old beard, needing a haircut sort of way. He'd always looked like a tough cop. Now he looked like the quintessential aging but wise detective who still had an edge.

"Babe, right here. Take a seat." Buck grabbed a stack of manila files off a torn vinyl chair and tossed them on the floor a few feet away from his desk.

"Nice filing system." Adela sat down, opened her full-length mink coat, crossed her knee high, high heeled booted legs, and showed plenty of thigh from under the short black leather skirt. The black cashmere sweater, with a deep V-neck, revealed the tops of her expensively augmented breasts.

Detective Milbank might not have a neat office or new furnishings but he did have a bank of state-of-the-art computers, printers, scanners, and phones spread across his desk. He slowly walked around to his chair, never taking his eyes off Adela. "We need to get together more often. You are a sight for sore eyes. Looking good, old friend."

"And you, also." Adela tossed back her head and gave a throaty laugh. "I guess we are just like fine wine. We're aging well. But first, down to business. "

Buck sat down, picked up his reading glasses, perched them on the edge of his nose, flipped on the computer, and started typing until he found the right file. "Believe it or not, I think I put your woman together. Just from her first name and the Kochevar last name. She's a real person with a long history and probably not much of a future."

"Really? How so?"

"Let's start with a rap sheet as long as my arm."

"I thought I was in shape." Natalie was huffing and puffing by the time she reached the top of the stairs. It was Saturday afternoon and Natalie had been released from the hospital. "Next time you build a house, how about a bedroom on the first floor?"

"Good idea." Julianne was doing the best she could to hoist Natalie up step by step with little or no weight on Natalie's left leg. "Almost there. Do you really want to shower this afternoon? It's been quite a day for you. But I'll run down and get a garbage bag to cover that knee brace thing if you want me to."

"Sorry, Mom, but would you mind too terribly much? I've got dried blood in my hair. Will you help me wash my hair?"

"Honey, I'd walk over hot coals barefoot for you. Just having you home safe and almost sound is all I need. Thank heavens the MRI was clear. Rest and time will take care of the healing."

An hour later, Natalie was settled in her old room, freshly showered, wrapped in one of her mother's thick chenille robes, propped up on a mountain of pillows, sipping a cup of tea and munching an egg salad sandwich. "If my knee wasn't throbbing and nose didn't hurt every time

I chewed, I could be enjoying this. Not my usual wild and crazy Saturday night."

Julianne sat across the room with a notepad and pen she'd found in Natalie's old desk. Together they made a list of all the phone calls and errands that needed to be done in connection with Natalie's accident. Natalie knew where her car had been towed. Her purse, briefcase, and cell phone were secured in the office at the lot. The nice policeman had taken care of that. The first and most important call was to Bruce, her next-door neighbor. He had a key to her unit and would go right over to take care of her cat. She was probably just fine as extra water and food were always left out but Natalie would feel a lot better if she were looked after and pampered a bit. Next, the insurance company, her father in California, her manager at work, two best girlfriends, and her personal trainer were added to the list of people to contact in the next day or two.

"I wish we had a television set in here for you," Julianne said, picking up the dishes to head downstairs.

"As soon as I get my computer back I'll hook up to ITunes or Netflix. This is the twenty-first century, Mom." Natalie was getting back to her old caustic self.

"That may be but tomorrow I have to get it together for another class on Thursday. So my computer will be drumming up recipes, menus, and such. You know, simple old stuff." Julianne shot back. Both mother and daughter enjoyed the familiar banter.

Burrowing down into the pillows, Natalie mumbled. "I could fall asleep right now. Go, do what you need to do."

"Yes, sleep awhile. I'll check on you about six. We'll have dinner together up here."

"Thanks, Mom. Hey, I love you."

The winter afternoon light was waning when Julianne got back downstairs. She set the dirty dishes in the sink and sank into the chair at her kitchen desk. Without another thought, she covered her eyes with both hands and sobbed and sobbed until all the fear, anxiety, and distress of the last forty-eight hours was cried out.

When the phone, inches from her head, rang, Julianne saw his name and weakly smiled. Finally she picked up just as the machine came on with her recorded message.

FIVE times Rob got up from his recliner and paced the length of the family room and kitchen. He usually liked Saturday afternoons in the winter, home alone, the television on ESPN, the volume turned up. Starting about noon, he huddled down in his favorite chair with a big cold meat sandwich, a beer, and a bag of chips to watch one college basketball game after another. He knew most of the coaches whom he had watched come up through the ranks as players. He never babysat the grandkids on the weekends so he felt free to holler, yell, and occasionally cuss out the players, coaches, officials, and even the fans. Life was good.

But this afternoon he couldn't settle down, becoming more than a little irritated. Long before now, he'd expected Julianne would call him. Sure, he had that brief conversation with her friend, Adela, and he was relieved that Natalie was doing okay, but he thought he meant more to Julianne than this. *What the hell, I'll call her at the house, not on her cell. I won't bother her if she's at the hospital. I'll leave a message. Thoughtful of me. Concerned. That woman is under my skin but what the hell!* Rob counted the rings. By seven, the recorded message came on. It was good to hear her voice. Rob cleared his throat and started to speak when Julianne picked up.

"Julianne? Hello? Is this a bad time? Is everything going all right?"

For the next thirty minutes, he listened. Julianne told him about the accident, Natalie's injuries, her release from the hospital, and how she would recuperate at Julianne's home. He was shocked to hear about Marta as he hadn't paid much attention to her on Thursday nights. Figured she was quiet, maybe antisocial, certainly not nasty or threatening.

"What can I do to help? Of course, I understand. Just give me a call if you need anything. Hey, what about the last class? You think you can? Thursday isn't that far away."

Before he hung up, Rob had many more questions to ask but he didn't because it didn't make sense. Why was Marta some kind of threat? What was the connection? Rob knew he hadn't been told quite everything, but with Julianne stressed, he wasn't about to press her for more details.

He looked at his watch and saw it was almost four o'clock and time for the Illinois Michigan State game. And time for another beer.

"Hey, beautiful, you don't have to go already?" Bucky sat up in bed and watched Adela scurry across the floor to her pile of clothes in the corner. "You look just as good from this side. Come on back over here."

"Bucky, I have to get home. I've got obligations. And, well, sort of a commitment." Adela had to laugh at that.

"Yeah, yeah, I know." Bucky crawled out of bed and pulled on his boxers. "Now listen up. I don't know your friend, this Janice Ann person, but I know you and you think you're invincible. And now you tell me her kid is chasing this Marta down the street. Getting hurt in a car accident."

Bucky walked over and helped Adela pull her sweater over her head. "Don't either one of you gals start messing with his Kochevar broad. Just cause she was denied a gun permit don't mean she don't got one. You know, kinda like the ten thousand gang-bangers on the South Side. Gun permits aren't a high priority item to a lot of folks."

"It scares me, Bucky. She'll probably be back at JULIANNE's, that's her name, house Thursday night. Any ideas?" Adela zipped her leather skirt. "Can I take the file? We sort of forget to make copies at your office."

"Yeah, I know, you were in a hurry to see my apartment," Bucky guffawed.

"You are so bad, Bucky."

"Hey, you just told me, not more than ten minutes ago, how good I was."

CHAPTER TWENTY-SEVEN

Monday morning was indeed a new day. The sun was blinding white on the snow; the temperature was in the high thirties, a January thaw in February to lift the winter weary spirits. After nine hours of sleep, Julianne was up before dawn. She left the house before seven to be at the collision shop the minute they opened to retrieve Natalie's personal belongings.

Home by eight, Julianne was busy fixing a breakfast tray for Natalie when she came scooting down the back stairs on her rear end. "What in the world are you doing? Natalie, stop. You're going to put that knee out again."

"Mother, I cannot and will not stay in that room another day. I called Enterprise and they're bringing a car by around ten. I can drive. I have my right leg in perfect working order. I'm getting some soccer-mom type SUV so plenty of room for ole leftie here to stretch out."

"But your office said to take all the time you need."

"Of course they did. But we know that was lip service. I won't go in until tomorrow after the car is picked up. I have reports at the condo that need to be taken care of. And, since I told you about my cat, I need to get back to her. Bruce can't look after her forever. Thank heavens I gave him a key to my unit. Hey, I really do have work I need to do today. Thanks a million for getting my stuff this morning."

"You are so stubborn. You can't take the L to work with that leg. You haven't thought this through, Girl."

"Mommy, dear. I'll Uber."

"Oh, good grief! I give up!"

After Natalie pulled out of the driveway, Julianne finished her shopping list. Next, she would be off to the grocery store to shop for Thursday night's class. This was the last session of *The Kitchen*. Sunday afternoon she retrieved three emails: Libby, Willow, and Carolyn, all asking instructions for a favorite food they didn't know how to prepare. The emails were the loveliest things. Each woman wrote about the love of a particular dish and what it meant, growing up, at a holiday, or at a fabulous restaurant now closed. The project for Thursday was a people's choice menu.

She hadn't heard from Rob but a quick text took care of that. Maybe this evening she would call him but then she remembered he would be taking care of the grandchildren.

As she was pulling on her most practical snow boots, the front doorbell rang. "Now what!"

Adela was walking in the house as Julianne got to the foyer. "The door was unlocked. Oh, is Natalie sleeping? I'll be quiet."

"No. Already back in the City." Julianne sounded short.

"Really? She's a tough gal. But, honey, I know your plate is full. Still we have to talk. Yes, now." Adela put her arm around her friend and headed her down the hall and into the kitchen. "Have a seat. This is important." Adela pulled a crumpled brown file out of her tote size Burberry bag, laid it on the table, and took a seat next to Julianne.

"Marta's last name is Kochevar." Adela laid a picture of Marta in front of Julianne.

"So she is connected by family to Jock. But this looks like a mug shot."

"It is. She's not got a pretty history." Adela shuffled through several pages before she found what she wanted. "She was born in the United States, 1972, somehow went back to Poland where she spent most of her childhood. Came back here as a young woman. Worked all sorts of miscellaneous jobs and then the trouble started."

"What trouble?"

"Seems she had sticky hands. Petty theft from cash registers, shop lifting small items, and then moved on to cashing fraudulent checks, and a little credit card and social security identification theft. Yes, after being given probation, or community service, she finally did a little time."

"I don't know what to say. In a way I feel sorry for the girl."

"Oh, but it gets much better, or I guess worse." Adela pulled out another piece of yellow paper. "She probably learned a new trade in the Dwight Correctional Center. And, it didn't take long to become successful at it."

"What?"

"I think these women prefer the name Escort rather than . . ."

"You mean she's a prostitute, a hooker?"

"Apparently not anymore. She was busted for that in '08. Her record shows she ran a pretty good size ring. Right here in Chicago. Did a plea deal. We can only imagine how many doctors, lawyers, and Indian Chiefs wanted her list of Johns to disappear. She served another year, cleaned up her act during her probation period and dropped off the police radar screen. Maybe that's when she found Jock. Found a new money hole."

Sitting dumbfounded, Julianne took a moment to think before she twisted in her chair to look directly at Adela.

"How do you know all this? Where did this information come from? And why are you in charge of solving the mystery of Marta? "

"Julianne! Are you upset with me?" Adela reached for her friend's hand but Julianne pulled away.

Adela gave Julianne the short version. "I know a guy. Ex-cop turned P.I., I asked a favor. I'm concerned about you. How about Natalie? Her, too. Gone chasing after a woman who may have a gun? A crazy woman who may want revenge or restitution from a dead husband or father or brother. Really! You can't be mad at me?"

"I don't know what I am." Julianne rose from the table and walked to the center of the room. "I think I need to work through all this."

"Well, then, I guess I'll go."

"Thank you, I think you should."

More than a little offended, Adela walked toward the front door but before she left, she turned to Julianne and said, "My mother, almost always halfway into a fifth of vodka by noon would say with some drunken wisdom, '*no good deed goes unpunished,*' pretty intuitive for a drunk."

After hearing the front door slam, Julianne grabbed the edge of the counter before her knees buckled. The room was spinning out of control and Julianne's life was spiraling unchecked. A cloud of surreal thoughts surrounded her, as if she weren't sure where she was or who she was. And why was she still here? She fell into the nearest barstool and tried to breathe.

Oh, Jock! Was it just a year ago we were in Naples, Florida, walking along Barefoot Beach picking up shells?

Was it just last spring we'd called an architect to design a gazebo, greenhouse, and new shed in the back yard? And later, a tree house for our grandchildren. How we laughed, betting which daughter would give us one first.

And then, Jock, right before you died in early October you mentioned Paris for our anniversary in November. "We'll have the City of Lights all to ourselves at that time of year," you said.

After a while, the air cleared and Julianne came back to herself. "And now I'm all alone. My daughter is hurt. Shelby is not happy with me. I'm running a silly cooking class. I need to sell this beautiful house we built together. And, as an added bonus, I've just alienated my best friend.

"I'm sorry I doubted you, Jock. I did love you. Our life was good! I adore our girls. We were all good together." Julianne walked to the prep sink in the center island and turned on the facet. "But now is now. I have to finish out this week. Fulfill my obligations. And then, we'll see."

While taking a long drink of water, Julianne decided

she might as well get on with her day, picked up the grocery list, and headed to the mudroom for her coat when another thought stopped her in her tracks.

And craziest of all, I was thinking of getting involved with another man! Stop Julianne! This is not the answer.

CHAPTER TWENTY-EIGHT

Twenty-four hours before the final class of *The Kitchen*, Julianne took time to re-read the emails from her four students. They each asked for the instructions to prepare their favorite food. The ingredients were purchased, the recipes printed, and by tomorrow afternoon the prepping would be completed.

Not surprising, the requests lent a peek into her student's inner lives, hinting at where they were, what they were thinking, and what they really wanted.

This morning she finally received an email from Rob. It warmed her heart as she looked at it again. The recipe was simple enough, she had everything she needed but the message made her sad.

Sorry I didn't reply sooner. But, honestly, I

had no idea what to ask for. But now I do. My sweet little granddaughter asked me again today after school if we could bake cookies. She said . . . I don't want to make you sad Grandpa but Nana use to bake cookies with us. Well, I couldn't believe she remembered Sara doing that. But me, being the slug that I am, missed out on that too. Can you help me? It might be fun to make cookies with the kids. I would like to keep the memory of their Grandmother alive. Sara loved them with all her heart. Probably more than she loved me.

Julianne thought that sugar cookies would be more fun than chocolate chips or ginger snaps. She would give Rob a couple of her cookie cutters, food coloring, sprinkles, and a recipe for frosting. The kids would have a ball and the mess would be at Rob's house. Julianne smiled at the thought.

Then there was Carolyn's.

Dear Julianne,

I'm thrilled we have this assignment. I hope my wish isn't too complicated or pricey.

My former husband and I traveled extensively and one dish we always loved to order in restaurants all over Europe and in the States was a Veal Marsala. I'm curious to learn the secrets of the velvety sauce and tender paper-thin fillets of meat.

Many of those past meals are lovely memories and it's time for me to focus on the good things in the marriage. I'm working on getting over my anger.

Thank you . . . I love my Thursday nights,

Carolyn

But the email that touched Julianne the most was Willow's. Little by little the woman was softening. Maybe Willow had been afraid or just shy at the beginning. Julianne saw the hard edges melting. Julianne sensed she was forming a friendship with Carolyn. The kind, wise, older woman, would be a wonderful blessing to anyone struggling.

Julianne,
Re: Caesar Salad

This may seem a bit strange but I love this salad. It's not fancy but I order it out all the time. I've purchased every dressing made and still it's not very good when I make it at home. I think it's one of those things that is best made from scratch.

Most nights I eat alone. The garlic in it won't bother anyone else. LOL. I could add shrimp or chicken and make it a different entree. That way I'm not too bored with the same thing over and over.

I haven't met a lot of people here yet but in the winter it's hard. I don't like the long dark nights. I want you to know I think everyone in the class is so nice.

It makes me unhappy that Thursday is the last night,

Willow

Then, of course, there was Libby's request. Julianne had to laugh.

Hi Julianne,

I'm kinda embarrassed. I asked my Timmy and I asked my husband if there was something they really, really, wished I would make them. Well, they both said the same thing. Sorry. It's BBQ ribs.

I know you cook fancy food. BBQ ribs aren't. But would it be too much trouble to give me a recipe? Thank you in advance.

I loved the classes but I don't like sitting next to Marta. Sorry. But she IS strange.

See you Thursday, ☺

Libby

Oh, my dear Libby, almost everyone loves BBQ ribs, especially here in the Midwest. And do I have a recipe? You bet the farm I do! And we will cook up a rack or two.

Marta remained heavy on Julianne's mind. Try as she might with shopping, class preparation, recipe hunting, and pre-cooking, Julianne could not shake the feeling of a threat. Now that they had a last name it wouldn't be too difficult to track down an address or phone number. Julianne had played with the idea of calling the police. But what for? They would not believe Marta Kochevar caused the accident with Natalie. And the last thing Julianne would want is to get Natalie a ticket.

Poor Natalie had enough problems right now. The BMW was in bad shape, something about the frame being bent, and the insurance company was reluctant to come anywhere near the cost to fix the foreign car. Plus, getting back and forth to work with the banged up leg was making Julianne's sweet daughter grumpy. So testy that Julianne dreaded her phone calls.

Back to Marta. Julianne went round and round. What would she do if she walked in here Thursday night? Would Marta make a scene in front of the others? Should Julianne head her off at the front door and ask her to leave? And what about this idea Marta could have a gun?

That's Adela for you . . . drumming up the drama. What choice do I have? I guess wait and see what happens tomorrow!

It was almost a week since the accident. Marta's Range Rover was in the carport next to her one bedroom apartment she rented month to month. She wanted to be flexible, not knowing how long she'd stay in the area.

The SUV was backed into the carport. The scraped and dented rear bumper didn't show.

The news on television was broadcast from Chicago and local accidents in Oak Grove didn't make the cut. Marta wondered if the woman behind her had been injured when she slammed on the brakes going over forty miles-an-hour. Marta didn't really care, she just wondered. Concern that the police might be looking for the car and driver who left the scene of the accident kept Marta home. The last thing she needed was the cops beating down her door.

It was a huge inconvenience not to drive. On the warmer days Marta bundled up and walked the five blocks to the 7-11. Thank heavens they sold cheap wine, milk, bread, canned soup, and the homegrown Oak Grove rag newspaper that came out on Wednesdays. A local accident would be reported in that paper.

Today was Wednesday and that's where she was headed. Forcing herself not to glance at the front page before the clerk bagged the few items she purchased, Marta quickly walked home. She took her time hanging up her coat, putting away the cheese and bread, and pouring herself a glass of wine. A quick look at her new Cartier watch made her smile ruefully. "Ten o'clock in America, a bit early for a glass, but Europe, probably not."

Page by page, column by column, Marta scanned every inch of the paper. Finally there it was. Not even four complete lines. A brief summary of a woman sliding into another vehicle, no serious injuries, the driver telling the police the other car was slowing for icy conditions and she couldn't stop in time. No tickets were issued. The driver of the other vehicle was not being sought but asked to come forward voluntarily for insurance purposes.

This was the all-clear sign Marta needed. Now she had wheels again.

"A toast to my little friend," Marta raised her glass. "Sometimes you don't get what you want, you get what you deserve. Salute!"

Two glasses of wine later, Marta decided, "Yes, why not? I'll go Thursday."

THE kids were settled in front of the television watching *The Bee Movie* when the front door bell rang. Rob was in the kitchen cleaning up the dinner dishes. He hoped he could get the casserole clean, this time, without soaking it overnight. When he made the macaroni and cheese recipe from *The Kitchen* class he had the same problem. The grandkids loved it but the baking dish was a crusted-on-mess. He forgot about spraying the dish with Pam.

The doorbell chimed twice. "Hey, one of you guys, go get the door for me,. Rob yelled as he shook off his hands and grabbed a kitchen towel. He heard his grandson interrogating someone. The visitor sounded like a woman, but Rob didn't recognize the voice.

"A pretty lady wants to see you, Grandpa." The boy yelled.

"Where is she?"

"Standing outside."

"Invite her in, knucklehead."

"You do it. The best part of my movie is coming on. The people trapped Barry the Bee." With that, he took off running back to the family room.

"Oh, for God's sake."

"Grandpa! Language!" His granddaughter shouted.

Rob walked to the door still wiping his hands. "Can I help you?"

"Hi. I'm Adela. We talked on the phone briefly last week."

"Of course. Come in." *This is a surprise.* Rob pushed open the storm door, stood off to the side, and let Adela pass. He gave her backside the once over and approved of what he saw. "Nice to meet you. Julianne has spoken about you often. I know you're good friends. But . . ."

"But why am I here?" Adela nervously looked around. "Can we talk?"

"Sure. My little den is down the hall. A messy man-cave but the kids and their silly show won't bother us."

"You're little grandson is a cutie. The movie sounds very ambitious." Adela tried to tune it out.

"Bees, very upset bees." Rob smiled as he led her into his office. "Jerry Seinfeld made it; he's the voice of the main Bee. The kids love it; the scary part scares them every time, as if they don't see it coming."

Twenty minutes later Adela rose to leave. Rob showed her to the door and closed it quietly after making sure

Adela got into her car and drove off. He was not happy. But it all fit together. This Marta sounded like trouble, maybe real trouble.

Adela's warning was fresh in his mind. *"She's a woman with a grudge and could have a gun."*

CHAPTER TWENTY-NINE

Very early Thursday morning, Rob was still tossing and turning. It was a lot to think about. He had real feelings for Julianne and thought their relationship was moving along at the right pace. Spring wasn't far off and he imagined them spending long days together, doing a little traveling, quiet late night dinners, early morning walks, and making love. But this might all change.

Getting involved with a woman with serious problems was questionable. He had his own family to think about. What did he really know about Julianne Girard? Not much. How much other baggage was there? More to the point, what did he know about her late husband? Only what Julianne told him.

Wake up, buddy, this is Chicago. Who knows what connections anyone has or had.

This brought him back to Marta. *Shit! An old hooker. What's that about? Maybe he should skip tonight.* Four weeks ago he didn't know Julianne existed and life was fine. Maybe pick up where he left off back in January. Possibly go see a movie or sit in a bar and drink whiskey neat. Rob knew he had choices but none felt quite right.

Damn weather. What I need is a good long run. The Y's better than nothing.

The grandkids didn't come after school on Thursday so Rob had the day to himself. After a two-hour work-out, shower, and light lunch back home, he crashed on the couch and slept soundly. When he woke at 4:30, the winter sun was down, the house was cold and dark, and he was a man with a purpose, not some grunt with no backbone.

Julianne is a woman I want to be with. I've been a competitor all my life. I'm in any game for one thing only: to win. Watch out, I'm in.

Rob dressed carefully, pleased to see the dove gray dress wool flannel pants still fit perfectly and the starched white Brook Brothers shirt was without wrinkles. Back in the cedar closet, safe from moths, was the royal blue cashmere sweater Sara bought him for Christmas. It had been their last holiday together. The memory hurt Rob's heart for a moment as he slipped the soft fabric over his head.

Where is that damn stuff my daughter got me for my

birthday? The Chanel Blue cologne hadn't been opened. Not knowing how much to use Rob liberally sprayed his neck and chin, then gargled, brushed his hair, and smiled at the man in the mirror. *Not too bad for an old guy.*

Before leaving the house Rob Googled florist shops in Oak Grove and found one close to Julianne's home.

LATE Thursday afternoon, Carolyn returned from that wonderful little chocolatier shop on the far north side. She wanted to bring Julianne something special tonight. Her first thought was More Bakery and several of the most divine cupcakes on the planet but then, wouldn't that be like bringing diamonds and gold to the queen? Julianne was the queen of cooking, why give her food, probably not a good choice. But chocolate, every woman loved a little rich dark luscious chocolate now and then.

Maybe next weekend she would ask Willow out to lunch on Sunday. The exotic woman fascinated Carolyn. Smart, chic, aloof, vulnerable, all this in one package. But more than that, Carolyn sensed Willow could use a friend. Decades in public education crafted a fairly astute judge of character and Carolyn sensed another Willow, one she would like to get to know better.

Dressing for the last cooking class made Carolyn a little

sad. But a red quilted vest over her white ruffled blouse and black checked slacks cheered her up. Carolyn wore a lot of bright happy colors as a teacher. She felt it set the tone for the day.

Maybe this isn't an end. Maybe this will create new beginnings. Carolyn always tried to see the glass half full.

"Avon calling." Libby opened the door to let her neighbor in. "I've got your order."

"Thank you so so much. I know it was on short notice but I really really needed a special gift and I think *Skin So Soft* is a present any gal would like to get. Don't you?" Libby babbled.

"I've been an Avon Lady for fifteen years now and I tell you that lotion is on every woman's wish list. You done good, Libby."

"Come see my new outfit. I've been trying to get a little fancy. You got me going on the cosmetics and I think there just might be a few less wrinkles than there used to be." Libby held up a purple flowered dress and blue rhinestone necklace. "I love those Glimmer Sticks too. They just line my eyes and lips like a real movie star. Don't you think purple eye shadow would be good tonight?"

For at least the third time, Libby told her neighbor the same story about the wonderful cooking school she attended every Thursday night. Libby went on and on describing the classy teacher named Julianne and her new friends, Willow and Carolyn, and how beautiful their clothes were. She brought up Marta only once and glossed over her saying she was a little weird. She elaborated about the man student in the class who might have the hots for the teacher or maybe not.

The Avon Lady tried to leave as soon as possible and still be polite. A customer was a customer and now that her neighbor had found her inner glamour, she couldn't be rude.

WILLOW never thought to bring a little something to the last cooking class. She had been brought up in a strict right-wing ultra-religious household where frivolous trinkets and unnecessary gifts were forbidden. As a young child, she'd envied those fancy girls in the public school down the street who wore bows in their hair and plastic beaded bracelets. In high school she secretly horded *Seventeen* magazine under her mattress and counted the months until her eighteenth birthday would bring freedom from parents, the church, and the small southern

Indiana town that was like a prison. In her senior year, Willow refused to go to Oral Roberts University and her parents refused to pay any expenses at Indiana State.

Some of her frugal ways remained. In college she worked two jobs, saving every penny for tuition and a few good designer pieces. She crafted her sophisticated style with vintage clothes and an inbred sense of fashion. Now a lucrative career with matching pay allowed Willow to buy couture pieces. But still she purchased only a few and chose fashions that would endure through the years.

Willow's therapist encouraged her to open up and deal with the stringent austere religious doctrine that had a hold on her inner core. The psychologist asked Willow if she felt responsible somehow for the actions of her attacker. Was guilt a viable part of her constant fears? No, of course not! Willow shot back at her. But still the analyst probed, as if she suspected there was more, something buried deep inside Willow.

And there was. A bigger issue Willow dealt with by herself. The decision she made eight weeks after the violent night, one the church would assure her a pre-paid trip to hell. No way could Willow be straddled with any reminder of such a terrible man. It was her decision. She would never tell anyone the secret. The doctor was gentle, kind, and supportive. The procedure was quick. The recovery was rapid. Compartmenting the incident and locking it away was the coping method that worked best for Willow.

But now it was time to get ready to leave. Willow enjoyed the Thursday night class. *The move to Oak Grove was the right one. Thank heavens.*

Willow gathered up five handwritten invitations and took them to the front hall to put into her handbag. The invitations were to a little cocktail party she would host the second week in March. The day of the week would be Tuesday, the start of Mardi Gras, Fat Tuesday. Willow would make all the low country hors d'oeuvres and serve hurricanes in tall tulip glasses. Everyone in the class was invited.

Calligraphy had long been a hobby of Willow's. The invitations were beautifully done with purple, green, and pink ink, the colors of Mardi Gras. The time would be six to eight, short and sweet. She and her therapist talked long and hard about the plans and emotions that would go into entertaining for the first time. Together they explored the levels of expectations and pitfalls. In the end Willow came away confident she could handle a small simple gathering, just *The Kitchen* group and a few office friends.

Not so much black. No more hiding. I want to be me again. Willow stood in front of the long closet spanning the length of one bedroom wall. Without giving it another thought, she grabbed the Helmut Lang jeans, pulled the cream-colored Escada hooded sweater on and zipped her feet into three inch heeled brown fringed suede boots. Keeping the kohl eyeliner and white lip-gloss to a minimum freed her spirit. In another couple of weeks, maybe her hair would be long enough to swing when she shook her head.

Hurrying out the back door of the condo into the attached garage, Willow patted the pocket of the large Gucci bag. It was a habit of hers every time she left the house or office or a store; any time she ventured out into the wide-open world.

The bulge inside the outside zippered compartment meant the 9mm Glock was tucked inside. The traveling companion she never went anywhere without.

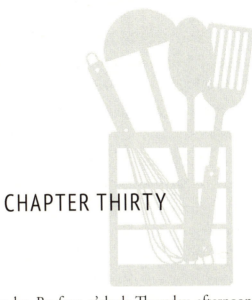

CHAPTER THIRTY

The day flew by. By four o'clock Thursday afternoon, Julianne was exhausted and edgy. Several times in the last eight hours she'd regretted this idea of asking the students to pick tonight's menu. Somehow working with their choices seemed more complicated and time consuming.

Taking fifteen minutes to relax with a hot cup of tea, Julianne curled up in the curve of the u-shaped sofa in the family room. Dusk was falling but Julianne didn't want to get up to turn on any lights. A million thoughts were circling in her mind each begging for a chance to be heard.

What about Rob? Can I go on with this relationship? Now? Jock's not gone for even a year.

It will be interesting to see how I feel tonight with Rob here in my kitchen and us working together.

Natalie? How did my daughter who lives in Chicago get

*involved? And get hurt? I've got to get her out of this Marta
business! Oh, dear. You don't suppose Natalie has shared any
of this with Shelby? Shelby doesn't need any trouble right now.
She's dealing with her dad's death, getting a foothold in the
design industry, making ends meet on her own. Enough. I'll
call Natalie tomorrow.*

*But that is a thought. Maybe Shelby's mother might know
something about this! Jock's first wife, or I think she was the
first, might even know Marta or know of her.*

*And that brings me to that woman! Marta! For once and
for all, I'm getting this over with. I don't care at what cost.
She's leaving my life and the life of my family and friends!*

*Oh! I almost forgot about Adela. That fence has to be
mended. After tonight. After I get this Marta off my back.
Adela, you'll forgive me. I know you will.*

*But tonight I still have to cook. I've liked this . . . actually
enjoyed these last weeks. For the most part it's been a success. But
do I want to go forward? Maybe. Here in the house? Not sure.*

The aroma of slow roasting ribs filled the kitchen and
great room. Julianne rose, put her mug in the dishwasher,
turned on lights throughout her home, and surveyed the
kitchen.

Three hours ago, Julianne rubbed two meaty racks with
her simple seasoning mix, spread a thin coating of BBQ
sauce, and topped them off with a layer of sliced onions.
They were wrapped, tightly sealed, in heavy aluminum

foil, placed on a rimmed cookie sheet, and put in a low oven at 300 degrees for five hours. When the class arrived she'd pull them out, go over the whole previous process, and let the ribs rest until the final step before they ate. It was an easy finish. Open the foil, discard the onions, heavily coat the fork tender ribs with more sauce, stick them under the broiler, wait four or five minutes and the result would be perfectly caramelized meat falling off the bones.

Caesar dressing was no problem. Julianne had been making this all her adult life. The old recipe had been tweaked a bit. Many cooks still made the dressing with a raw egg which made a difference, the flavor and consistency was much better. But fear of salmonella changed the process. Now the egg was either eliminated or hardboiled. The middle of the road approach was to coddle the egg by boiling it until the yoke was starting to set. Julianne planned to have Willow, at the center island, actually prepare the dressing with her guidance. They would also make homemade croutons.

Next it would be Julianne and Rob mixing sugar cookies. There was no way around it. The only way for Rob to learn was to actually cream the butter and sugar, add the eggs as the mixer ran, roll out the dough, and cut it. The cookies could bake while Carolyn and Julianne started on the veal Marsala.

After deciding not to pound the veal beforehand, Julianne assembled all the ingredients for the superb entree on a large tray and put it on the back counter. There were several steps to this wonderful dish but simple ones and it would be fun to see Carolyn involved. Julianne knew she would enjoy participating.

By five o'clock, Julianne was dressed and with nothing more to do, wandered around the house. It surprised her how nervous, jumpy and preoccupied she felt. Usually at this time, before a class, Julianne would be focused on the food to be prepared, rereading the recipes, adjusting the prep ingredients, and mentally going over the procedures. Not tonight. She paced between the front door and the kitchen, a sense of trepidation keeping her moving.

So when the doorbell blared, followed by rapid pounding, Julianne jumped. *WHAT?*

Startled and somewhat fearful she crept down the front hall. Even though it was impossible to clearly discern who was on the other side of the beveled glass door, Julianne was sure it was a man.

"Julianne, it's me, open the door, I'm going to drop this damn vase."

"Rob, what the hell?" Julianne turned the deadbolt, flung open the door, and collided with the man and his flowers. "What are you doing here?"

"Is that anyway to greet a guy bearing gifts? And, excuse me, but it is Thursday night." Rob stepped around Julianne and put the vase on the Bombay chest that lined the long hall wall. He turned to Julianne and saw distress, fatigue, and anxiety written all over her handsome face. "I know. It's been a rough week. So I thought some flowers?"

Julianne walked over, held onto the crystal vase with both hands, and buried her face deep into the lush bouquet. It was filled with hydrangeas, sweet peas, camellias, and stargazer lilies. "Rob, they're beautiful!" Julianne gently touched the petals and breathed deeply.

When she turned around Rob was in front of her. In one swift movement, he cupped his hands on either side of her face, and kissed her long and deep. Julianne started to cry.

"It's all so damn complicated." Julianne wiped the tears away with her fingers. "So much is going on. It's crazy out of control. I'm sorry."

"I know, I know." Rob took her in his arms and held her tight. "We've only known each other for a month. But I feel like you've been right here waiting for me for the last two years. I walked in this door four weeks ago and it was right where I was supposed to be." Rob held

Julianne out at arm's length and grinned. "Did that make any sense?"

"No. It didn't. But that's okay because nothing is making much sense these days." Julianne laughed, looked at her watch, and yelped. "Look at the time. I've got to pull this together. Rob, stay here, answer the door, I'm running upstairs to fix my face."

"Juli, what if Marta comes?"

"Oh, my God, you know, don't you?" Julianne stopped and spun around.

"Yes."

"How?"

"Later, we'll talk later. No time now. What do you want me to do?"

"Drag her sorry ass in here! Make her stay after tonight! And then, then I'm getting it all out of her once and for all." Julianne screamed as she took off up the stairs. "Who is she?"

When Julianne came back downstairs, Rob was ushering Carolyn in the front door. She heard them exchange pleasantries and Julianne met the older woman just as she entered the kitchen.

"Oh, it smells so good. What is cooking?" Carolyn exclaimed.

"Those, my dear, are Libby's ribs." Julianne reached over to take Carolyn's hand and walked her to her stool. "And I'm thrilled to make veal Marsala. I love that dish."

"I was worried. I thought it might be too fussy. By the way, I left a little something for you on your hall table, right next to those gorgeous flowers. A secret admirer? Don't tell me. A girl can have her mysteries."

"How nice of you to bring me something." Julianne ignored the other question.

"These Thursday nights have meant the world to me."

"Thank you. I hear Willow, excuse me."

The foyer was full of activity. Rob was busy helping Willow with her coat. The door was wide open and Libby was bent over struggling with her boots while balancing a bright foil gift bag and a purse the size of a small suitcase.

"Come in, come in. Libby let me close that door behind you before we all freeze." Julianne decided Libby needed the most attention and stayed with her to chat up the new dress, necklace, and gift bag.

Rob and Willow walked down the hall to the formal living room to leave her coat, scarf, and fuzzy mittens. But the large Gucci bag slung over Willow's shoulder slid off and bumped Rob's hip. He reached over to grab it before it hit the floor. "Here we go. No harm done. That's a heavy sucker."

"Sorry, Rob." Willow took the handbag and hastily tucked it under her arm but it was too late. She saw the surprised look on his face. She knew he knew. Rob walked off to the kitchen and took his place at the counter, too stunned to greet the others.

I'll be damned! She's got a gun in there. Right there in the side pocket. I can see the outline of it. I felt it myself. What the f . . .!

At five minutes after six, Julianne cleared her throat, exchanged eye contact with Rob, and started the class. "Shall we start? We have an empty stool at the counter and I don't know if it will be filled or not but since we have a full night ahead of us, we'll begin." Rob nodded in agreement. Somehow, by not saying Marta, Julianne kept her voice and face neutral.

"The wonderful smell filling the air is thanks to Libby and her menu request. Yes, I'm sure you all guessed . . . ribs." Julianne walked over to the double ovens, pulled on oven mitts, and brought the hot pan to the island. When she pulled back the foil, they all exclaimed their approval. Libby sat beaming. This was her moment. Julianne went on to explain the final steps and once again thanked Libby for her selection before moving on to the salad.

"Willow, let's get our dressing made for tonight's Caesar salad." Julianne motioned for Willow to join her and put on the apron Julianne was holding. The others seemed to like Willow's choice.

"Willow, I have a four cup Cuisinart over here for you to use. It's a convenient way to blend all our ingredients. Everything you need is in the ramekins in front of you so, as I describe what we're doing, please add each item. The romaine lettuce is washed, torn, and in the refrigerator. We can toss it all together right before we eat."

The mini food processor made short work of chopping the seven anchovies and three garlic cloves. Next, blending together with the paste, Willow added Worcestershire sauce, dry mustard, lemon juice, olive oil, red wine vinegar, and a coddled egg. "It's finished. How easy was that?" Julianne said, scraping the dressing into a glass jar and moving it off the island.

"There really is no comparison. Crisp homemade croutons are delicious and so simple to make."

In less than five minutes, Willow tossed the bread cubes with a combination of melted butter and olive oil, sprinkled on onion powder, garlic powder and sea salt, spread them on a cookie sheet and put it into a 300 degree oven for approximately ten minutes.

"Our bachelor grandpa wants to bake cookies with the kids. Is there anything better than being in the kitchen cooking or baking with the little ones? Rob, the best way to learn something is to do it. While Willow watches the croutons, I want Rob to start a batch of sugar cookies."

Rob did what any man would do in such a situation. Made jokes, teased Julianne, created a mess, made everyone laugh but somehow mixed it all together. Next he rolled out a sheet of the dough and cut out stars, circles, bells, and birds. Julianne told the class she'd been using these cookie cutters since she was a little girl baking with her Grandma.

Rob forgot himself and almost kissed Julianne when she presented him with a box of Disney character cookie cutters for his grandkids. Julianne wondered if the others noticed.

Rob and Julianne heard it at the exact same moment. Someone opened the front door. In an instant, Julianne realized she hadn't locked it behind Libby.

As casually as he could, Rob walked back to his place at the counter, put down the cookie cutters, caught Julianne's eye and nodded toward the front of the house. In one quick movement, he slide off his loafers and sneaked silently to the foyer.

In the meantime, Julianne made a commotion with the dirty cookie bowls, telling the ladies to take a quick break, and asking Carolyn to join her at the center island before the next demonstration. No one seemed to notice Rob disappear.

Rob cracked open the door to Jock's office and crept inside. Standing off to the side and behind the other unopened door he had a full view of the hall and formal living room where he could watch Marta.

Standing at the front, she looked all around. Rob thought by the tilt of her head, she was closely listening to the goings-on in the house. *But wait*, Rob said to himself, *of course, she's a convicted felon. Probably knows how to case a joint.*

Swiftly and soundlessly, Marta moved down the hall and stood out of sight at the entrance to the kitchen. Rob saw that she hadn't removed her coat and she wasn't carrying a purse or wearing gloves and that her shoes were a sturdy pair of black rubber soled oxfords. No one in the kitchen noticed her but what bothered Rob was the way she kept patting the large bulge that was in her coat pocket.

Could she be packing? What the hell! Everyone brings a pistol to a cooking class?

Out of nowhere Libby appeared, rushed toward Marta, and greeted her like a long lost friend. "You're so late. But hurry in, we still have a lot to do and wait until you see my ribs. I can't wait to try them."

Marta didn't move.

"Are you cold? You can leave your coat on." Libby took her arm and attempted to drag her over to the counter and the stools. Reluctantly, Marta followed her.

Julianne continued to talk with Carolyn but Libby and Marta were in her peripheral vision and she heard every word. *"Who better than Libby to handle the situation?"*

After Marta was pulled into the kitchen, Rob eased himself out of the office, crossed the hall to the front room over to Willow's handbag. He couldn't remember going through his wife's purse, or anyone else's purse, least of all a woman's bag he barely knew. It was a simple act once he flipped it over, unzipped the outside pocket, and exposed the gun. Gingerly lifting it out, Rob was surprised how cold and heavy the gray metal Glock felt in his hand. It was several years since he had handled any type of firearm but the old feeling of control came back. Holding a gun gave the potent authority of power. He lifted up the back of his sweater and shoved the gun inside the waistband of his pants. The belt held it in place.

Nonchalantly, Rob walked back into the kitchen, grabbed a bottle of water, and took his seat. Looking casually down the row of empty stools, he said to Marta. "When did you sneak in? Glad you could make it. Nobody wants to miss the grand finale of *The Kitchen*."

With a cold stare, Marta looked over at Rob, "Good things do seem to end. Don't they?"

Julianne cleared her throat and asked everyone to take his or her seats. "Why, Marta! Welcome. I hope all is well. I was concerned, but glad you joined us, even a bit late."

A half smile and icy glare was Marta's reply.

Not missing a beat, Julianne resumed. "We are finishing up this amazing evening with much good food but I'm going to say veal Marsala might rate as one of the kings of the main course at any dinner. The recipe is in front of you. Please read it over so we all know where we're going with this. This was Carolyn's pick and she's going to assist."

Libby clapped, Willow gave Carolyn a little pat on the back, and Rob gave Julianne a non-verbal high sign that said *I've got it covered.*

Preparing the veal went smoothly. Carolyn was impressed and pleased that it wasn't at all as complicated as she thought. There was little or no mess pounding the meat as Julianne demonstrated by layering the floured salt and peppered strips of veal between two sheets of parchment paper. Then they were moved to a platter next to the range as Carolyn sautéed the shallots, mushrooms and finely chopped garlic in a large skillet.

Using the same pan after removing the vegetables, olive oil was added to recoat the surface and the veal was browned gently on both sides and set aside again. Julianne helped Carolyn make a roux with equal parts butter and flour in the same skillet, added beef broth and the Marsala wine. The mixture thickened as it boiled and reduced.

"Everybody back in the pan!" Julianne exclaimed. "Now it all comes together to cook slowly for ten minutes or so. Carolyn, please add the meat to the skillet. Nestle the fillets into the sauce. Now cover the meat with the mushroom mixture. Let's drop a lid on all of this, turn the heat to low, and let the meat simmer and mingle with all that wine goodness and deep flavors."

The kitchen was bursting with rich aromas, happy chatter, and busy people. The sugar cookies were cooled on a rack. Rob was about to slide them into a zip lock bag and take them home to his grandkids to frost and decorate. Libby slathered the ribs with BBQ sauce and set them under the broiler to finish. Willow was tossing the salad in Julianne's favorite wooden bowl. The room hummed with activity. The entire class was engaged.

All but Marta, she hadn't moved.

As the group had done for the previous three classes, they ate together. But tonight it was casual. Julianne cleared off the back counter, put out a stack of white plates, silverware wrapped individually in a lemon yellow linen napkin, several bottles of opened wine, stemless wineglasses, and the platters of the food they had all worked to prepare.

"Help yourselves, sit anywhere, I'll light a fire in the fireplace so the big couch in the great room might be a good choice. Go ahead, put your drinks on the coffee table, it's glass. Sometimes it fun to eat off our laps," Julianne proclaimed.

There weren't a lot of choices for Marta. She could stay glued to her stool at the counter, walk back out the front door, or reluctantly join in. She finally rose and put a small amount of food on a plate. As fate would have it, Carolyn took it from there. "My goodness, Marta, look, you barely have a thing to eat. Are you feeling well? I see you're still in your coat. Come sit by me, dear. Tell me what you've been doing." Carolyn took Marta's arm and led her to the far end of the long circular couch.

That was it. Marta was handled. Rob could relax for a minute.

Julianne poured herself a glass of wine and got busy cleaning up, chatting with Willow and Libby, and trying to ignore Rob as he stood off to the side balancing and eating a plate of food. *What is with him? He's being such a prig.*

To say Rob was uncomfortable would be an understatement. He couldn't join the women on the deep cushioned couch because he was scared stiff the damn gun would come out of his pants. So he stood. Plus he liked this vantage point. With his back up against the column that divided the kitchen from the great room, he saw everyone. When he looked to his left, Julianne was putzing with the pots and pans. When he looked to the right, he clearly had Marta square in his vision. She was sitting on the very edge of the sofa. The right side of her coat hung almost to the floor with the weight of the fat pocket. Marta and the gun were directly in Rob's view.

Long after the food was gone, Libby, Willow, and Carolyn lingered, not wanting the evening to end. When Willow passed out the invitations to her Mardi Gras get together, the spirit of the night no longer seemed so final. It was a relief that they would be together again soon. Julianne was touched by the visible effort this strange reclusive young woman had made. She smiled tenderly when Carolyn put an arm around Willow and gave her a quick hug. Libby was ecstatic. Rob polite. And Marta turned the other way when Willow tried to hand her one of the beautifully addressed envelopes.

Finally it was time to leave. Julianne ushered Libby, Carolyn, and Willow to the front room, helped with the coats, wished them all well, and thanked them profusely for making her first cooking class session a success. They promised to keep in touch before Willow's party.

Unfortunately, all that gushy goodness wasn't totally sincere. Julianne could only guess what was going on with Rob and Marta and she wanted to get back into the kitchen.

MARTA had made up her mind. Tonight would be Marta's last night in Oak Grove and possibly her last night in Illinois. The final work with that weasel attorney, Maxwell Marconi, was over and done with. After his fees and various expenses, she walked out with less than three fourths of a million. That was a start.

Quite by accident last week, Marta had been channel surfing and landed on a special about the Florida Keys. The area looked warm, sunny, eclectic, and most important, anonymous. The kind of place a person could blend in. The residents seemed a little wacky and no one appeared to give a damn what anyone else was doing, where they came from, or if they were staying. The Keys looked like as good as any place to reinvent oneself.

Marta didn't take much from her apartment. The Range Rover was packed and the G.P.S. set to the first destination, Indianapolis, if the weather held. Marta had no experience driving long distances and even though she Googled the trip, the concept of fifteen hundred miles from Chicago to the end of Florida was lost on her.

But first, tonight, Marta wanted to tell this arrogant, stuck-up socialite a few things about her precious dead husband. It was time to let the perfect Julianne Girard know whom she'd been sleeping with all those years. The lies Julianne's life was made of. The man her husband pretended to be. The sins he died with on his damned soul. True, he tried to atone in the end. The money was nice.

But what about my poor mother? The life she was forced to live because of him! How it wore her down and killed her in the end. He owed us so much more. I should have this house! And everything in it! And all his money!

My father's condescending arrogant wife won't push me around. I won't be denied.

"MARTA, take a seat at the table. Please!" Rob walked over to the fireplace and stood next to Marta. She'd been standing, staring into the flames, since the others left the room to gather their things and leave. "I'd like to take your coat. Surely you must be warm by now."

"Don't touch me," Marta snarled, then looked him in the eye and challenged. "Why aren't you leaving? I'd like to speak to Julianne privately. As in not with you here, Frat Boy."

"First of all, I'm not leaving you and Julianne alone. Secondly, you are one tough cookie and you're not fooling anyone. We know quite a lot about you. It's not attractive. But there is much more we'd like to hear."

Marta slipped her hand into the bulging pocket.

"Oh, no, you don't." Rob grabbed her arm. "Get your damn hand out of your coat."

"What's going on?" Julianne's voice cracked in alarm as she walked into the kitchen.

"Tell your tough boy boyfriend to beat it. You and me are going to have a little talk." Marta twisted away from Rob.

"Rob, maybe that would be best. Just Marta and me. I'll make us some coffee." Julianne turned toward Marta. "Is that good?"

"I think she has a gun."

Hearing that, Marta pulled out the pistol and let it hang in her hand facing toward the floor.

"Oh My God! Marta, don't be a fool. We know you're just off probation. That thing could put you back in jail. Come over here and sit down. Put the gun on the coffee table, walk over to the counter, and sit down." Julianne's voice was steady and clear. She surprised herself.

Rob didn't move. He never took his eyes off the gun. Julianne kept talking and he kept watching.

"Tell me about Jock." Julianne took a seat at one of the empty bar stools and turned toward Marta and motioned

293

for her to sit next to her. "What was he, to you, I mean? Marta, I found pictures. Buried in his office with other things he never, never, intended me to know about. Do you know why?"

That did it. Marta moved toward Julianne. "I want all that. He promised me he would bring me my baby picture and picture of my mother when she was very young. The next time we met but . . ." Marta drifted off.

"My husband was your father? Am I right?"

"If you mean, was he a sperm donor? Then yes."

"Sit. Marta, sit down. I want to know this story, your story, and Jock's story. Can't you see what not knowing is doing to both of us? I see your anger. But for one teeny second think of my grief, my dismay. I need to know about the man I married." Julianne nodded at the empty seat next to her. "That is, the truth about the man I married. I have another whole story but it is a pack of lies, apparently."

Slowly Marta made her way to the counter and stood behind the stool next to Julianne. The gun was back in her pocket. Rob deliberately inched his way from the fireplace to the column where he stood before. The women seemed not to notice.

Gradually, he moved his right arm behind him and lightly placed his hand on the handle of Willow's Glock tucked into his pants.

CHAPTER THIRTY-ONE

"**M**omma died a scrub woman." Marta spit out the words.

She'd finally sat at the counter. Not next to Julianne but at the far stool. Her coat stayed on. Refusing to look at Julianne and staring straight ahead, she folded her hands and rested them on the granite. It was as much of a peace offering she was willing to give.

"Look around you." Marta softened her tone to bitter resentment. "How many times have you ever scrubbed a floor? Look at that range, six burners. On that wall, two ovens and a drawer to keep food warm. We had a hot plate to cook our meals. In the little cottage there was only one bed. But that was okay because we needed to sleep together to keep warm when the wet wind howled through the paper thin walls." Marta wrapped her arms around herself, remembering the bone chilling cold. It seemed she had nothing more to say.

"Where was this? How old were you?" Gently and slowly, Julianne asked.

"Growing up. Not in America. Not in your land of good and plenty. Oh, no. Uncle Tomasz had long sent us back. He would have nothing to do with a pregnant teenager. Well, let me see. He did wait until after Momma gave birth. I guess that would be a gift he gave me, American citizenship. There would be no father for me. He also made sure of that. Especially when he found out my father did visit us at the run down boarding house he put us in, waiting for Momma to be able to travel. That's when the picture you have was taken. Momma thought everything would be okay. When he held me," Marta put her chin on her chest and didn't move.

Almost in a whisper, Julianne asked. "Who is Uncle Tomasz? Why would he do such a thing?"

Rearing up, Marta shouted. "You are so naive! Living your wonderful life. Never giving a thought to leaving your homeland, learning a new language, trying to stay under the immigration radar. Lucky woman.

"My father, your husband, wasn't about to be allowed to be straddled with a silly girl who spoke no English and a baby that was somehow her fault for being born. You know his real name? It was Slavomin, not that made-up

Jock. He was Uncle Tomasz's pride and joy. Uncle Tomasz had a wife, three grown daughters, but no sons. Slavomin was an apprentice at his printing shop. He was grooming him to take over the business. He took him into his home, treated him like the son he never had. Momma fell for his good looks, charm, tall tells. She was just sixteen, he nineteen. For many months she hid her shame well. When Uncle Tomasz discovered her secret, he hit her hard. I came early."

Marta looked like she might cry.

"As soon as possible he sent us back to his brother in Poland, my grandfather. He told Matka, my Momma, we were dead to him."

"Why could this Uncle Tomasz send you anywhere? Marta." Julianne reached across the counter as if to lay a hand on her arm. "Please, start from the beginning. Tell me about your mother, coming here, how she met your father . . ."

"Don't touch me." Marta snapped. "My uncle had sponsored my mother, so he just unsponsored her. Momma was sent home in disgrace. I heard that can't happen anymore."

Rob moved toward the kitchen never taking his eyes off the pocket with the gun. Julianne saw him, held up her hand to motion stop and continued talking to Marta. "It's all fine. Can I get you something? Water? Tea? There is no rush. We'll talk when you're ready." Marta didn't answer but Julianne went to the back counter where the buffet had been set up and poured them each a glass of water. Rob caught her gaze, raised his eyebrows questioningly, but Julianne gave a positive nod back.

Accepting the water and taking a sip, Marta sneered. "My Matka would love this kitchen. I was about six or seven when Momma finally got a good job. Or so it seemed at the time. We were living in that cottage on the back lot of JaJa's farm. Grandmother was dead. Grandpa was humiliated with a prodigal daughter that shamed him with her bastard baby. A neighbor lady took pity on us. She found mother a job as a housekeeper for a rich English Language professor at the University and his very sick wife. They lived in a big house in town."

Marta turned in her chair and look at Julianne. Her voice was cold as ice. "He seemed to not teach too much. He was home a lot. I was sent to the local grade school and Momma would tend to the ill woman, cook, clean. We lived in their attic but it was warm and nice. I loved school. I was smart. The professor delighted in teaching us both English and insisted we speak only that in his house. We did. Then, the wife got sicker and finally died. My mother was so frightened. Where would we go next?"

The story was taking a toll on Julianne. There was so much she wanted to say to Marta. She felt she needed to apologize for the sad life Marta and her poor mother lived. The Jock she married was kind, sometimes generous to a fault. Why would he have deserted his new family, shirked his responsibilities, permitted them to be as good as deported? Julianne took several deep breaths, made herself keep quiet, and encouraged Marta to go on.

And Marta did. But it only got worse. Marta told how the professor allowed them to stay. He convinced Marta's mother that her daughter needed to continue her schooling. He would pay for a higher education when the time came. He needed a housekeeper, a cook, and a gardener for his dead wife's prized roses. What he really wanted was her. Marta remembered pretending to be asleep in their third floor room and Momma quietly sneaking out of bed, not returning until dawn, crying softly, and scrubbing herself by the commode.

"How awful. I'm so sorry for you and your mother." Julianne was almost in tears.

"Save your tears," Marta sneered. "I was next."

"Oh, dear God."

"He grew tired of Momma. I was twelve. I'd grown strong and pretty under his roof. We had nutritious food to eat. I walked to school in the fresh air and sunshine. I had warm winter clothes. In the summer, I swam in the creek with my friends. All this is why Mother stayed and did what she had to do. Where else could I have such a good life? Until, until he got ahold of me."

"No! You were a child." Julianne covered her face with her hands.

Rob shuffled back and forth, shaking his head and wondering when it would all end.

But Marta went on with eyes staring straight ahead that only saw the past. "At first he would invite me into his library. Said he would help me with my studies. Then little by little he was sitting too close to me, put his arm around me as I worked the math problems, give me a kiss for a right answer, hug me too long when I left. It scared me. I thought it was because I had no father or brothers in my life. I didn't know the way of boys or men. But when he put his hand up my skirt I knew it was wrong. He whispered in my ear if I tell anybody he would put me and momma out on the street and make sure we lived in a ditch the rest of our lives." Marta swallowed hard. "On the afternoon of my thirteenth birthday, he sent my Matka to town for my birthday cake. Then he took me to his room. That night at dinner he handed me a red velvet box. Inside was an 18-carat gold cross on a chain. He put it around my neck. I refused to thank him. Momma said I was a selfish girl."

"But you had to tell someone. Surely you did!"

"You are a spoiled rich woman. You have no notion of what hunger, cold, being poor and disgraced is like."

"No, I don't."

"Four years of this, then I ran away. I knew where the passports and birth certificates were hidden. Since I was a little girl I'd been taught their importance. I took mine and tucked them down the front of my camisole. I left Momma there. I learned later he threw her out. I didn't care, how could she not know what he was doing. I found my way to my Grandfather's farm; I waited in the bushes by the road until he went to the barn to milk the cows in the early morning. I snuck into his house and knew enough of his miserly ways to know he hid money. It took a while but I found his stash. I stole TaTa's cloak, best dress, her handbag and shoes, a suitcase. I walked to town, went to the bus depot, and got on the next bus. When night came and the bus stopped, I got off. For a year, I lived with three strange women in one room at a cheap boarding house. I slept on a palette on the floor. I worked in the back of a kitchen, ate the scraps off plates, and saved my meager pay. On my eighteenth birthday, I renewed my passport and bought a ticket to America."

Marta turned and glared at Julianne. "I came to find my father."

"What a brave girl." Julianne could barely whisper.

It seemed they were all to numb to go on. Julianne sat in stunned silence.

Just as Julianne was about to insist fixing a pot of coffee, the doorbell blared again and again. Someone started to knock then pounded and pounded even harder on the front door!

Julianne startled, jumped up, flung her arm across the counter, and smashed into her glass of water. It flew to the floor and crashed.

Marta bolted off the stool, backed up into the kitchen, and went for the gun in her coat pocket.

Rob pulled the Glock out of his pants, gripped it with both hands, and pointed it at Marta.

Marta screamed at them, "It's a set up, you called the police."

"No such thing." Rob lashed back, not taking his eyes off her.

"Then who's at the door?"

Rob has a gun? Julianne was shocked. "It could be anyone. Could be my daughter, or my friend, Adela. Don't panic! And both of you. Put those damn guns down! Now!"

Looking around the room Marta counted her options. "How do I get out of here? From the back I mean."

"Through the mudroom, into the garage. The light will go on automatically, walk around my car to the side door. No one will see you." Julianne pleaded. "Go. You'll be fine."

Julianne hesitated. "Wait. Marta. There is something else. Please give me a minute."

"What? I'm leaving. Now."

The knocking continued. Rob had the gun pointed at Marta and wouldn't leave the room to answer the door until Marta left. "Julianne. Let her go. It's over."

"No it's not. Marta, you have a sister. Well, I mean a half-sister."

Marta stopped, spun around, but didn't say a word.

"You father had another wife, before me. They had a child. She is here in Chicago. Here name is Shelby, she's thirty-one, you remind me of her. Around the eyes, and that thing you do with your hair . . ."

"Juli, do you think this is a good idea?" Rob interrupted.

"Give me a second. I'll write her name on a piece of paper and her phone number." Julianne ignored Rob, scurried to her desk and scribbled the information, ran over to Marta, and thrust it into her fingers. Julianne held Marta's hand and her gaze for a second. "Take care, be well, try to be happy. I am truly glad you did find you father."

Marta pulled away, tucked the paper into the pocket with the gun, and bolted out the door.

The last cooking class had been so much fun. Well, more than fun. It was pleasant, filled with lovely people, and it made Willow feel good about herself. The psychologist was right. She'd gained confidence, learned a new skill, and met people that she could interact with comfortably.

Everyone seemed thrilled with the invitation to a Mardi Gras party. Willow couldn't wait to share that success story with her therapist. Maybe, just maybe, she might ask a couple of the women from the office. What about that good looking guy that worked in the department across the hall? Willow smiled, parked the car in the attached garage, and grabbed her purse.

Swinging it over her shoulder, Willow knew immediately. It was too lightweight. Why hadn't she noticed it before? That's right, Carolyn walked her to the car because her arms were full and Carolyn wanted to help. Julianne had loaned Willow four of her southern and low country cookbooks for recipes for the Mardi Gras party. The books were big and bulky. Carolyn had grabbed Willow's purse and a bag of Mardi Gras beads that Julianne thought would be fun to give the guests. They laughed and chatted all the way down the driveway to Willow's car. Willow pulled the car keys out of her winter coat pocket, flicked the button on the key fob, opened all the doors and per Willow's instruction, Carolyn put the big purse on the front seat. The women hugged and promised to keep in touch.

Willow's usual habit, when she arrived home, was to unzip the side pocket and rest her hand on the gun's handle as she made her way into the condo. From there, Willow would walk through every well-lit room, look into every open closet, recheck all the double locked doors, and finally drop her car keys and purse on the dresser. Later, she would remove the gun from her purse and leave it on the nightstand while she slept inches away.

Not tonight. She never made it out of the car. Willow locked the doors, turned on the interior light and searched under the two front seats, between the seats, and behind the seats.

She was frantic. Willow shrieked, "It fell out of my purse! Must be in the living room. I have to find it! I have to have my gun!" Willow started the car, backed out of the garage, and gunned it down the street in the direction of Julianne Girard's house. "No, someone wouldn't steal it, would they?"

SPRING

CHAPTER THIRTY-TWO

The monotony of March finally gave in to the magic of spring. All of a sudden, the afternoon temperatures were flirting with seventy. Birds were calling for a mate before the sun rose and buds on weary winter tress seemed to grow fat and green overnight. Everyone's mood changed as April was just a day away.

The month of March had been a healing time for Julianne and Natalie. Natalie's knee brace came off and she started walking laps at the gym, promising herself she'd be running by the end of April. She'd only seen her mother once the entire month. They met one Saturday for lunch at the big mall near the airport. Julianne told her daughter how the last cooking class ended. Natalie was relieved that the woman she saw with Jock was his daughter, not his lover. Her stepfather hadn't betrayed her mother which was good to know.

Both Julianne and Natalie weren't a hundred percent satisfied with the little they knew of Marta. Marta's confession led to more questions than answers. They might never know any more. Julianne didn't tell Natalie that Marta had a telephone number for Shelby. Julianne decided she would handle Shelby. It was time for Natalie to butt out.

For much of March, Julianne rested. She hadn't realized how much time and energy preparing her class plans, shopping, and giving the demonstrations had taken. Now all she wanted to do was watch a couple of her favorite television shows, rent a movie whenever she felt like it, and read the new best sellers. Many days she stayed in her pajamas, ignoring the time, eating when she was hungry, and napping when she was tired.

On occasion, a burst of energy propelled her out of the house and she'd call her friend or Rob to meet for a drink or a meal. That kept her from being too lonely.

After several long lunches with Adela, the bridges were mended. In fact, they had a good laugh or two about it all. Adela said she was not only astounded but also proud that sweet Julianne had finally found her inner bitch again. Like the old days before Jock, Adela added.

Of course, there was Rob. Dear protective Rob. Julianne knew this was a special guy. He'd taken Willow's gun, stood guard over Marta, and made sure Julianne was safe. It did cross her mind and she did speculate on what could have happened that last Thursday night of her cooking lessons. It made her sad to think of it all.

The scene with Willow was almost as dramatic as the confrontation with Marta. She was hysterical. Pounding on the door, screaming at Rob when she discovered he had her gun and babbling out of control about her welfare. It took an hour for the two of them to get her composed enough to drive home.

The Sunday after the last class, Julianne invited Willow out to lunch, apologized prolifically, and hit a few of the high spots regarding Marta's story and Julianne's connection to her. She did the best she could to defend Rob taking the gun out of Willow's purse. Willow was astute enough not to ask any more probing questions because Julianne didn't ask her any. Normal people don't become panic-stricken and terrified the way she did unless there is a deep-seated reason. Willow would never tell her story again no matter what her therapist recommended.

Lunch went well so Julianne and Rob attended Willow's Mardi Gras party, which turned out to be pleasant. Julianne had to chuckle when she realized the food was catered. "Oh, well," she whispered to Carolyn, "Rome wasn't built in a day." Carolyn whispered back, "But she's having people at a party, in her house. We have to crawl before we walk." Julianne took her cookbooks back home with her. Willow was a little embarrassed when she gave them back but Julianne smiled and told her it was a wonderful party and the secret to entertaining is not to be all stressed out. "So hire a caterer and enjoy your own party."

Willow didn't forget to invite the realtor who sold her the lovely condo. There was Adela all decked out in a skin tight purple, green, and yellow Harlequin print sheath mini dress, painted sequined cat eyes around her eyes and matching violet and gold plums cascading from her hair. Yes, she was the hit. By the end of the evening everyone knew Adele's name and left with a business card describing her real estate company.

When Julianne shook her head and wagged her finger at her friend, Adela laughed at her and said, "It's all about the marketing, baby. And by the way, girlfriend, we need to start thinking about your May cooking class. Need to advertise, get the word out."

Not wanting to discuss or even think about that Julianne muttered, "We'll see. Too soon to tell." She walked away before Adela could add anything more.

THE month of March meant only one thing to an ex basketball coach, March Madness. Rob tried to justify this to Julianne but gave up attempting to explain the bracket he was filling out. Apologized in advance for evenings and weekends he would be unavailable. Maybe wouldn't even answer the phone during a game.

The few times they were together, he sensed Julianne's mood. The last six months had been full of life changing events for her. Rob knew the world had to stop and let Julianne off. She needed to heal. She needed time to figure it out. He wasn't going anywhere. Often when they parted, he would hold her close, stroke her hair, and reassure her of his loyalty.

Julianne was sorry she wasn't making the effort to cook Rob dinner or make fun plans and think of things for them to do together. She was exhausted mentally, emotionally, and physically.

For days after she'd told Marta about her half-sister, Julianne would reach for the phone to call Shelby. She needed to explain to her about Marta, Shelby's father's relationship with both women, and Jock's past life but it was overwhelming, Julianne couldn't do it.

Then came a lifesaving email from Shelby. She was invited by her boss to travel to Los Angles for a week at the spring design show. From there, she and another gal were driving north up the coast on Highway 1 to San Francisco and wine country. She would be gone for eighteen days. Shelby wrote she needed a break from the Chicago weather, work, and grieving for her father. Her boss understood and said it was a good time to take off.

March was a slow month. Julianne sent back wishes for safe travel and positive reinforcement for the benefits of getting away.

Best of all, Julianne knew Marta couldn't reach Shelby. In her haste that night to write down Shelby's number, Julianne only gave Marta Shelby's home number, didn't add her cell. At the time, it had been in error but now it was a blessing. Shelby could enjoy her trip. Julianne wasn't about to tell Shelby a thing until she returned.

THE morning of April first Julianne woke up with a smile on her face. She'd slept with the window open a little and the fresh spring air carried a whiff of wet earth, crisp dew, and greening grass. She smiled. Spring was a new beginning, a fresh start.

Mother Nature was smiling along with her. Spring was also her favorite time of year.

CHAPTER THIRTY-THREE

"This is very good." Rob picked up the French boned slice of lamb and took another big bite. After he savored the perfect medium rare piece of meat and wiped his mouth, he asked, "You are one-hundred percent sure it's okay to eat this with one's fingers?"

Laughing, Julianne assured him, "Yes, it's called a lollipop, the exposed bone being the handle and that's how it's done in France even at a three star Michelin restaurant. Trust me. I run a cooking school."

They laughed together tucked away in a quiet corner booth at Julianne's favorite bistro. The French restaurant only accommodated thirty-six patrons per seating, four nights a week, six o'clock and eight-thirty. The menu was very limited. The wine list was extensive and expensive. The maître d', hotel, and wait-staff were abrupt and curt, the chef strolled through the dining room expecting only accolades. It was quite French.

Rob Murphy had never been here. Julianne wanted to return the favor of his dinner reservation on the cold wintery Saturday night they drove out to the country and had prime rib at the old tavern. Well, it had been fun. The beef was delicious and the night loving and sweet. It was a Rob kind of place. So tonight was a Julianne kind of place. She'd been flexible, would he be?

Julianne called him the afternoon of April first. It seemed appropriate to start spring and a new month with a fresh idea and an invitation from her. She felt great. The gloom had lifted.

After Julianne described the upscale restaurant and its dress code, Rob retorted, "You almost had me there! April Fools, right? No!" It took a minute but he caught on. "Okay. Only because you sound so good and I'm ready to spend all the time I can with you. I'll eat frog legs in a jacket."

"The lamb. You have to try the lamb." Julianne was enjoying the banter.

"Texans eat beef."

Here they were on a warm Saturday night and the evening was progressing beautifully. They'd decided no Marta talk, no dead spouse's memories, and no children or grandchildren stories. With the first glass of wine, they toasted to themselves and a lovely evening with just them, no ghosts or baggage.

"You know, Lady, this sport coat hasn't gotten out much lately. You about gave me a heart attack when you suggested . . ."

"Wait a minute, Mister, you asked. As I recall it went something like this. *I suppose this fancy-smancy place has a ridiculous dress code.*"

"Yes, and then you made some rude comment about letter jackets and how it was time to trade it up for a sport jacket."

"Hey, I said for just one night! Furthermore, I happen to be quite fond of one particular such jacket that landed in my living room more than once last month."

Rob reached across the table and took Julianne's hand. "You look so good. Are you happy? Is all that 'stuff' behind you now?"

"You know, Rob, I feel like I slept a month. March is a blur. I think I needed that down time to heal and recover. Natalie sensed it. She just let me be. And you, well you were a doll. Thank you. I wanted to spend more time together, but I couldn't somehow. You understood, didn't push. That was special to me."

As the dinner plates were cleared, Rob let go of Julianne's hand and being the guy he was, not being able to take a compliment, gruffly said, "I got preoccupied myself.

Basketball, babe, it's in my blood and the March sweet sixteen starts a transfusion. Every year, got to have it."

"Stop it! Really? I've got a lot to learn, I guess." Julianne grinned.

"How about we start with bathrooms, sinks, and toilets?" Rob teased.

"What?"

"The trip we talked about. Kohler, Wisconsin, plumbing capital of the world. The American Club. A weekend away when you're ready. It's a beautiful spot. We can hike down to the Wolf River and have lunch at the hunt club. You'd like that. Every item on the menu is native to Wisconsin. Now that I've had a piece of sheep, your turn. Maybe a smoked pheasant salad or nice elk tenderloin."

Amused and pleased, Julianne winked at Rob, raised her glass to him, and saluted. "Bring it on, big boy. I'm game. I think we have a lot to learn about each other."

"Maybe we have the rest of our lives to learn it all." Rob winked back, lifted his glass, and clanked it against Julianne's.

Both of them were quiet on the ride home which was inevitable. What to do at the door? Kiss, or come in. Rob took control when they pulled into Julianne's driveway. "I'm going to walk you to the door. See that you get in and locked back up. I've had a great time, my jacket's had fun, and we know when the party is over. But just for tonight. Right?" Neither one made a move to get out of the truck.

"Robert Murphy, you are a gem. I think the old term was 'keeper.' Thank you for being a good sport. Maybe, just maybe, we can do that restaurant again?"

"Never again with your credit card. Gee, what do you suppose that waiter thought?"

"Toto, we're not in Texas now. I'm not the 'little lady' and you don't have a white steed. We women can pick up the tab. Did you hear? We get to vote, also."

"Good. I vote we do this again next week. What's your vote?"

"Yes. I vote yes. Oh, I should go in." Instead, Julianne leaned back in her seat, rolled down the window, and inhaled. "I can smell it. The April air is fresh and clean and it brings a change to every living thing."

Without saying a word, Rob got out of the truck and walked around to the passenger side, opened the door and took Julianne in his arms. "You're bringing a wonderful change to my life."

SHELBY had been back in town for almost a week but busy with work. Her boss had contracted to decorate three new homes by June 15th for a builder in the bedroom community of New Bedford. The houses would be part of the annual Parade of Homes. It was prestigious and exciting work. Shelby was thrilled to be part of the project. By the time she got back to her apartment at night, it always seemed too late to return Julianne's numerous calls.

On Sunday morning Shelby wanted to sleep in but her phone rang again. A bit groggy, she answered on the fifth ring. Ten minutes later, she felt she didn't have any choice but to meet with Julianne for coffee. The other option was a thinly masked threat that Julianne would come to her apartment.

Good grief, what could Julianne have to tell me that sounded so important. Probably another story about dad leaving us all less money. Well, I got mine. He took care of me with his life insurance policy. I'm sure Julianne has all the rest, to say nothing of that beautiful house they lived in. That's hers to keep forever. Really, I like the woman. She's never been anything but good to me. I just don't want to see anybody today!

To show her discontent with being forced to make an appearance at a coffee shop she couldn't stand, Shelby dressed in sweat pants, tank top, flip flops, and her oldest hooded fleece jacket. *No jewelry, no make-up, but I'll be there.*

The Kitchen

From the beginning, it was evident that Shelby wished she were back in bed. First of all, she arrived ten minutes late. Then, to be contrary, she wouldn't order anything to drink. Julianne was seated at a table in the back with her latte almost finished by the time Shelby sauntered over and plopped down in the metal chair.

"Good morning. You look sleepy, Shelby. Late night?" Julianne tried not to sound annoyed.

"No." Shelby slumped back in the chair and crossed her arms over her chest. "I'm working. Every day, ten hours at least. Three big houses to decorate. Really Julie? You look surprised. College drop-outs do find work, can make a living." Shelby yawned. "Really wanted to catch up with my sleep today."

"Honey, don't be cross. We have to talk. I'm sorry to pull you out of bed. I didn't know. Let me buy you a coffee." Julianne rose from her chair and headed for the counter. "Tell me what you want."

"If I must. Plain black coffee. A large. It's obvious I'm here for a while."

As patiently as she could be, Julianne let Shelby take several sips from the big white mug before speaking. "This is difficult and complicated. Please let me start from the beginning. I want to lay out the whole story before you. Then have at it. Ask me any questions you want and I promise I will be as honest and forthcoming as possible."

Shelby sat up straight. "What the hell?"

"It started with your father's death. Where he died . . . in that hotel room . . ."

"Did you finally find out? Why was he in a room in Chicago? Who with and . . ."

"Stop. Let me finish. A lot of those questions will be answered. There is so much to tell."

It wasn't comfortable but Julianne thought she covered everything in the long fifteen minutes she didn't stop talking. Anxious lines formed around Shelby's mouth and she seemed tense and jittery. Julianne wanted to literally get up and go to Shelby and put her arms around her. It wasn't easy for Jock's daughter to hear her father was a phony. Harder still to learn about a baby, who was deserted and abused as a child, and who turned to crime and prostitution. Then to find out she was back here, found their father, and confronted Julianne with a gun was shocking.

"Why didn't you call the police? For God's sake, she had a gun."

"I don't think she wanted to hurt me. Marta is a damaged bitter angry woman. Some part of her believed if she discovered her father, maybe the horrible things that happened to her would go away. Can you imagine seeing how Jock lived? How enraged that made her, thinking of her mother in poverty, and imaging what might have been."

"Daddy never told her about my mom and me?" Shelby asked softly.

"I don't think so. When I told her she had a half-sister I could see she was stunned."

"Oh!" Shelby gasped. "I never thought . . . a sister. She is my sister!"

"Honey, I had to tell you everything. You need to know. And it's possible she may try to contact you. You see," Julianne swallowed hard, "not only did I tell her about you I gave her your telephone number."

CHAPTER THIRTY-FOUR

By the end of April, Julianne had the yard raked, the flower beds mulched, the dead branches on the bridal wreath and mooch orange bushes trimmed, and the bird houses cleaned out and rehung. In previous years, Jock hired a landscaping company to do the work. Not this spring. She canceled the appointment. Julianne couldn't wait to get outside and into the warmth of the sun.

The physical labor felt good and her aching muscles the next morning made her smile. It was pure joy to see the tender young buds growing fatter by the day and new green life appearing on the brown shoots of the shrubs. The tulips and daffodils were up. The tall stems were still weeks away from flowering. She gave special care to her beloved peony bushes and lilacs. But it was the birds that had her lifting her face to the sky and rejoicing. The call of the crimson red male cardinal to his not-so-pretty brown mate had her laughing out loud several times.

As Julianne worked, she flashed back to previous springs. Jock liked to get away in April for one last warm vacation before his club opened and the golf courses in Illinois were ready for play. Cabo San Lucas was sunny, hot, and sexy in April. At one of the most up-scale resorts, Jock rented a villa for two weeks with a private Jacuzzi, outdoor kitchen, and a double lounge chaise the size of a bed on the wide deck. All this was hidden behind tall walls on the top floor of a three-story building high above any prying eyes. Jock liked to call it the "clothing optional" unit. Below was a huge salt-water pool with a swim up bar with undisturbed views of the ocean and wide white sand beaches. They seldom left the complex after a morning walk on the beach and a quick swim in the pool. Jock had the concierge stock the kitchen, the bar with tequila and California wine, and deliver fresh fish several times a week. Julianne prepared simple gourmet meals or Jock grilled on the lanai. The Mexican heat made Jock amorous, passionate, and romantic.

Julianne enjoyed the time together but by the end of two weeks, she was ready to come home to spring in the Midwest. She was secretly upset if she missed her early blooming flowers or Easter with the girls and her mother when she was still alive. One week would have been plenty of time away but there was no arguing with her husband about his time in Cabo.

Being at home and connecting to nature this spring was another important healing step for Julianne.

On rainy days, she worked inside. Everything in the sun porch was covered with a thin layer of winter grime. After the cooking school ended, Julianne dismissed her weekly cleaning ladies. She felt bad because they probably depended on her work for a steady paycheck but now was the time to cutback. How dirty could the house be with just her in it? So the re-opening of the porch also fell on Julianne. It had been years since she'd mopped a floor and washed windows. What was it that Marta screamed at her on that awful last night of the classes? *How many times have you ever scrubbed a floor? Momma died a scrub woman.* Julianne quickly pushed the memory away and carried on.

Dusting, brushing, sweeping, was almost fun. After she uncovered and wiped down the furniture, Julianne ran out to the florist. She needed to surround herself with living things. She bought a big Boston fern in a hanging wicker basket, several philodendrons for the side tables, and couldn't resist a tall Peace lily in a bright yellow ceramic pot to put in an empty corner.

"ADELA, hi, I'm returning your calls. I know, but I've been working outside and I refuse to bring out my cell. I don't care. Mother Nature doesn't like to be disturbed by people taking irritating phone calls while she's busy doing Spring. Oh, stop nagging, you sound like my daughter. No, I won't have a heart attack or something and have to call 911."

Adela and Julianne continued to chat as only good old friends can. Julianne invited Adela to come for lunch the following day. The weatherman pledged to deliver an almost eighty-degree afternoon. Julianne promised a light strawberry chicken salad, served on the freshly cleaned porch, and a pitcher of her specially brewed peach ice tea.

April was the busiest real estate month. People were out looking for a new house after being cooped up all winter. Parents with kids wanted a family room or finished basement. They needed more separate spaces. Apartment dwellers never wanted to leave a car out again to pile up with snow and ice. Garages were their priority. And pregnant mothers wanted a nursery and a laundry room. All men felt they needed an office, known as a man-cave, with a door and lock. It was a seller's market.

Lunch wasn't something Adela needed to take the time for but, as she grew older, her priorities shifted. Years ago she'd flatly said no, call me in July when things slow down. Now she would rearrange her schedule, turn off her phone, maybe put it on vibrate, and enjoy a leisurely part of the day with her best friend.

Ten minutes before twelve the next day, Julianne's doorbell chimed. Laughing and rushing to the front of the house, Julianne said out loud, "You can depend on a good realtor to always be early. They know how to keep an appointment. And this one only likes my front door."

"It's so good to see you." Adela and Julianne fell into a long hug. "I brought you flowers." Adela handed over a bouquet of white ruffled Parrot tulips. "Happy Spring!"

"Oh! Look at these. Adela, they are gorgeous! Come with me, out to the sunroom, and this will be our centerpiece. Now I feel like it's really a spring day."

The lunch was delicious, the chatter benign, they talked of having Easter brunch together, just girlfriends enjoying each other's company.

Over a cup of fresh strawberries and cream for dessert Adela thought it was time to ask some tough questions. "Marta? What have you heard? Any idea where she is?"

After flatly denying knowing anything else, Julianne decided to come clean. Adela had heard about the final evening of *The Kitchen* class seven weeks ago. She knew all about the guns, Marta fleeing, and Adela thought that was it, end of story.

"I might have made a terrible mistake." Julianne averted her eyes to the yard outside. "I did something so spur of the moment, it flew right out of my mouth, didn't think, didn't use my head . . ."

Sitting perfectly still, Adela looked across the table to her friend. She knew well enough to keep quiet, knowing Julianne would continue when she was ready.

"I felt sorry for the poor woman. She'd had such a terrible time of it. Okay, she was a criminal and I guess a hooker but with her childhood, did she have a chance to be anything else? I knew she was all alone in the world, especially after she found her father and lost him too! So sad. I guess I felt sorry for her." Julianne drained the last of her tea, turned to Adela, looked her directly in the eye, and spat it out, "I told her she had a sister, half- sister, and I gave her Shelby's phone number."

Adela's mouth fell open. "Julianne! Oh, no!" In a flash, she backtracked. "What's done is done. What did Shelby do? Is she all right with all of this? Has she heard anything from Marta? What's next?"

"Shelby was naturally shocked at first. Then it was questions, calls, and more questions. I only know so much. Finally, I had her come over and I gave her everything. The pictures, the documents, Jock's birth certificate, old driver's license, everything."

Throwing up her hands, Adela exclaimed, "What! You didn't make copies?"

"No. It was like a sin on my soul. I got rid of it all."

Julianne paused. "You know, I feel better. It's gone. Think about it, all of it is really Shelby's history, it's her father."

"I suppose you're right." Adela didn't agree but said nothing more. She waited another minute before glancing at her watch. "Look at the time. I've got to run. Showing a house for the third time. Nicest couple, he's back from Afghanistan about to be discharged and she's pregnant with twins. They have to use his V.A. benefits and the credit is a bit sketchy but I'll put it together even if I have to throw in part of my commission." Adela stood up and grabbed her keys off the coffee table. "They deserve this chance for a home."

"That is wonderful. Good for you." Julianne said, as Adela started to clear the table. "Put those dishes down. I'll walk you out. Here, let's go out the porch door."

The two friends walked arm in arm around the house and down the driveway to Adela's car. With the car door propped open the two hugged and promised to do this again soon.

Just as Adela was about to drive off she rolled down her window and yelled out. "I forgot to ask. What about your Rob guy? What's up with that?"

Waving her off Julianne hollered back. "That's a whole OTHER story!"

CHAPTER THIRTY-FIVE

Coming out of a deep sleep just before dawn, Julianne felt disoriented for a brief moment. She knew it was Sunday morning but her head was pounding and her mouth was so dry it felt like her lips were stuck together. Slowly, it all came back. The night before, actually the entire day before, Saturday, working in the yard together, martini's on the deck, light jazz throughout the sound system, grilling the rib eyes, another bottle of wine, slow dancing in the dark. Then here. The guest room.

With an easy smile, Julianne rolled over and watched Rob sleep. The thin morning light cast a golden glow on his warm skin, his once blonde hair was equally gray, and the stubble of his beard had a reddish cast. He slept quietly and soundly, flat on his back. What Julianne wanted to do was wake him with kisses and caresses but she silently scooted out of bed and down the hall to the master bedroom and bath. She returned wrapped in a taupe silk dressing gown and carrying a robe for Rob, one she recently found in the back of the bathroom closet with the tags still on it. Her late husband was a fussy man and apparently a royal blue terrycloth wasn't his thing.

Rob moaned and sat up. Julianne perched on the edge of the bed. "Good morning, pretty lady." He reached up and stroked her cheek. Julianne bent over and softly kissed him. Rob rose up, put his hands under her arms, lifted her up and over until she was across from him and back in bed. Her robe fell open and Rob gently covered her willing body with his hands and mouth.

THE previous day had begun with another great spring morning, the first Saturday in May. Julianne was all about getting out in the yard. The grass needed mowing and there was a perfectly good push mower in the back shed. Jock had used it once, put it away, didn't like being hot and sweaty, and hired a landscape crew. Julianne wheeled it out, filled it with gas from the red gallon can, and pulled the rope.

As a teenager, Julianne always mowed the lawn. If she had to choose between household chores or being outside working in the yard and garden or even shoveling snow, Julianne chose outside. Today that darn mower wouldn't start no matter how many times or how hard she pulled.

Discouraged and disgusted she went in the house for a glass of water. That was all it took. The phone rang.

It was Rob asking her to go out to dinner but before he could get another word in, Julianne let loose with a tirade about busted machines, bad luck, wasted days, and long grass. "I'll be right over," Rob replied, hanging up before the distraught woman on the other end could argue with him.

And so it went. After Rob checked out the Husqvarna mower, noting it was the top of the line, he made a quick trip to Lowes and back. Ten minutes later the machine was running and Julianne was sailing around the yard. Rob snooped about in the shed and wheeled out two Trek bicycles, both with flat tires, found the air compressor, and fixed the flats. He thought they might take them to the river trail and have a nice ride in the afternoon. Next, he hosed them down and proudly parked them in the driveway. Julianne gave him a thumb's up as she walked by, still pushing the mower.

The fun of cutting grass lasted a little over an hour. "I'm pooped," Julianne sighed, collapsing into an Adirondack chair on the deck. "That's a lot of walking." Secretly, she didn't blame Jock for also throwing in the towel. "I guess

I'd better reconsider my lawn guys. But I'm doing the flower beds myself and I'll have them till a small garden space over there in the corner." Julianne realized she was talking to herself when the mower motor kicked in and Rob smartly waved good-bye as he took to the side and front yards. Julianne recovered, manned the pruning shears, and started on the back hedge.

By four o'clock they finished. Sitting side by side in the big wooden chairs on the deck they heaved a tired sigh in unison. Chuckling, Rob turned to Julianne, "Where do you want to go for dinner tonight? I think I asked that very question seven hours ago. Man, a lot has happened in between and I still don't have an answer." Grinning he reached over to take Julianne's hand.

She closed her eyes and thought a minute. "Well. I'm too tired to do my hair. Look at these nails! I'd also have to figure out something to wear. Na! No dinner out."

"Hey. I've got an idea. The grill is in good shape. How about I haul it out of the shed, you run to Angelo's, grab us a couple of thick prime steaks and whatever. We grill, chill, and relax."

"Love it!" Julianne squeezed Rob's hand. "Rob, think about it, Angelo got us together. He actually came to the house with your phone number, said you needed a cooking lesson and I was to call you." Julianne rose to go inside, walked over to Rob, bent down, and kissed his forehead.

"I'm going to take a quick shower first. Asparagus is so wonderful this time of year. You okay with that?"

"Sure, surprise me. Give the old Italian a big hug and kiss for me, you're the best thing I ever got at that store!" Rob got up, too. "Juli, I've got clean sweat pants and a tee shirt in my gym bag in the truck. Got a bathroom I could use while you're out?"

When Julianne returned to the house, she brought in two grocery bags and put them on the island. A fresh and casually dressed Rob was on the deck cleaning the grill grates with a wire brush. He saw Julianne through the French doors and came into the kitchen. "I've been a busy boy. You'll like this." Rob walked to the freezer, took out two frosted martini glasses and a silver shaker.

"Oh, just what I need! Thank you." Julianne's hair was pulled back into a ponytail. She wore faded blue jeans, a chambray shirt, and practically no make-up.

"You are beautiful! Plus a good little worker. Here's to our day." Rob poured the chilled liquid and toasted. Julianne reached up to smooth back his still wet hair.

While Rob grilled, Julianne made the side dishes, turned on the music, opened the wine, and set the small round table in the sunroom. Just as they finished the meal and the 2009 Silver Oak Cabernet, the sun went down and the smooth jazz station switched to mood music. Julianne found the lighter and lit the decorative candles that were scattered around the porch. Rob carried the plates to the kitchen and returned with another opened bottle of wine.

Soon they were slow dancing to Burt Bacharach singing, "This Guy's in Love With You."

After another glass of wine, Julianne belted out with Tina Turner's "What's Love Got To Do With It." Rob, fascinated by Julianne's inner rock star, applauded loudly when she put down the microphone/wine bottle and took a bow.

It was the power of Rod Stewart singing "The Way You Look Tonight" that was too much. Julianne blew out the candles one by one, took Rob's hand, led him through the dark kitchen, up the back stairs with the music still playing, and into the guest room.

It was still early in the morning as Rob and Julianne came downstairs and entered the kitchen. "Oh, I guess the Sunday paper will stay in the drive a little longer." Julianne looked down at herself then over to Rob. Both were in robes.

"I'd go get it but the neighbors might not want to see a man in a bathrobe coming from your house this time of day." Rob started to rinse last night dishes piled in the sink as Julianne was grinding coffee beans. "Wouldn't bother me."

"What was it the girls called it? When you had to sneak in the next morning with last night's clothes . . . *the walk of shame.*" They both chuckled.

Within fifteen minutes the kitchen was clean, the coffee brewed and poured, and Julianne was pulling bacon and eggs out of the refrigerator. Rob had the heavy Lodge pan heating on the stove. He turned to Julianne and grinned, "I'll handle breakfast. Grab a seat at the counter and pretend you're in some cooking school."

As Rob carried two steaming plates to the counter, they heard it at the same time. Only Rob didn't know what the sound was and Julianne couldn't believe her ears. "Oh, good God. No!"

"What the hell is that?"

"The garage door."

"Who could possibly be opening it?"

Julianne slid off her stool and started toward the mudroom when Natalie burst through the connecting door, a pink bakery box in her hand, and calling out. "Hey, Mom, there's a big pick-up truck in the driveway . . ." Natalie froze in her tracks. First, she saw her mother in a sexy silk gown and then her gaze took her across the room to Rob standing by the counter, wearing the robe she bought Jock two years ago for Father's Day.

"Honey, I'm surprised. You usually call," Julianne stammered.

"Well, excuse me! I thought I would surprise you with fresh croissants and palmiers. But I can clearly see you are busy, very busy." Natalie sneered and walked toward Julianne thrusting the bakery carton into her hands and turned on her heel. "I'm out of here!"

"Natalie, please. Give me a minute."

"Really, Mother! Really?" With that, Natalie walked toward the garage, grabbed the mudroom door handle and slammed it as hard as she could behind her.

THE breakfast was ruined. Julianne never ate a thing, just sat and sipped her cold coffee and tried to make polite conversation. Inside she was seething. Rob picked at his food, took the dishes to the sink, and said it was time to get going.

After Rob changed into sweatpants and yesterday's tee shirt, he told Julianne he was sorry and, frankly, didn't know how to proceed. He, too, was privately angry. Yesterday, last night, this morning, it was all so wonderful and now what? He didn't want this to end. He left, telling Julianne to call him. He'd let her have all the space she needed.

Hours later, Julianne had remade the guestroom bed, unloaded the dishwasher, swept the sunroom, brewed ice tea, and was still looking for anything to keep busy. All she wanted to do was call her daughter. But she felt it was Natalie's place to call her; *own up, be an adult, and apologize to me for acting like a jealous twelve year old.*

The phone didn't ring all day. Emails were the usual junk. Nobody texted.

CHAPTER THIRTY-SIX

By seven that evening Julianne felt like she was climbing out of her skin. She hated unresolved issues and couldn't stand the thought of not clearing the air with her daughter. How would she spend all next week not texting or phoning Natalie? They connected every other day or so.

At seven fifteen, the phone rang. Julianne was trying to watch a PBS special but she couldn't concentrate. Startled, she ran into the kitchen to the phone on her desk. It was Adela. At first, she didn't intend to answer but with Adela it was hard to be evasive.

"No, I'm okay." Julianne didn't have it in her to make any kind of conversation, heavy or light. "Trust me on this one. I don't want to talk right now. What? No, I cannot make any kind of commitment for another cooking school." Julianne was pacing with the phone. "I'm going to go now."

That's it. My daughter has to talk to me. I'll never sleep tonight and tomorrow will not be any better. I know she's home. She's obsessive enough not to change her schedule because of this morning. My Natalie uses every Sunday evening to prepare and launch her week ahead. Balancing her debit card, ironing clothes, washing her hair, doing her nails, grooming the cat, putting her schedule on her iPad and who knows what else.

It was a quick decision. She punched in Natalie's number and listened to it ring six times. On the last ring, Natalie picked up. "Yes Mother."

"Honey, we need to talk."

"About what? I saw it all. Eight months after your husband's death, you take another man into his bed. You let your new boyfriend wear his clothes. He's prancing around the house like he owns . . ."

"Please let me explain. You have it all wrong . . ."

"What I saw this morning made me sick. Mother! Do I need to tell you I loved Jock? Yes, I love my father, too, but he lives in California and Jock was here. He was here for me. There are things you don't know about our relationship. For instance, we played this little investment game. When I was in college and majoring in finance, he gave me money to buy and trade stocks. I never let him down. I loved the man. He was a great father figure. I don't care what he did when he was nineteen or twenty. I miss him every day. Apparently you DON'T!"

"STOP!" Julianne screamed. Natalie very seldom heard her mother yell. She quit talking.

"I loved Jock. Don't you doubt that for one minute, Natalie Bennett. But he betrayed me. He broke our trust. He ripped my heart out with his lies, his other life. He could have told me it all. Preferably, before we married. I would have helped him look for his long lost daughter. I would have welcomed her into our family. Yes, you're right. Things we do at nineteen and twenty should sometimes be forgiven, overlooked, but why hide it in a metal box behind bricks in our home? He left her a large share of our money. I was deceived. I couldn't even mourn the man decently." Julianne sat down to take some deep breaths.

"I get all that," Natalie conceded. "But what bearing does it have on your new lover?"

"I'm alone." Julianne's voice was almost a whisper. "Rob is a nice man. He's kind, funny, and good. He's practically raising his grandchildren. He's doing the best he can to help his daughter through a bad divorce. He's alone, too."

"So?"

"Grow up girl! People need people. We needed each other. Last night was the first time we were together and, not that I owe you any explanation, we were not in my bed and I'm sorry to hurt your feelings but Jock never wore that robe. I took off the tags before I gave it to Rob." Julianne stopped rambling. "Can we just be two grown women about this? It wasn't a one-night-stand. Your mother is still a respectable, decent, moral human being. I don't think I need to wear the scarlet letter."

Natalie finally broke the long silence. "You know, I never read that book. Way back in high school I thought the whole idea of a big red A was stupid, even for colonial times."

Both mother and daughter laughed. It was over. Humor is a good way to draw a peace agreement. Neither one needed to say any more about the subject.

THERE was one more thing Julianne had to do before she could put this Sunday in May to bed and this was indeed a day that needed to end. But not before one more unresolved issue was resolved.

Rob came to the door only after Julianne pressed the doorbell repeatedly. It was obvious he'd been sleeping, probably in front of the television. As a man would, he yanked open the door, more irritated than cautious, and his reaction quickly turned to surprise. "Juli, what's the matter? Everything okay? Come in."

"No, I won't come in. I just have to tell you something. I think I woke you, sorry, so I'll be brief and to the point."

All this felt like a gut punch to Rob. "No, no don't stand out there. It's a cool night. Please come in." He couldn't let her cut and run. He needed to stall for time. He couldn't bear to hear they were over when they'd just begun.

As he reached for her hand, Julianne threw her arms around his neck and kissed him hard. Rob stepped outside and wrapped her in a tight embrace. He never wanted the kissing to end especially if it was a goodbye kiss.

Almost as quickly as it started, Julianne pulled away, put the palm of her hand on Rob's cheek, and whispered. "I'm sorry. But I will be honest with you. Always. And this is what I have to say. I'm falling in love with you, Rob Murphy." Julianne turned to leave.

"You can't leave! Not now!" Rob gasped before starting after her.

She was practically running down the sidewalk to her car. "Yes. I can. The last twenty-four hours have been the best and the worst. I'm going home and going to bed. Will you call me tomorrow?"

"Yes! And the next day, and the next day, and all the days after."

"Maybe I should sell the house." Julianne and Adela were power walking on the river front trail the following Wednesday afternoon. Adela tried to take one day off during the week. The weather was warm and balmy and the women agreed they needed to be outside instead of sitting in yet another restaurant eating. "The time is now. Right? The spring market."

"Geez, I'm out of shape." Adela was huffing and puffing, trying to keep up with her friend. "I should not have let my gym pass expire. I was a faithful member at the new Y for years. How come you're doing so well?"

"My winter was busy. I do all the yard work now and I also clean my own house. I hardly had a spare minute to my name with that cooking school deal and now all the chores fall to me. But answer my question about selling the house. What do you think? What would I list it for? Have the prices rebounded?"

"Hold it." Adela came to an abrupt stop. "It's always the same with you. You've got to think this through. Where will you go? Buy? Rent? Do you qualify for a mortgage? Rates are the best in decades but that takes verification of repayment, usually called a job. I'd love to talk money with you, that is, your money situation, but it's not my business. First things first . . ."

"Let's keep moving. I'll slow down." Julianne began

walking again but at a leisurely pace. "I agree with that part. I'm floating along with my finances and I suppose I need to buckle down and figure out exactly where I stand."

"Right decision." Adela could talk and walk now. "Let me put you together with a good guy. Yes, he's a financial planner but he's honest and fair. He should have retired years ago. I don't know why he keeps working, doesn't need the money. He's like a wise uncle who takes care of his clients. His advice will be practical and sage."

"Maybe I should start there. I think I'm managing." Julianne paused. "I need a long range plan, don't I?"

"Yes. We're a long way from marketing your house. Remember Julianne, it's your home! Not to be easily disposed of."

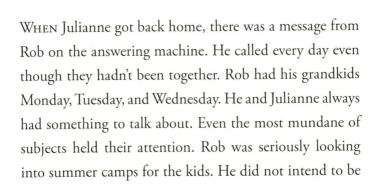

WHEN Julianne got back home, there was a message from Rob on the answering machine. He called every day even though they hadn't been together. Rob had his grandkids Monday, Tuesday, and Wednesday. He and Julianne always had something to talk about. Even the most mundane of subjects held their attention. Rob was seriously looking into summer camps for the kids. He did not intend to be the full-time babysitter for three months after school let out. They made plans for the weekend.

It was all good.

Thank heavens Natalie was herself again. Shelby stayed busy with her new job and pretty much out of Julianne's hair.

SUMMER

CHAPTER THIRTY-SEVEN

June 21st was Summer Solstice, the longest day of the year and the official start of summer. The sun is the furthest north of the equator. The Latin word for this event is *sol sistere* and it means the sun has stopped. Pagan rituals abound on this day. Massive bonfires burn through the night to ward off the evil spirits set free when the sun stops. It is also the time of the first harvest. Fruits and herbs ripe and ready to be picked are said to hold potent powers from the extra time in the sun.

The village of Oak Grove held their annual community Summer Solstice picnic, outdoor concert, and bonfire. Julianne hadn't gone for years and Rob had never attended. They decided it would be fun. The town square had a perfectly maintained concrete band shell from the 1950's and the two blocks of surrounding lawn soon filled with folding chairs and blankets. The city allowed people to bring food and drinks to the concert. The concert started an hour before sunset to celebrate the extra twenty minutes of daylight.

Rob and Julianne, nestled together, were sipping wine, munching on crostini's and Mezzetta olives. The band played classical and contemporary numbers while a light breeze kept the bugs at bay. The night was perfect.

"Why did I even bother to bring that thing?" Julianne whispered to Rob as she disengaged herself and reached for the tote bag. Her iPhone was buzzing softly indicating she had a text message. She intended to turn if off but saw it was from Shelby and the mother in her said to read the message.

I HAVE to talk to you ASAP!!!!!

What can this be? Now? Shelby can be a bit dramatic but . . .
"Excuse me. I'll be just a minute. Sorry." Julianne mouthed to Rob as she turned the other way and sent a short text back. Immediately, Shelby replied.

No, I'm okay. But something really strange happened. Can I come over tonight?

It would take Shelby almost forty minutes to drive out to Oak Grove. Julianne was concerned and worried. She texted Shelby to come as soon as possible. She would meet her at the house. The concert would be over in another half hour and Rob had parked several blocks away to avoid the exit traffic. *That should work.*

Shelby was there when they got to Julianne's. She'd used her key, had the kitchen lights on, and was pacing around the center island looking more than a little upset. Shelby and Rob hadn't met. She politely shook Rob's hand and said she'd heard all about him.

"You have?" Julianne asked.

"Of course. From Natalie." Shelby answered but Julianne didn't have time to react before Shelby went on. "I had the strangest, weirdest phone call tonight. The phone in the kitchen rang. Nobody ever calls me on that phone. Well, you do sometimes. So I almost didn't bother answering, figured it was a telemarketer or robo call. I looked at the I.D., some strange area code, 941, and Julianne the rest is so mind-boggling. I'm blown away."

"Come. Let's sit on the couch and you tell me everything," Julianne said, as she led her stepdaughter into the great room. Rob walked by her with the newspaper heading to the sunroom giving her a brief wave that said call me if you need me.

By now, Shelby was almost shaking. Julianne took both of Shelby's hands in hers and quietly said, "Start from the beginning, tell me very word." The knot in Julianne's stomach was growing.

"This woman tells me her name, asks if I'm who I am, then goes on about what she does. She is a hospice nurse. I'm about to cut her off cause I'm watching a movie and figure she's calling about some charity to give to. Then she asks me if I know Marta Kochevar. At first I said no. Then it hits me. I say yes, well sort of." Shelby looked at Julianne. Julianne shook her head, squeezed Shelby's hand a little harder, and nodded for Shelby to go on.

"The nurse proceeds to tell me Marta is very ill. Well, go figure. She's in hospice. So I say something like that's too bad and then this woman told me Marta was all alone in the world and after some counseling finally Marta told her she had one relative. Me!" Shelby quit talking, pulled her hands away and ran them through her hair. "Me, her half-sister."

"Yes. I know. It is you." Julianne sighed. "Remember? I gave her your number. Now what?"

"Now what? Listen to this!" Shelby glared at Julianne. "This hospice lady, by the way I wrote it down, her name is Thelma, I have her number here." Shelby handed Julianne a crumpled sticky note. "She was very nice, thinks I should come to Florida to see my half-sister! Because Marta has no one. No one visits. Marta is dying . . ." Shelby raised her arms in frustration. "What the hell am I supposed to do?"

With one quick movement, Julianne firmly pulled Shelby's arms down and held them right above the elbows. "Shelby, this is a huge decision. It's life changing. There's only one opportunity left to see Marta. It's now. Decide what to do with your heart not your head. Because for the rest of your life you'll wonder."

"What about work? Take off time. Tickets are expensive. Hotel. Car rental. I don't know."

"Shelby, from your heart. *Family Leave* for illness or family crisis is a law, your job is protected. I'll help you with the rest."

"What will I say? How will I act?"

"Do you want me to come with you?" Julianne offered.

"I don't want to upset you but Thelma told me Marta specifically mentioned you and Marta didn't ever want to see her father's wife again. Sorry."

"That's okay. I get it."

"Listen, Shelby, take a deep breath. This is how it works. Thelma will guide you through the entire process of dealing with a terminally ill patient. Those volunteers are angels on earth. Thelma will tell you what to say, how to handle any situation and prepare you and Marta for the end."

Julianne and Shelby sat quietly. There was nothing more to say.

Finally Shelby spoke. "If I don't go, I'd have never met my half-sister."

"That would be very sad. For both of you."

Shelby started to cry. "I'd better go."

JULIANNE asked Rob to help her. Jock always arranged the travel details and Shelby was too distraught. So Rob jumped on Julianne's computer, used her American Express card, and took care of everything.

There was a direct flight from O'Hare to Destin, Florida the following afternoon. From there Shelby would drive to Panama City. Rob made sure the rental car was equipped with GPS. He called Thelma and explained the situation, got all the necessary information for Shelby to find the Hospice House, and booked a hotel nearby. Thelma was pleased to hear the news and said Marta would be eager to meet her sister but time was of the essence.

Julianne took the phone, identified herself as Shelby's stepmother, and asked Thelma if she could ask a few questions. "How did Marta end up in northern Florida?"

All Thelma shared was that Marta was driving to Key West, took ill, couldn't go any further, checked into a motel, and a maid found her. The hospital transferred her to Hospice. Julianne asked about her condition. Thelma said Marta was holding her own right now, hospice was keeping her comfortable, and when Shelby arrived, they'd share all the information with her, as she would be next of kin.

Shelby washed her face, pulled herself together, called her boss, cancelled appointments by email, and texted several friends to change weekend plans.

When it was time to leave, Shelby and Julianne hugged long and hard. Julianne lifted Shelby's chin and promised she would be a phone call away. Day or night, she would have her cell with her. She assured Shelby she was strong and brave and most importantly was doing the right thing.

Rob gave her a kiss on the cheek, wished her safe travels and good luck. He offered to drive Shelby to the airport but it would be easier for her to use Uber.

Two hours later Shelby left Julianne's house. With her, she had a one-way airline ticket, car rental confirmation and hotel reservations.

It was a long time before Julianne fell asleep that night. Her mind churned. Over and over, she thought about all that had happened in less than a year. Rob sensed her sleeplessness, moved closer, and wrapped his body around hers.

With several deep breaths, Julianne closed her eyes and sleep came.

CHAPTER THIRTY-EIGHT

Five days later, Julianne and Natalie were on the way to the airport. Shelby had called Julianne the day before to tell her it was over. Marta had died peacefully in the night. The hospice nurse called the hotel very early the same morning to let Shelby know Marta had passed.

Natalie sat in the passenger seat looking out the window, then turned to Julianne. "Mother, sometimes I think you are the most generous person I know. What a comfort for Shelby to know her father and Marta, her half-sister, will share the plot at Oak Grove Lawn. I suppose somehow, someway, Jock would appreciate this, also. After all Marta was his family, just like us. Well, not quite . . ."

"That's enough, honey. I know what you mean." Julianne reached across the console and patted Natalie's hand. "Oh, there she is." Julianne steered the car toward the curb at O'Hare. "I think the best way to handle this is to let Shelby take the lead. She may not want to talk. It's been a lot. We're here to support her in any way we can."

"I was surprised she wanted me to come with you."

"You're her sister, too!"

THE trendy chain restaurant was almost empty in the middle of the afternoon. Julianne insisted they stop somewhere when Shelby told them she hadn't eaten all day and couldn't remember if she did the day before. After exchanging pleasantries, the women were quiet on the ride from the airport.

Although Julianne and Natalie weren't hungry, they each ordered a small salad to keep Shelby company as she tried eating soup. By the dark circles under Shelby's eyes and the pallor of her skin, it was evident it had been a tough five days. "I'm so tired. I feel like I could sleep for a week," Shelby said, looking down into the barely touched bowl of Minestrone. "But, it's like I don't really want to go to my apartment. I don't know."

Without missing a beat, Julianne jumped in. "I think it's because you don't want to be alone. I know that feeling. Please come home with me. Stay a few days. After some rest and good food, you'll feel stronger. Home cooked meals help heal." Julianne smiled and Natalie laughed.

"Shelby, do it," Natalie encouraged. "Mom's right. Take some time."

"I will. Thank you. Both of you." Shelby looked across the booth at Julianne and Natalie. Tears slid down her face. "I always took family for granted. I figured there would be years to spend more time with Dad. I kinda resented you, Julie, and I guess I was jealous of you, Natalie. But poor Marta. What a life! So sad, so all alone, damaged. We have so much and we were a family. All the holidays and parties. I was so lucky to grow up that way. I guess Dad tried to make up as best he could when they found each other."

"I think he would have." Julianne added, "He was a good person."

Shelby put down her spoon and dried her eyes with the napkin. "Marta said they'd meet somewhere, try to talk, try to be father and daughter but they were strangers. I suppose they were. I think it was because there was no history. Nothing to share. No past memories together. And then she said she got angry. She hated all of us because we had Dad. We had him for a long, long time and she had no one."

"Oh, my. You're right. Of course she resented and despised us," Julianne exclaimed. "By why did she come to my cooking school?"

"Can we go?" Shelby asked reaching for her purse. "I'm beat. There is so much more to tell but not now."

"She's in the shower right now. She slept until 2:30 this afternoon. Yes, she was starved when she came downstairs. You know, Rob, I think she ate more than even you could have," Julianne teased. "Three scrambled eggs with fresh chives and cheese, two pieces of wheat toast with my strawberry jam and a huge glass of milk. Then two sugar cookies."

Shelby had been back from Florida for a little over twenty-four hours and the healing process had started. She was sad, a little numb, felt a sense of loss, but relieved. Waking up in the home that meant so much to her father gave her great comfort. Julianne was kind and caring. She fed Shelby's body and soul with nourishing food and motherly compassion.

Julianne hung up the phone and took her novel and a glass of iced tea out to the sun porch. She never opened the book. Bits and pieces of her interaction with Marta flashed across her mind. She couldn't put it to rest.

Shelby found her gazing out the windows looking at nothing. "Am I interrupting?"

"Good heavens, no. I brewed some iced tea. Can I get you a glass?"

"I'll get it. I know my way around your kitchen and you've waited on me enough today." Shelby walked back into the house and took her time fixing a glass of tea. Underneath her left arm, she'd tucked the manila envelope. Standing tall with her chin up, she took several deep breaths, turned, and went back to the sun porch.

"Come sit by me on the couch." Julianne patted the bright sunbrella cushion next to her. "There is a lovely breeze coming in from the western windows. What's this?"

Shelby laid the brown package on Julianne's lap. "Wait a minute to open it. There is a long story that goes along with it." Taking a slow drink, Shelby closed her eyes as if she were praying. "Marta had so much to say. Her stories took days. They came in bits and pieces as she tried her best to stay lucid, shooing off the nurses with the morphine patches, sometimes talking until her voice gave out."

"Oh, honey, I'm so sorry for both of you."

"No! Don't be. Marta wanted to die with a clean slate. I was the vehicle she used to get there. What if I hadn't gone? What if she died how she lived? So alone. This was a gift, both to me and her. We share a father, genes, blood type, eye color and like the hospice priest told us, *God works in mysterious ways.* He felt God put us together, even if it was on death's doorstep. Now do I buy into all that? Maybe. Probably not. But I do feel being with my sister at the end was meant to be."

As Shelby talked, Julianne watched her face, the light in her eyes, and her mouth turn into a small sage smile. Shelby was now older, wiser, and Julianne sat very quietly, listening, and letting the dark package rest on her thighs.

"I didn't know looking death in the eye could change a person like that. I mean, listen to this Julie, she wanted me to tell you and Natalie how sorry she was for the trouble she caused because Dad told her how much he loved you and how happy you made him. Daddy wanted her to meet all of us. He told her we would welcome her, especially you, just like you did me."

"Really?" Julianne breathed.

"Yes, but then Daddy died and she turned cold and bitter toward us. You know how he died? He was resting in her hotel room after they had lunch, said he had indigestion, so Marta went to get him a 7-UP from the hotel bar and when she returned, he was dead. She fled, she was scared."

"I always figured something like that. At least I hoped it was as innocent as that."

"So, now this." Shelby took back the manila envelope and slid her finger under the seal. "Daddy left Marta $750,000 in his will. She gave it back to us, minus a donation to Hospice. I'm to pay her medical bills, then we split it three ways. You, Natalie, and me. Marta said we were her family."

"Oh! Oh, my God." Julianne was visibly stunned.

"I know. I was shocked, too. The Hospice people arranged a paralegal to draw it up, notarize, and record it. The money was transferred into an account with my name. I'll disperse after I handle the other stuff." Shelby passed the documents to Julianne to read for herself. When Julianne was finished, Shelby looked upward and murmured. "The priest gave her Last Rites the evening before she died. She was baptized a Catholic as a baby."

Tears streamed down Shelby's face and soon they turned to sobs. Julianne took her in her arms and rocked Shelby back and forth.

Soon Julianne started to cry, too, and together they held each other and wept until all their tears were gone.

CHAPTER THIRTY-NINE

"It's a tradition!" Natalie exclaimed. "It's our family tradition."

"Oh, honey, not this year," Julianne lamented.

"Come on, Mom. It will be a way for us to honor Jock. With Shelby just back from Florida, she could use a party. In fact, I think it would give her a feeling of family again. At least this family. Sure, she has her biological mother and grandparents but they're far away. Let's do it. I'll do most of the work if that's your reason for hesitating."

Julianne and Natalie were on the sun porch spending a lazy afternoon avoiding the heat of the day. "We'd only have a week to put this together. People have made other plans," Julianne tried to explain. "Plus the fact my entire social circle has changed or we could call it what really happened, it disappeared. Couples are hesitant to include a single woman. I see almost none of our old crowd. I don't think so."

"Well, be honest, Mom. Your so-called social life pretty much revolves around Rob now. Period. End of story." Natalie had been reclining on the rattan love seat, her feet dangling off the opposite arm, when she suddenly swung her legs around and sat up. "That's the point. Let's make it a new party. Let's invite our new friends. A signal to a new life. We got that whether we wanted it or not. So, we're moving forward but still honoring your husband who was Shelby's father and my step dad with a great party. Mom, Jock would like that!"

"What about Rob? I'd want him to come," Julianne asked. "His daughter? The grandkids? I'm feeling a little funny about that situation. Rob at Jock's celebration."

"So what? You're not marrying the guy. He's a past student from the cooking class, now a friend, bringing his family. Nobody will even give it a second thought. Hey, what about the rest of the cooking school people?" Natalie's eyes lit up as she went on. "Of course, Adela, and her guy. I know Blake, Makenzie, and Chelsea would love to come here again. They could bring dates. We'll add that to all the invites for the singles."

"If we do this, I'm asking the neighbors. They've always been here for the 4th. Actually, I'd like that. It's been too long since I've been neighborly and they were so wonderful right after Jock died."

"Perfect! It's all coming together. You get me the email addresses of your guests and I'll send out an Evite invitation card today."

"How will we know how many to plan for?" Julianne was reaching into the drawer of the side table for paper and pen. If this were going to happen she'd need to start making lists of food, beverages, paper plates, cups, plastic ware, and the list would go on and on.

"Mom, they email the RSVP right back on the invitation." Natalie shook her head. "It's a new world out there."

"Don't you start on me." Julianne shook the pen at her daughter before she thought a minute and questioned Natalie. "Shelby will be ready for this? I couldn't stand the thought of her alone all day on the 4th. When you talked to her last night did she mention going down to the farm to see her Mother?"

"No she's not going to see them. Well, not yet. I think she needs time to digest the Florida thing. Thank heavens, Marta went quickly. They had several good days together before she was mostly unconscious. You know all this. I don't have to go into detail. Shelly really appreciated you picking her up at the airport and bringing her here to spend the night."

"It was good." Julianne smiled ruefully. "I think she needed to talk it out. It was no easy thing she went through. Add to that fact, the circumstances of their relationship, meeting on Marta's deathbed! Yes, being with family and people would be good, important to Shelby's well-being and healing. I'll leave it up to you to make sure she comes."

"I'll ask Shelly to invite anyone she wants to, that way, she'll be comfortable." Natalie was thoughtful for a quiet moment. "We've grown closer since Jock's been gone and we met Marta. All of us, we seem to be closer, don't you agree?"

"Yes, we have. We've bonded over our troubles these last months." Julianne turned to her daughter with a tender look. "I haven't heard you call your step-sister, Shelly, in years. My father would say 'every dark cloud has a silver lining.'"

By late afternoon, mother and daughter had moved into the kitchen, each busy with their tasks. Natalie sat in front of Julianne's computer sending out the Evites while Julianne tore lettuce for a salad and blended fresh raspberry vinaigrette to dress it.

"Look! Answers already," Natalie shouted. "It's the

Cooper's next door. Helen added a note saying they're delighted to hear you're carrying on the annual event and she'll be happy to bring her usual Smokey Baked Boston beans."

"Quick, send a thank-you and we'd love the beans. One less thing on my list." Julianne was pleased.

Natalie piped up again, "Willow LeClair says she would love to see us all again and she will bring a guest but her guest has his seven year old son for the holiday. Would that be an imposition?" Natalie said she'd answered immediately. "No, the more the merrier and there will be other kids."

"Good job, Natalie! This is going to be fun." Julianne carried the bamboo bowl to the counter where she'd laid out two place settings. "I'll serve the salad. Now call Shelby, make sure she got the email and she's up to it. After our supper, I'll call Rob and get his daughter's address so we can send an invitation directly to her."

"Another reply. This is from Chelsea. She's going to stop by, say hi, and then off to another party. Two more neighbors responded. One's bringing nachos and the other deviled eggs. Wow. These guys must have been holding their breath waiting to see if you'd do this shindig again."

Natalie laughed. "Surprised it took Adela this long to add her two cents. The answer is all smilie faces and she says, 'You Go, Girls!! Me & boy-toy wouldn't miss it! Will Stud-Muffin be manning the grill??? I'll bring my Margarita machine. Cheers!!!'"

Julianne didn't know whether to laugh or cry. It was bittersweet to remember all the good years and all the fun on the 4th with Jock. So here they were again, planning the same party. Only this time a new family member stepped up to the plate and headed up the festivities.

By noon the following day, Julianne had heard from almost everyone.

Carolyn Deaver phoned in the morning to say she would be delighted to come. It was cute how she made small talk about seeing Julianne's lovely house in the daylight and not surrounded by snowdrifts before finally coming to the point and saying she would bring a guest. A new old friend, she explained. He'd been a college sweetheart and just imagine this social media stuff, they found each other on Facebook.

The email from Libby Ellis was a bit troubling. She thanked Julianne for thinking of her but she would have to wait and see. Libby explained in great detail how she was divorcing her husband. His drinking had gotten way out of hand. Timmy was now a troubled pre-teen. She was forced to sell the house, had found work at Target, but didn't know what her schedule would be on the 4th of July. What could she bring if she did come? She would be by herself as Timmy was away at a camp for kids in conflict.

As supportive as possible, Julianne wished her well and said she'd love to see her again but understood and assured her not to bring a thing if she could make it. There would be plenty of food. Dear Libby, Julianne thought to herself, and then sent a prayer hoping the poor girl would get a break soon.

"Are you sure about the grandkids?" Was the first thing out of Rob's mouth.

"Of course, it's a BBQ, a picnic, and at least another little boy is coming. I'll have Natalie come up with a game or two. She's so good with kids. I do wonder if she'll ever have any of her own the way she's so career driven." Julianne was on her cell phone driving to Costco. "Rob, I've never asked you, because it's none of my business, but what does your daughter know about our relationship? We'll do whatever you want us to say to make her comfortable."

"Oh, she knows a lot," Rob replied. "Our weekend trips, evenings and mornings when she would call me here at home and no answer, it didn't take long. Quite frankly, I told her the same thing. I'm still the parent not the child, and I didn't feel the need to answer to her interrogation. Yea, it was a little harsh but she needs to act like an adult about my love life." Rob took a chance with the next statement. "I think you would certainly know about that situation."

"Touché." Julianne was about to say goodbye when she added, "Dinner tonight at my house? It will be gourmet Costco. I'm too busy to cook."

ON the morning of the 4th Julianne and the sun got up together. All kinds of emotions were mixing just below the surface. She was excited to see the neighbors, the cooking class students, meet Rob's daughter and her children, and watch her beautiful daughter and stepdaughter together. A minute later she felt sad and for some reason sorry. When that passed, it was contentment. This was now. This was her new normal. The fall and winter had been tough but somehow the summer sun healed and soothed and now it was time to go forward right into the future.

It hit her. Clear and concise, the decision was made. She would sell the house. Buy a townhouse or condo. This big house really wasn't hers any more. It truly was Jock's with a few of her touches. Yes, she had loved living here but not without Jock. He was the missing piece that had made this house a home. It was time. Time to find something she could make all her own.

She would start a business. Perhaps a small storefront on Main Street filled with upscale cookware, unique kitchen accessories, and beautiful glasses and dishes. There would be a room in the back, seating for fifteen or twenty, a raised stage with a mirror over it reflecting her cooking techniques as she chopped and stirred and sautéed on the commercial cooktop. She would name it *The Kitchen*.

All of a sudden, Julianne felt as light as a feather. The party today took on another whole meaning. For her and her alone, she'd not share her decisions until she was ready.

Today was a celebration of new beginnings and a farewell to an old friend, her former life.

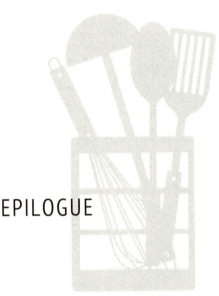

EPILOGUE

"What a lovely day for a ride." Julianne looked out the passenger window of Rob's high truck and took in the gently rolling countryside miles west of Oak Grove.

It was early fall. The corn in the black fields had turned brittle gold. The ditches were filled with ruby red sumac. Farmers were out in the fields harvesting the last of the seed corn to store for silage. A v-shaped flock of Canada geese flew over honking their hearts out. Fat white clouds meandered across the blue sky and a gentle breeze wafted in the cab as Rob slowed down and opened his window. He was searching for something as he squinted into the sun and scanned the horizon.

"Ah. There it is!" Rob exclaimed as he pressed on the accelerator and took off down the narrow blacktopped road then turned into a gravel lane.

"There is what? Why are you turning into this farm?" Julianne asked.

Rob stopped the truck. "Hold on. In fact, will you stay right here for a minute?" Rob didn't wait for an answer. He hopped out and walked toward the old farmhouse. Carefully stepping over the rotted boards on the porch, he hammered on the front door. When it was apparent there would be no answer, he went over to the closed window and peered in. Satisfied the place was deserted, he jumped down and came back to the truck and opened Julianne's door. "Come on. I've got something to show you."

"What are we doing here, Rob? Aren't we trespassing? I don't think I'm real comfortable with this . . ."

"It's not trespassing if you own it. Right?" Rob grinned.

"This Sunday afternoon ride is turning into quite an adventure and I might add some real surprises. Did I hear you say you own this place?" Julianne carefully picked her way through the tall weeds.

Rob shushed Julianne, put his arm around her shoulder, guided her past the old house and broken down abandoned chicken coop and stopped. They were standing high on a ridge. Beyond them was a valley and a winding creek meandered into the distance. On the other side of the brook, the land rose into soft hills. Recently mowed, bales of hay dotted the hillside.

"It's beautiful," Julianne whispered, as a red cardinal flew over their heads and landed on a gnarly tree nearby. "Oh, look. Isn't he beautiful? Rob, that's an old cherry tree he's in."

"Actually, if you look further that way," Rob pointed past the cherry tree, "you'll see a small orchard. Some apple, some plum, and more cherry."

"How do you know all those trees? They don't have leaves."

"The appraiser listed them in his report." Rob grinned. "I'm not that smart."

Julianne could only stammer. "What . . . I don't get it . . . this land . . . the old house . . ."

"Come over here. How about we sit down, right over here, on this old log bench, and I'll tell you the whole story." Rob pretended to dust off the warped wood, sat himself down, took Julianne's hand, and pulled her next to him. "It's safe. I think."

The entire story took a while. The sixty-acre farmette had been in Rob's wife's family for four generations. Rob's mother-in-law inherited it from her parents, then willed it to Rob's wife. When Rob's wife died, the will was changed so the property would go to Rob's daughter upon her grandmother's death. A year ago that happened and the land, house, and barn belonged to the young single mom but Rob arranged to lease it out to a neighboring farmer. They made enough income to pay the taxes and insurance but now Rob had come up with this idea.

"I'm buying it from my daughter. She has no use for this farm. Plus she sure could use the money. I've had two appraisals done and with the proceeds she'll be able to move out of the crummy townhouse she rents and buy a little home for her and the kids. We'll start a couple of college funds and maybe she'll be able to cut her hours and be a stay-at-home mom a little more. The best part is we keep this land in the family. Maybe my grandkids will want it someday."

"Okay." Julianne turned in her seat to look directly at Rob. "Excuse my French, but what the hell are you going to do with all this?"

He couldn't help himself. Rob grinned from ear to ear. "Build us a house and you a studio for cooking classes. We'll do some organic vegetable gardens, we'll get an arborist to bring back the orchard, raise a few chickens . . . I love those blue eggs the Easter Egger lays and Rhode Island Reds are so cool . . ."

"Hold on, mister. Don't we both own our own houses now? And, let me get this clear. You did say build a new house? Right?" Julianne turned to look at the weathered and dilapidated farmhouse.

Rob leaned back, spread his arms across the back of the

bench, crossed his long legs at the ankles, and smugly said. "Yes, my dear, I will build us a big spacious country home. By the way, my house goes on the market tomorrow."

"No kidding!"

"Seems we know a super realtor named Adela. Wow. Is she a mover or shaker or what? I've been cleaning out, sprucing up, rearranging. She takes no prisoners. That woman is hard core saleslady."

Julianne stood up. *Really, Adela, you do business with Rob and you don't share this with me. I'm not too happy about that!* Turning a full circle slowly and taking it all in, Julianne mumbled. "I don't know. It's a lot to wrap my head around. I've got to think this through."

Rob was on his feet. He walked to Julianne and took her in his arms. As he held her tight, he whispered into her hair, "Take all the time you need. It will be well over a year before I get it all up and running. But I do want you to be part of the planning and building whether you ever live here or not. I need a woman's touch."

"Alright. I think I can do that. It is a beautiful spot!"

"Hey, do you have enough energy to see the barn? I think it can be saved. This idea really came to me after you shared your secret dreams about a new business." Hand in hand they walked toward the gray timeworn old building. "Look at the fabulous barn siding on the old girl. With a whole new interior, floor and roof, I thought maybe you could have the cooking school out there, your own office, and indoor garden during the winter. Maybe we could find a corner for a little retail shop. Kinda like that cooking channel woman, Barefoot Somebody."

Julianne laughed. *With the sale of my house and the other money, this could be **The Kitchen**.*

She reached up, kissed Rob, and then kissed him again. "You're quite the salesman yourself! You sure can close a deal!"

THE END

Join the Cooking Class

Favorite recipes prepared by

THE KITCHEN

Bolognese Sauce

2 Tablespoons olive oil

2 Tablespoons butter

1 small onion chopped

1 carrot chopped

1 celery rib chopped

2 garlic cloves minced

4 ounces pancetta diced

1 pound ground chuck

1 cup milk

1 cup red wine

1 teaspoon oregano & basil to taste

1 28 ounce can whole tomatoes

In a heavy pot heat oil and butter. Sauté onion, carrot, celery, garlic about two minutes. Add pancetta and beef, cook until meat is no longer pink, season with salt and pepper. Add milk and cook until milk is absorbed into meat and vegetables. Add wine, stirring until wine evaporates.

In a blender or food processor coarsely puree tomatoes and the tomatoes' juices. Add to the mixture, simmer one hour or more.

Chicken Pot Pie

1 large chicken breast

1 ½ cups chicken broth

3 Tablespoons olive oil

½ cup celery, chopped

½ cup onions, chopped

1 cup carrots, chopped

1 cup frozen peas

1 cup turnips, chopped

2 Tablespoons butter

2 Tablespoons Wondra fine flour

1 prepared pie crust

sprinkle of thyme and parsley (optional)

In a heavy skillet heat 2 Tablespoon olive oil, add chicken breast and sauté until cooked through. Remove chicken to a platter. When cooled, dice into small pieces.

In the same skillet add the other 1 Tablespoon olive oil, heat on low, add celery and onions, sprinkle with salt. Cook for about three minutes until onions are translucent.

Add the remaining vegetables. Cook until almost done. Remove to another platter.

Add butter and flour to the same pan. Heat and stir until a paste forms. Add remaining broth and stir until a thick golden sauce forms. Combine the meat and vegetables into the pan, stir until blended together.

In a greased 9 inch pie pan pour the mixture. Cover with the store-bought piecrust, cut in small slits, brush with butter, sprinkle with thyme and parsley.

Bake in a 400 degree oven for 30 minutes or until crust is golden brown.

Honey Mustard Salad Dressing

¼ cup honey
¼ cup stone ground mustard
¼ cup extra virgin olive oil
¼ cup champagne vinegar
1 teaspoon dill

In a small jar with a lid add all of the ingredients and shake vigorously. Store in refrigerator until ready to use. Shake again before pouring on salad greens.

Swiss Onion Dip

1 cup mayonnaise
1 cup finely chopped onions
1 cup shredded Swiss cheese

In an oven proof dish add all ingredients. Bake in a 350 degree oven for 30 minutes or until the top is starting to brown.

Lemon Rosemary Chicken

4 boneless skinless chicken breasts
4 Tablespoons olive oil
4 garlic cloves
2 Tablespoons crushed rosemary leaves
1 lemon

With one tablespoon of the oil grease a 12 x 8 baking dish. Lay the breasts side by side, not touching.

In a small bowl add the zest of the lemon and its juice, the remaining oil, 4 finely chopped cloves of garlic and the rosemary. Pour over the breasts. Season each with salt and pepper.

Bake for thirty-five minutes at 325 convection or 350 standard. Meat should register a temperature of 165 degrees.

Lemon Cream Pie

1 store bought graham cracker pie crust
1 14 ounce can sweetened condensed milk
1 cup fresh lemon juice
1 8 ounce carton Cool Whip

In a large mixing bowl, combine the milk and lemon juice. Fold in the Cool Whip. Scoop mixture into pie crust. Chill at least one hour before serving.

Macaroni & Cheese

3 cups uncooked penne pasta

¾ cup cheddar cheese

¾ cup gruyere cheese

¼ cup romano cheese

6 Tablespoons butter

¼ cup Wondra flour

2 1/3 cups milk

6 drops Tabasco

pinch of dried mustard and nutmeg

¾ cup Panko

Cook pasta according to package directions. Drain and set aside.

In a large saucepan melt 4 Tablespoons of butter, add flour, stir to make a paste, add the milk. Cook until thick. Add the cheeses, Tabasco, and dried spices. Combine with pasta. Pour into a 2 quart casserole coated with a cooking spray.

In a small saucepan melt the remaining butter, add Panko. Spread over the casserole.

Bake at 375 degrees for 30 minutes or until bubbly.

Home Style Meatloaf

¾ pound ground beef

½ pound sausage

½ pound ground chicken

1 small onion

½ green pepper

2 garlic cloves

17 saltine crackers

1/3 cup milk

1 egg

1 Tablespoon ground mustard

1 Tablespoon Worcestershire sauce

1 Tablespoon thyme

½ (more or less) 8 ounce can of tomato sauce

In a 7 cup Cuisinart chop the garlic, onion and green pepper. Scrape out the veggies and set aside on a plate.

In the Cuisinart add the crackers and milk. When blended add all three meats. Pulse 20 times.

In a large bowl (use your clean hands) mix the meat mixture with the veggies, egg, mustard, Worcestershire, thyme, tomato sauce. Add optional salt & pepper.

Form into a loaf. Bake in a greased bread pan at 350 degrees for 90 minutes.

Red Velvet Cupcakes

2 1/2 cups all-purpose flour

1/4 cup unsweetened cocoa powder,

1 teaspoon baking powder

1 teaspoon baking soda

1 teaspoon kosher salt

1 cup buttermilk, shaken

1 Tablespoon red food coloring

1 teaspoon white vinegar

1 teaspoon pure vanilla extract

1/4 pound (1 stick) butter

1 1/2 cups sugar

2 eggs

In a small bowl, sift together the flour, cocoa powder, baking powder, baking soda, and salt. In a large measuring cup, combine the buttermilk, food coloring, vinegar, and vanilla.

Using an electric mixer beat the butter and sugar on medium speed for 1 minute. Add the eggs. With the mixer on low speed, add the dry ingredients and the wet ingredients alternately, beginning and ending with the dry ingredients, and mix until combined.

Scoop the batter into the lined muffin cups. Bake at 350 degrees for 25 to 30 minutes.

Red Velvet Frosting

8 ounces cream cheese, at room temperature

12 Tablespoons (1 1/2 sticks) unsalted butter, at room temperature

1/2 teaspoon vanilla extract

3 1/2 cups confectioners' sugar

Mix all ingredients and frost when cupcakes are completely cooled.

Stuffed Pork Tenderloin

1 1.5 pound pork tenderloin, butterflied

2 cups breadcrumbs

1 celery rib, chopped

¼ cup chopped onions

½ cup beef broth

2 Tablespoons butter

1 egg

1 teaspoon sage

salt & pepper

Lay opened tenderloin on a flat surface. Salt & pepper the inside.

In a medium skillet melt butter, sauté onions and celery then add bread, broth, egg, sage. Heat thoroughly until the stuffing forms a cohesive mixture.

Scoop the stuffing on to the meat. Fold the meat closed and tie with butcher's string.

Bake in a shallow roasting pan at 400 degrees for 40 minutes or until internal temperature is 160 degrees.

Smashed Roots

4 medium potatoes

2 carrots

2 large parsnips

2 Tablespoons butter

½ cup half & half (more or less)

salt & pepper

In a large pot boil the cubed peeled potatoes, diced carrots, peeled and cubed parsnips until fork tender.

Drain the veggies, return to pot, add butter and milk and mash until smooth. Adjust the flavor with salt and pepper.

Pear & Blue Cheese Salad

2 firm pears cut lengthwise and cored
2 Tablespoons butter
4 heaping Tablespoons blue cheese
½ cup brandy

In a heavy skillet melt butter, add brandy. Bring to a slow boil, reduce by half. Add pears, face down and lower heat for 3 minutes.

Turn pears over, spoon cheese into center and heat just enough to soften the cheese. Remove and place pears on small individual salad plates. Spoon brandy liquid over each pear.

Veal Marsala

1 1/2 pound veal cutlets (also called scallopini; 1/4 inch thick)

3 Tablespoons unsalted butter

1 pound mushrooms, quartered

1 large garlic clove, minced

1 shallot, chopped

1 1/2 Tablespoons olive oil

1/3 cup all-purpose flour + 2 Tablespoons

2/3 cup sweet Marsala wine

1 cup beef stock

Heat 2 Tablespoons of butter in a 12-inch heavy skillet, sauté mushrooms, stirring frequently. Add garlic and sauté, 1 minute. Transfer to a bowl. Pat veal dry, salt & pepper each.

Heat 1/2 Tablespoon oil with 1 teaspoon butter in skillet over moderately high heat. Dredge 2 or 3 pieces of veal in flour, shaking off excess, then sauté until just cooked through, 1 to 1 1/2 minutes on each side (meat will still be slightly pink inside). Transfer to a platter. Sauté remaining veal in two more batches using remaining oil and butter. Transfer to platter.

Add Marsala to skillet and deglaze, stirring and scraping up brown bits, until reduced by half. Stir in beef stock. Add mushroom mixture and veal juices accumulated on platter, then season with salt and pepper if necessary. Simmer 2 minutes more and spoon over veal.

ABOUT THE AUTHOR

BETTY FELLERS BARRY writes under the pen name of Elizabeth Fellers. Her first book of fiction was *The Club*.

She and her husband divide their time between Arizona and Wisconsin.